When her abusive father
year-old Rayne Kennedy finds that her savior is far from an angel. Lost and alone she is completely enraptured by the beautiful but murderous, Scarlett. Taken on an adventure by the vampire's well-intentioned sister, Rayne is drawn into Vires, a dark and dangerous vampire world, where humans are little more than natural resources to be exploited.

In a society that has been turned upside down while learning to live inside its constraints, Scarlett Pearce may not be much more than a slave to a power-hungry Government and the violent bloodlust that consumes her may be all her own. Before she loses herself in a world unlike anything she has ever known, Rayne needs to find Scarlett and the answers to those questions.

BLOOD ECHO

L.E. Royal

A NineStar Press Publication

Published by NineStar Press
P.O. Box 91792,
Albuquerque, New Mexico, 87199 USA.
www.ninestarpress.com

Blood Echo

Printed in the USA
First Edition
December, 2018

Print ISBN: 978-1-949909-57-9

Also available in eBook, ISBN: 978-1-949909-53-1

Warning: This book contains sexually explicit content, which may only be suitable for mature readers, and depictions of captivity and torture, bloody violence and death.

Chapter One

BLOOD. THERE WAS so much blood. It tasted metallic and sticky as it flooded my mouth. My back was uncomfortably warm, wet, and screaming in agony. A high-pitched sound filled the air, piercing, shaking me to the center of myself. My frantic blue eyes searched through spinning space, looking for him. My father was three steps up our staircase and wasted, drunk on his beloved infusion of cheap apple cider and vodka that smelled like drain cleaner on his breath.

The siren kept on wailing. I searched his eyes, so similar to my own, for any of the fear I felt, anything to signify that he too knew, this time, he really had gone too far. I saw none, and the panic settling over me was ice cold and heavy, crushing down on my chest.

Warm wetness was all around me. Only when the siren stopped, and I sucked in a deep and frantic breath that sent white-hot pain shooting through my torso, did I realize I had been screaming.

Lying there, my body strewn across the entryway of the house where I grew up, I considered that I'd never thought much about death. Bleeding at the bottom of the stairs, my ragingly drunk father staggering toward me to either save me or hurt me more, I wished I had.

At least I might see Mom. That's what I told myself as the edges of my vision began to bleed, the colors mixing together and fading out. My father's expressionless face swam into focus as he stared down at me. He almost looked sorry, then he ran the back of his hand across the midnight shadow on his chin and I was drifting away again as he started to shout.

"Stop looking at me that way, Marion! You left..."

The words drifted to my ears like I was hearing them from miles away, through a thick-fogged glass of space, time, and pain.

"You left me! You left us... You left us behind... So don't you dare..."

I was dragged back to myself, back to the agonizing sting where the cool air hit the gashes in my skin as, with a wet thwack, a glob of my father's spit landed on my cheek.

He's going to kill me. The thought spun in my head, a carousel doomed to run endlessly. I tried to find the words to tell him I wasn't my mother; she'd left us both when her long fight with cancer was finally lost.

This was how I would die, after six years of watching the man who had raised me sink further and further into an abyss of alcohol, emptiness, and violence. The occasional "accidents" had escalated to flat-out beatings, and tonight, I realized it would all come to an end. The minute he had thrown me down the stairs, sending me crashing through the glass door below, it was over.

"Rayne... Marion..." I heard low mumblings in the familiar voice that had come to foster a sick and unnatural fear in me. I told myself the lie I had lived by since my mother's funeral—my father had died with her. I would remember him for who he was, not the grief-crazed murderer wearing his pajamas.

Tears flooded my eyes. I felt everything, but I couldn't move. I didn't want to move. I wanted to sleep and to not hurt anymore, not like this.

Shouting woke me again. I listened to my father's voice, the click of the front door closing, blowing cold air on the bare skin of my side. My shirt was still wrinkled around my middle from the fall. The words made no sense. The questions floating to me came from a voice I didn't recognize. His replies were suddenly uncertain. The aggressor was gone, and I opened my eyes just in time to watch him become the victim.

I don't know where she came from, how she found me, or how she knew the exact right time to walk into my life.

A woman stood in our entryway. Slender and petite, softly waved brunette hair hanging loose around her shoulders, and a form-fitting and deep crimson dress riding dangerously high up her thighs. A smooth leather jacket molded to her small form like a second skin.

I had no time to wonder who she was, but I knew from the minute she appeared like an omen in my darkest moment she was someone.

Dark eyes looked down at me, and I looked back, though I could not prevent my own closing. I shivered against an invisible cold and the action was exhausting. The warm pool I had been lying in was cooling and everything told me to close my eyes. It was curiosity that kept me alive, it was her, and those haunting dark eyes, searching mine, looking down at me so intensely, yet she was unreadable.

I was a captive audience, powerless to look away from her, and I saw it all.

Full lips parted, and I watched in awe and almost complete detachment. The way she moved was animalistic, fingers twisting roughly into my father's hair—his head yanked right, while hers dipped left. When she turned back to me, letting his body fall to the floor with a heavy thud and pushing it away as if he was a wooden puppet, not a two-hundred-pound man, her lips were marred with blood.

She was beautiful and she was terrible, this killer, my angel of death. I wondered with the last of my strength if she had come to save me or just to take me away. By now, they were the same thing.

Her eyes as she crouched beside me were unforgettable, one brown, one green, though the irises seemed to be alive. The colors swirled, rich and bright, moving like flames, spinning into their own constellations. Suddenly, I was glad this beautiful killer would be the last thing I'd see.

Those strange eyes peered down at me, perfectly shaped eyebrows arched, and I stared back up at her. The only sound breaking the silence was my own rasping, rattling breaths.

This was it. It had all been for nothing, my father, my mother, me... This was the end of the Kennedy family, but somehow, I couldn't feel sadness. Looking into those swirling eyes, light-headed, I couldn't feel anything.

I sucked a gurgling breath through my bloodstained lips as I watched my father's blood drip down her chin. Somehow, I forced out my last words.

"Thank you."

I WOKE UP alone, disoriented and confused, lying on the old threadbare sofa. The only other piece of furniture in the living room was the large flat-screen TV I knew my father had sold the last of my mom's jewelry to buy.

The nightmare felt so real, I still felt the large shard of glass sticking out of my thigh at an odd angle. I remembered the smell of my father's breath on my face when he grabbed me at the top of the staircase, every bump on the way down, and the killer with the galaxy eyes.

The thought of her stayed with me, haunting me, following me around the empty house as I walked from room to room, lost. My father, or at least his body, was gone. I found the glass shards that had littered the floor in the trashcan beside our back door, the only proof all this was real. Everything was the same, but everything had changed.

My feet took me back to the sofa where I had woken up, my fingers played with the comforter that had been taken from my bed and draped around my body. It seemed as if I was looking down at myself, watching from a distance, unable to feel or to process the situation as I should.

My father was dead. I reached out for the remote. He'd been murdered by a strange and merciful killer with eyes that moved like something from one of the science fiction books lining my bookcase. I flicked through the channels until I found a news station, noting the time and date in the corner of the screen with disinterest. Two days were gone, yet the panic I knew should follow this realization remained absent.

Something clouded my emotions—relief, fear, maybe even shock? I didn't have the answer, and I didn't look for it. Deciding instead to fall into my usual routine, I went up the stairs to dress, then leave on the hour-long walk to school. I might still make it for my afternoon classes, during which I'd forge another note to explain my absence. At least this time I wouldn't have to try to explain the bruises.

The realization hit me hard and fast, knocking all the air out of my chest, leaving me empty, my blood running cold. I looked down at my arms, my legs that ran long below my blood-stained pajama shorts. Nothing hurt. There were no bruises, no scars, just my skin, as pale as ever, unblemished.

The impact of every stair came back to me, and I flinched. The agony of the glass tearing into my skin, lodging into my thigh, my back, my arms crashed over me, a tsunami that stole my breath and finally instilled some of the panic I knew I should be feeling into me.

I was alive. Inexplicably unharmed after what seemed like certain death. My father was dead, gone, and though it meant the beatings would stop, staring at my rain-streaked windowpane, I realized I had a new problem. Without his disability allowance, without him, how would I pay the already grossly overdue bills? How would I keep the house and finish school and escape to college?

I had no answers to my own questions, so I pulled on my worn blue jeans and old sweater and wrapped my long hair into a braid with shaking fingers. I set off, unable to escape the thick fog of shock still shrouding me. Leaving the house behind, I tried to ready myself to do what I always did—to carry on. For years, I had learned to leave home problems at home and disappear into the crowd. Nobody noticed me or cared much for me at school, or anywhere, really—facts I wore like a cape of invisibility.

Chapter Two

THE WORLD MOVED around me.

My father was dead. My mother was dead, though that was nothing new. I existed, living between the cracks my death—my almost death—had left in my version of reality.

They were knocking at the door again. It was another Tuesday night spent sitting in the bathtub, my chin on my too-bony knees, waiting for them to leave. The faucet dripped pitifully on my sneakers and I almost wanted to cry.

I traced shapes in the thin sheen last night's bath bubbles had left on the discolored porcelain beneath me. My father was a man I had come not to know, someone who I lived with, and lived in fear of, yet knew so little about—the men banging on the front door of the house proved that.

The first time they came by, I had answered their insistent knocking, a mistake I wouldn't make twice. The one who had spoken to me was full of quiet anger I could sense brewing behind that polite façade, and it scared me. I didn't have the money they mentioned in the message for my father, and sooner or later, they were going to realize he wasn't really in the hospital after falling down the stairs either.

I closed my eyes, leaning back against the cold, hard side of the tub. Once again, I was amazed and dumbfounded by myself in equal parts. I should be terrified, falling, breaking into a million pieces. Since the accident, my usual easily panicked demeanor seemed to have faded out. It felt muffled now, not quite absent.

Rather than being consumed by the mounting bills and the men who came knocking at the house at all hours, I was consumed by *her*. An unremarkable week had passed, and she monopolized my every available moment. I dreamed of her, of those liquid irises, the blood dripping down her chin. My thoughts drifted back to her when making the long walk to and from school, sitting at the back of geography class, walking through the lunch hall to my usual seat, alone. I felt as if she could just disappear, nothing more than a dream, an imagined savior to slip through my grasping fingers, and so, my mind clung to her. I relived every piece of her, and pulled together more, from that frantic, blood-stained memory at every opportunity.

I studied my sneakers, still filthy from the time spent looking for my father's body, in the backyard, the small shed he kept, in the trunk of his beat-up old van. I had looked for answers yet found none. Although she was the thing that held my focus, I never tried to find answers about her. Part of me was afraid if I did, my greed for knowledge would somehow cause her to disappear forever. Another part of me thought that was stupid, but it wasn't enough to convince me to look.

Of course, I had drawn my own conclusions. The neck biting led me immediately to believe she was a vampire—if such a thing existed. Yet she had broken through the door before the sun was fully dead behind the woody skyline of our quiet little New Hampshire town. When she looked down at me, I didn't see fangs. I just couldn't rectify something so beautiful, the thing that had saved me, with something so...dark, any more than I could understand my own rose-tinted view of this murderer.

My breath left me in a sigh. The shouting and knocking had subsided, I didn't know exactly when. The faucet dripped on and I was content to study the dirty tiles.

She was palpable in my mind. Sometimes, I thought I sensed her, three steps behind me. It was ridiculous, but those eyes haunted me. I'd watched her kill my father, but she fascinated me, grossly so. *If not for her, my father would have been the murderer that night, and the victim...* I couldn't finish the thought.

Everything inside me pulled and strained, and I ached to be close to her again, to look into those oddly colored magical eyes, and know her. Somehow, I felt like I already did, or had. Morbid curiosity was killing me, but she was gone, and so I clung to her in my thoughts, my dreams, blocking out the knowledge that I was fixated, probably unhealthily so, because it was the easier alternative.

I drifted closer to sleep, lulled by the steady dripping of the faucet. As my eyes closed, I felt her presence again, as if she was close to me, watching over me, thinking of me. It made no sense, but sense wasn't what I searched for.

The intensity with which she had looked down at me that night, the way she had saved me without a moment of hesitation, her nearness... I fell into a vivid and dream-riddled sleep, where once again I had all these things I knew I had begun to covet.

MY NECK STILL ached. One of my favorite books was open on the table in front of my lunch tray, and although my eyes lingered on its worn pages, I wasn't reading. I loved *Romeo and Juliet*, and I hated it. A love like that seemed to belong exactly there, in a storybook, yet the way it was all lost, all twisted and broken and tragic in the end—that seemed more like real life.

I jumped as the chair across from me was drawn back. The cafeteria was loud, but I wasn't expecting the sound.

Nobody ever sat with me, and that was the way I had come to like it. My lunchtimes were the smell of fried food, the clamor of footsteps and voices, fading in and out of my awareness as I disappeared into a book, or lately, into her. They were never shared.

My eyes automatically shot up, then up some more, and I imagine the color drained out of my face. She was tall and pretty—beautiful, actually. Softly tanned skin and thick dark hair, plump lips and expensive clothes left me wondering how she had stumbled into my humble presence.

I offered her a weak smile, though I was sure she had either come to mock me, or to ask to copy my English homework.

"Would it be okay if I sat with you?"

The way she spoke was strange, I couldn't place her accent to either coast, but the request seemed genuine enough. I nodded, blushing furiously before I looked back to my book. She must be new, that's what I told myself. She was new, and her presence would be a short-term inconvenience and novelty in equal parts, until she realized I was not the go-to lunch crowd if you wanted to be anybody at Jaffrey Public High.

I could feel her watching me. Discomfort crawled down my spine.

"My name's Jade Pearce..."

I was forced to look up again.

"Rayne... Rayne Kennedy."

I paused, waiting for her to speak, but she just looked at me with brown eyes that seemed too dull for the rest of her dazzling self. I cleared my throat.

"Are you new?"

She nodded, twirling her fork with slender fingers, pushing the salad on her plate into a neat little mound with a finesse that seemed misplaced on such a menial task. I had no idea what else to say, so I went back to pretending to read.

"*Romeo and Juliet*?"

I just wanted her to leave so I could go back to thinking about *her*, about the angel of death—that's what I called her in my mind now. Ever polite, I looked up and gave her half a smile and a nod.

"Do you like tragedy, Rayne?"

It was an odd question. She watched me with an intensity that made me want to shrink, and I considered my answer carefully.

"I think it's realistic." I leaned back in my seat, resigned to having this conversation. "Life is tragic, love is never straightforward... Or least not from what I've seen," I added quickly, not wanting to say too much on a subject I had experienced so little of. "There's light and dark in everything, the story doesn't fall into the light for the sake of a happy ending. Things end badly, imperfectly... Like I said... Realistic."

Realizing I was talking a lot, or at least a lot for me, I gave an apologetic shrug and took a token stab at one of the soggy fries on my plate. I didn't even bother to raise it to my lips. Jade seemed pleased with my answer.

"I agree, it takes a certain kind of person to be able to find beauty in tragedy, to see light in darkness."

Her voice was rich and smooth, velvety. She was obviously American, but I still had no idea where she must have moved from to come here, and it seemed rude to ask. I liked her, though, the way she spoke about the book, the fact she had spoken to me about anything.

"I like Greek mythology and vampire books."

The mention of the V word made my blood run cold with guilt as I offered her what I was sure was a watery smile. I was out of practice with all this, but curiosity drove me to pursue the conversation.

"Some of the myths are interesting, the stories of all the gods and goddesses," I agreed with a nod. "I don't know about the vampire stuff, I prefer to stick with more...realistic things."

I had to say it. Somehow, I had to defend myself from the unspoken accusation that I was a liar, that I knew too much.

Jade Pearce arched one perfectly sculpted eyebrow, and I wished I had never spoken, though her expression quickly cracked into a smile.

"You think it's impossible they exist somewhere out there? Or are you just scared?"

Her tone was even, and unreadable as anything more than just casual chit-chat, curiosity, but it made me nervous. I wanted to get up and leave, to protect my thoughts from this girl who seemed to have an unnervingly accurate feel of them, although I knew it was impossible.

"I'm not scared. I mean... If they did exist, they're just people with a specific diet. Some people eat dogs, doesn't mean every dog should be afraid of a person..." My metaphor was tactless, and it made me cringe, heat crawling up my neck to color my cheeks a little deeper.

"I... I don't eat dogs, I love dogs...it's just...the same thing, you know? I don't know...." I hoped she would drop it.

My bumbled answer seemed to amuse her, as she continued to twirl her fork between her fingers with a dexterity that forced me to watch the movement until she spoke again.

"For my next class, I have politics."

Her smile was infectious, and though I wasn't sure how the watered-down, washed-out politics course the school taught was anything at all to be excited for, I nodded in recognition.

"Rayne, could you show me the way? I don't want to be a nuisance, so..."

I was already shaking my head.

"It's right on the way to my English class, it's no problem."

I shoved my book back into my backpack. Eyes followed us, Jade and me, as we began to weave our way out of the cafeteria, the foot traffic only just starting to thin ready for next class. We were polar opposites. She was tall, taller than most of the students we passed, and her perfectly proportioned features and smooth dark hair turned head after head as we walked side by side down the corridor. I was shorter, my long blonde hair twisted into a thick braid, hanging down to my waist, my clothes plain, the jeans and T-shirt that were my regulation school wardrobe meant to draw as little attention as humanly possible.

Jade lurched beside me. I reached out without thinking, catching her around the arm, as she steadied herself on her feet. My heart was racing and sinking all at once, and my chest felt too tight. The amount of panic propelling my hand forward in that split-second, the aversion I felt to any kind of harm coming to her caught me by surprise. I had known her barely half an hour. My cheeks were flaming on her behalf, but as I looked up at her, she didn't seem quite as affected by her stumble.

"Thanks. I'm the clumsiest dancer you'll ever meet..."

Even raised to find me over the swell of conversation around us, her voice was still so ethereal, and I thought I could listen to her all day long.

"You're in 209, right?" I paused as best I could outside the doorway, though elbows and backpacks continually bumped my back, my shoulder, as bodies continued to push by us. Nobody seemed to run into Jade that way, but Jade hadn't spent the last four years at the school making herself invisible.

"I believe I am." She looked down briefly at the palm of her hand at neat, but smudged, blue scrawl. "Thank you, Rayne, meeting you has been a pleasure."

I nodded, trying to keep the heat out of my cheeks—a constant struggle.

"Me too. I'll...see you."

With one last smile, I left, disappearing back into the crowd, heading toward English, and back toward my invisibility. This month was so full of the unexpected: my lunch companion, my father's visitors, my visitor... Of course the last one, she was the only thing that stayed on my mind. I settled back into my seat, content to think of her and gaze at the empty chalkboard, as Mr. Wattley talked about the themes in a book I had read close to twenty times already.

Chapter Three

THERE WERE A hundred other things I should be doing. Letters were becoming my enemy. Unpaid bills formed a neat stack of doom on the kitchen counter, and I didn't dare to open any of them.

My father had kept what little money he had stuffed in a sock down the back of the air conditioning unit in his room, money that was now in my wallet and was lasting fairly well, mostly thanks to how infrequently I remembered to eat. I was holding myself firmly in my regular routine, but such trivial things as food had lost all importance. If my energy wasn't so consumed by other things, I might have been worried.

His debit card was there too, along with three shiny credit cards I was sure could help with the bill situation, and probably with sending me to jail for card fraud. So instead of using them, or looking for a way out of this, I headed back to my room for another night of pretending to read when, really, I was just thinking about her.

The crash that came from downstairs made my blood run cold, icy panic spreading from my chest through every piece of me. The fear was white-hot, and it froze me in place, perched on the end of my bed, a book still in my hands. I knew the sound. Somebody was in the house.

I had to hide. Call the police. Climb out the window and run screaming to the neighbor, though he smoked so much marijuana I wondered if he would be conscious enough to help. My heart hammered, pounding against my ribs painfully, driven by fear so salient that for a split-second I was lying at the bottom of the stairs again. Then, now—this was the same feeling, waiting to die.

I had to hide, but my body refused to move, fear-frozen as I heard dragging, staggering footsteps, the crash of a glass breaking in the kitchen. My father. He was my first thought. Somehow, he had survived, somehow, he was back for me now, back to finish what the angel of death had stolen from him.

My hand covered my mouth with a soft slap. I realized I was shaking, my whole body vibrating with nervous energy dying to pour out of me. I couldn't let myself scream.

I had to move.

Counting down, I waited, ready to bolt... *Three, two, one...* But still, I didn't move. Those fumbling footsteps were headed for the stairs, and I tried again. This time, on one, I ran, running for my life, not quietly, just fast, my half-laced sneakers thudding against the carpet as I ran across the hall and into the bathroom. I slammed the door shut and locked it behind me—that was one of the first changes I had made after my father's death. I looked at the little lock now, the alloy fresh and bright against the faded paint and dirty tile of the bathroom. I silently pleaded it would be enough to save me.

He was coming. Faster now, desperate, the cadence of his footsteps was all wrong, but he was hurt, I could almost feel that he was hurt, a wounded animal, come to take me down with the last of his strength. I was in the tub, pressed back behind the shower curtain, my shaking hands still clamped over my mouth, and I wanted her. I wanted her to be here again, to save me again, but he was in the hall now, coming for me.

Six years to die like this. Six years without my mother. I hoped it was fast, I hoped it didn't hurt. It was going to hurt—it always hurt. He tried the handle and I shook my head, desperate, as if that had ever stopped him—as if it ever would.

My little lock was holding fast, my final defiance, and I wished I'd tightened the screws more, bought a bigger one, but it was all I had now. Though the handle turned, the door rattled, it held out for me, keeping me in, keeping him out.

A blood-curdling scream filled the air. It stole the oxygen from my chest until I tasted the very bottom of my lungs. It pierced my mind and blanched my vision into a muted, faded television scene. I watched the door, the last barrier between us, buckle in on itself until it was broken open.

It was her.

I stopped screaming because it was her... She must have chased him away, thrown him aside, perhaps down the stairs, but she was here, and she was hurt.

Dark hair was plastered to her face, soaked from the rain, clinging to her skin. Her eyes were hollow, and I rushed toward her, because he had done this, he'd done this to her and she had come here for me. I tripped out of the tub, falling painfully on my knees, but I got back up as fast as my adrenaline-hobbled legs would allow—I barely felt them. My stomach seemed to fall through the floor as I came closer.

She was covered in blood, gashes down her bare arms, chunks of flesh missing from her neck, her legs, and to my horror, a deep crack running down her cheek, almost as if she was made of stone. I couldn't even find the words to apologize for what he had done. I tasted my own tears as, fear-drunk, I reached for her. To my surprise, she reached back.

We were kindred flames, opposite poles, and she pulled me to her while I pulled her closer. She was safety. She came in my darkest moments to save me, she followed me silently through the mundane wreckage my life had become ever since she had walked into it. She was my savior, my lifeboat in the cold dark waters I had long since learned to swim in, though I knew I wouldn't have survived much longer.

I knew her, I could feel her, her presence made something burn bright in my chest. I ached to speak her name, to taste it on my lips. Cold fingers locked around my wrist in a vise grip, dragging me forward, closing the last of the distance between us.

What happened next should have surprised me, but it didn't. Life hurt, the things I loved hurt me, and by now, I was sure I loved her somehow. I needed her; she was the only thing I had left.

The way she yanked my wrist upward sent pain searing through the joint and down my fingers. The bones breaking, twisting and tearing as they grated over each other, was audible to me. It only got worse as I fell to my knees, still looking up at her, at the sunken dark eyes that were nothing like those from my dreams.

I cried, pleading silently. She wasn't supposed to hurt me. She wasn't supposed to be hurt like this... She fell when I fell, and we struggled for just a moment. She was stronger, unnaturally strong, and as soon as she twisted my wrist back up to her mouth, lunging for me sloppily, everything went quiet, still.

I sobbed, my breath hitching, my chest jerking, tears wet on my cheeks, soaking my ashy pale hair as it splayed on the tile around me, though the action was losing momentum. I felt young again, six years old, finally giving up the fight to uphold the tears when my mother soothed me.

Where her mouth connected haphazardly with my wrist, there was a dull ache that intensified as, with a dragging sensation, she drew more from me. Then, like the tide, the drag stopped, and I was able to catch my breath. This was what she needed, I could tell, and that feeling filled me up, beyond my broken bones, beyond the strange pull or the way my fingers were alarmingly cold.

She was here, looking at me, and I stared back at her, my cheek against the cold hard tile of the bathroom floor, while she half lay, half crouched beside me. Tears were still falling, though my breathing was evening out, and they felt like relief, like the first rain after a scorching dry summer.

Her mouth wasn't flush against me, but I knew she was drinking my blood. Somehow, the knowledge didn't scare me. I lay there anesthetized by her presence, a silent audience as her mismatched eyes regained their brilliant colors and began to dance for me. She watched my face intensely, emitting soft little noises of approval into the silence, now and then.

I flinched when it was over. The way she jerked my broken wrist away from her mouth hurt, but I didn't make a sound. My hand hung limply in her grasp, and I studied the odd angle at which my fingers hung in comparison to the rest of my arm. Everything started to move, the room around her, the colors in her eyes, one green, one brown, and I was dizzy and sick.

I tried to cling to the present, to her, watching as she raised a finger to her mouth and pressed hard against a spot on my wrist that stung like a tiny speck of fire. I wanted to ask her what she was doing, but I couldn't find the words, so I continued to watch, trying to cling to consciousness. Brilliant eyes were studying my ruined arm intensely, and her face was half veiled by her long dark hair as she leaned forward and gave the limp limb in her grasp a soft shake. The pain the motion caused made my stomach roll; I grit my teeth so as not to interrupt whatever seemed to be fascinating her so.

Then I screamed.

In one swift motion she jerked my hand up straight, and again I felt it, the bones grating against each other as she snapped the joint back straight and held it there, though I tried to pull away.

Pain. It swallowed me up, and I twisted and writhed, trying desperately to escape her iron grasp, but she held me still. Her breath smelled of whiskey, and that surprised me. What surprised me more was she gazed at my face now, though I was too delirious to really look back at her, to decipher her expression.

"Stop."

It was a single word, a single command, undeniable, and in spite of myself, I did. My shoulders lifted rhythmically from the floor under the force of my breathing. It still hurt, but I tried to stay silent, the pain squeezing tears down my cold cheeks.

The only sign of approval she gave was a small nod, yet she watched me intensely. I looked at her, struggling to breathe and remain still.

By the time I noticed the pain subsiding it had let up substantially. She hovered over me now. For the first time, I could really take her in. Her face was almost impossible to read, though I sensed she was uncomfortable, or at least thought I did, but what did I know about her?

She was so different from the single dimensioned thing she had become in my dreams, so vibrant, so vivid, and so intense as she loomed over me. Her presence alone was enough to rob me entirely of my voice. I knew I wouldn't be able to speak to her, even if I had the nerve to try.

Eventually, she lowered my arm to rest against the cold tile, and although it ached, the horrible burning was gone.

"Don't..."

My voice was too pitchy, too laden with panic as I called out. Immediately she began to get up. She had just come back to me, and I wasn't ready to let her leave again, not yet, not until I had answers, maybe not even after. Her presence was a drug now, and I craved it, I wanted her to stay, to remain close to me, and somehow, I sensed we needed to be near each other.

Bloodied black patent heels were sleek and shining, close to my head, and I studied them for a second before I looked back to her face. She seemed to be considering, her galaxy eyes tumultuous, and I felt the war inside her. I desperately wanted her to stay, but I didn't dare to ask her again.

The way she lowered herself down beside me was slow, repentant, and I waited, my heart hammering in my chest; although I was unsure, I wasn't afraid. The pads of her fingers skirted across my stomach as she slid her arm around my waist. She settled her head on the tile, and I turned mine so I could look at her face. All I tasted was the whiskey and iron on her breath.

Dark eyes looked back at me. All the wounds were gone now, her skin was flawless, though still stained with blood. I reached up without thinking, the fingers of my good hand running over where the crack in her cheek had been. To my surprise, she leaned into the touch and pressed her body closer against mine.

For a split-second, the gravity of the situation dawned on me. I was here, and she was holding me, the woman who I was sure had just broken my arm, who had killed my father. I didn't care. Her embrace was cool, but it filled me up, and as the adrenaline subsided, I found myself breathing easier than I had in a long time.

There was no denying she was terrible, my blood still drying at the corners of her lips; but with her, I was safe.

We lay like that for a long time, my legs numb from lying on the floor, but when I finally let my mind drift from trying to soak her in completely, I flexed my fingers and realized my broken arm didn't hurt at all.

"You fixed me?"

My whispered words sounded like gunshots in the silence, and it felt strange to be so nervous to speak to the woman who held me so intimately, unlike anything I had ever experienced.

"I broke you..."

Her voice was black coffee and dark chocolate, rich and smooth, low and heavy. I shook my head, even though what she'd said was true. She ran her tongue over her lips, and I sensed the moment to talk had passed.

Butterflies danced on the edges of my ribs and tumbled down into my stomach when she reached up to touch my face. I lay very still, afraid to break the moment, afraid to do anything but savor it. The pads of her fingers were cool against my skin, not unpleasant, but definitely tepid, as they ran over my cheek.

Questions loomed, threatening to spill from my lips and ruin this moment, but I held them at bay. The intensity with which she watched me scared me, and it made me feel alive, visible, and for once, I didn't mind.

One cool hand cupped my cheek, and she looked at me as if I was her most precious possession. I wondered silently if this was what love felt like. She cared for me, something was warm in my chest, but it wasn't my own emotion. Never in my life had I been able to sense someone's mood like this, to taste what they felt with so few words exchanged—if this was even real outside my head. That thought stung. I wanted her to care for me like I thought she might.

"Are you afraid?"

Her voice was hypnotizing, and I almost answered no by default, before I forced myself to fully consider the question. Somehow, my every answer felt important, heavy, and for a second, I was reminded of Jade at lunch with all her questions.

"No."

I held her eyes, refusing to look away, because her eye contact wasn't the uncomfortable affair I found the rest of the world caused me. She laughed, and the sound was so bitter that, for a moment, my answer changed, yet she held me still, gentle.

"You will be, eventually."

Her tone was final. She hid her sadness well, but the twinge in my chest was as sharp as if it was my own. I watched my fingers graze delicately across her cheek again, marveling for a moment at how effortless reaction was around her. I didn't have to hide because she already knew me.

"The things you've done, they scare me."

I whispered the words into the silence, pausing as I realized when I held my breath, the room was completely silent. She wasn't breathing. I'd been quiet too long, not wanting to leave my explanation unfinished, so I added that question to the growing pile in my mind and continued.

"But you don't scare me, I'm not afraid of you."

"Aren't they the same?"

I could taste her trepidation, feel so much was riding on my answer, yet it was easy to deliver the truth, and my reply came out on a soft half-sigh.

"No."

We lay there, still beside each other on the floor of my bathroom, the murderer, and me, though it was becoming impossible to think of her like that. I played with her hair and her eyes narrowed slightly as she leaned into my touch. Everything else slipped away until we were all that was left, until all my worry and all her torment was gone, and we were peaceful; she felt peaceful as she held me.

"Go to sleep now."

She seemed to always speak that way, commands and demands, though her voice was soft, scratchy in the back of her throat.

"Will you come back?"

I tried to keep the desperation out of my voice. I already knew she had to leave. Though she lay perfectly still beside me, I felt her emotionally peeling herself away, pulling back from me, from our little bubble of peace. It made no sense, but I knew she was putting her armor back on and this soft side of her was slipping away. She didn't answer for a long moment and my heart beat so hard I was afraid she would hear it.

She moved quickly, until she hovered over me, looking down on me, leaning on her elbow. I could have sworn in that moment the colors inside her mismatched eyes became impossibly more vivid.

Her face came closer and closer to mine, and I watched her eyes until my own fell closed.

I'd always thought the metaphor about fireworks was...well, a metaphor, but when she kissed me, I felt them, exploding in my chest, on my lips, in the pit of my stomach. Her lips pressed against mine, light at first, tentative, though it faded quickly. The emotional feedback loop between us forced my lips to part, so I could taste the moment, steal as much of her as she'd give.

Her tongue touched the inside of my lips, but the slick of it, cool and smooth, sent hotness plummeting through my veins, a heat that bounced right back to me from her. I knew she felt it too, and soon after, she pulled back, just barely.

"Tell me your name?"

My request was breathy and my lips tingled, still reliving that perfect first kiss, as she leaned down again and quickly gave me my second. Her restraint slipped, and this time her tongue pushed itself between my lips a little further.

"Scarlett."

She left the word against my ear. Her breath on the suddenly sensitive skin there made my body burn. She pulled herself away from me inhumanly fast and was gone.

I didn't hear her walk down the stairs or out of the door.

"Scarlett..." Her name tasted holy on my lips, still tasting so very faintly of whiskey and rust.

Chapter Four

SINCE THE KISS, time had moved in strange increments, flying and stalling, and I was driftwood, caught in its waves. After Scarlett's visit, my nights were sleepless.

I worried about my lack of dreams. I worried about any small and insignificant change that could signify she was disappearing out of my life. I missed her as soon as she was gone. All I had left of her was the fading ache and the single rounded puncture scar on the inside of my left wrist. But I knew her name. Before, she was a question mark, thin smoke leaving too soon on an unwanted breeze, but now, she was real, she was Scarlett.

"Miss Kennedy!"

I jumped in my seat and my cheeks flamed instantly, though I cared less than I usually would about gaining the exasperated attention of my teacher and the rest of the class.

There was a question, and he was waiting for an answer, they all were, but I was clueless. The thought of speaking in front of my suddenly large audience was horrifying but continuing to say nothing and humiliate myself further seemed worse, so reluctantly I scrabbled for my voice.

"I'm sorry, could you repeat the question?"

The words came out horribly, pitchy and broken with nerves, and there was nothing I could do but wait for it to be over. He did as I asked, and I answered easily, though it took the entire remainder of the class for the blush on my cheeks to finally die.

I ate my lunch in my usual solitude. There was no sign of Jade today. I gave up wondering if she would come, sure she'd probably found more suitable acquaintances to eat with. Like many things, it had been sort of nice while it lasted.

My thoughts drifted back to Scarlett, though the book my English class was currently deconstructing, painfully, was open on my desk. Her kiss haunted me, and I was dragged back to the way she'd looked at me, touched me, imperfect as I was, tears wet on my cheeks.

Here I was nothing, nobody, because that seemed like the safest bet. Secrets were easier kept when you had no one to share them, no one to notice the bruises or ask about the frequent absences. Somehow, I just didn't belong here, and I couldn't remember a time when I felt like I had. Perhaps before my mother died? I didn't waste my energy struggling to sieve through my memory. It didn't matter now, because with Scarlett, finally, I fit.

She was terrible. The thud of my father's body hitting the carpet, the snap of my breaking bones—I knew she was terrible, but she was everything. Nobody had ever looked at me the way she did, nobody had ever held me like she had, and I hadn't imagined they ever would. It made no sense. She was beautiful, and she was powerful, raw, yet underneath that, there was softness, almost a brokenness I tasted in her kisses, and felt radiating from her when she was still.

She was everything, and I had spent my whole life trying to be nothing. Her actions, the fact she had come to me at all, it was almost like a vote of confidence, like a wake-up call, and for the first time in my life, I wanted to step into the light, to be noticed, to mean something to her.

The thought made me ache. It filled me up until I wanted to stand up and shout out, to shed my skin, shed my invisibility cloak and somehow make myself worthy. I wanted so desperately to be good enough for Scarlett.

My mind caught between imagining her as she was after she'd drunk my blood, strong and sure and undamaged, and the way she had been when she'd staggered through the door. The thought of my father made my blood run cold. The fear of him being alive seemed illogical—he had looked dead, he had been dead in my mind for days—yet it refused to fade. Who else could have done that to her? Who could do that to her, as strong as she had felt when she was hovering over me, breaking my bones and setting them straight?

"Rayne?"

I looked up to see who had joined me.

"Hi, Jade, are you okay?"

My voice sounded bolder, even to my own ears, though I told myself I was being ridiculous. Jade looked uneasy. Her brows were pulled together, two perfectly arched lines, and she worried her lip. She perched on the table beside me, closer than I was comfortable with, though I was too caught up in what could be troubling her to move away.

She nodded and continued to hover there, wordless. I waited as long as I could stand before I spoke again, turning slightly in my seat to try to catch her eyes.

"Jade?"

Tentatively I reached out to touch her arm. When the pads of my fingers brushed her bare skin, I yanked them away. Immediately, those oddly dull, dusky eyes turned on me.

"Sorry, static shock."

My lie surprised me. My thoughts were reeling. Maybe I was imagining it. Maybe I was so caught up in Scarlett and my fascination with her that I was somehow projecting her now into my mundane school life. Maybe the air conditioning was to blame, though it was fall and I knew for a fact it wasn't on. I had no rational explanation for it.

Jade Pearce's skin was cool, tepid, the exact same temperature I remembered so vividly from Scarlett's.

The realization made my stomach churn, yet I looked at Jade and found nothing out of the ordinary. Her eyes weren't like Scarlett's, there was no blood at the corner of her lips. She was sentenced to senior year, or what was left of it, at Jaffrey High, just like the rest of us. There was no way she could be anything like Scarlett. Yet her words came back to me, her love of vampire books, and I was conflicted, fighting with what I knew and piecing together a puzzle I only had half the parts for, far too fast. I was aware of her watching me. And I knew I had been quiet too long.

Only a few seconds had passed, but I felt as if I'd spent a half hour staring at her face, my brain moving painfully slow, yet breakneck quick over all the little pieces I was either imagining or putting together totally wrong. Jade Pearce was just another girl from school, there was no way she could be like Scarlett.

"I have to go."

Her voice dragged me back to reality, back to the part of me that cared about something other than Scarlett, and all the questions that swirled around her existence and her presence in my life. Jade had seemed uneasy, sad even. Maybe she was having trouble at home, or with some of the unfavorable kids at school. All I'd done was pull away from her and then stare at her as if she had two heads.

"Jade... Wait..."

I called after her, but she didn't stop or look back. Concern bubbled up in my chest, but it was also curiosity, and I hated myself for it. The closest thing I'd had this year to a friend was clearly upset, and although I wanted to chase after her for that reason, to comfort her or help, a larger part of me wanted to go after her for another reason, a selfish one.

For the first time, I was really afraid of my own curiosity about Scarlett. I was afraid of how I let it consume me so violently that I dreamed about her at night, thought about her for most of the day, and let myself live inside the temporary reprieve her memory offered. I avoided the mounting bills, the late-night callers at the house, and dealing with my current situation now my father was dead.

Realization was like waking up, lifting my head from the sea of brilliant browns and greens that had swum in those haunting eyes on the night she walked murderous into my life, and taking a long breath.

Suddenly everything stung. Jade leaving the way she had, my father's death, the mounting bills, the men who came to the house, and the dozen voice mails on the phone I was ignoring. It all hit me at once, falling on top of me like concrete blocks. Jade walked out of the cafeteria, and I watched her go, stunned. Tears pricked my eyes.

Voices roared around me, swallowing me back into my nothingness, yet the blind comfort Scarlett's memory used to bring me was gone. I was alone in so many things, alone now every time she left, and she always seemed to leave, with never a promise to return. Tears choked me, yet the world continued on, and just as I had always wanted, nobody seemed to notice.

Jade was gone. Whether it was for the loss of an almost friend, or finally for the loss of my father, or the fear of the future, I had no idea, but the tears were coming now. They chiseled their way up through my chest and filled my eyes, red-hot and eager to pour down my cheeks, but it was no time to cry.

My book was still open on the table, and so I lowered my gaze back to its pages, quickly swiping across my lower lids and catching the drops before they could fall. I swallowed the emotion down, forcing myself to read the same sentence, forcing my eyes over the little line of black print again and again until I had myself in check.

For now, as hollow as I felt, there was nothing left to do but carry on.

THOUGHTS OF JADE Pearce followed me home, though she wasn't what worried me, not really. I was obsessed, dangerously so, and the way I had treated Jade today had painted a picture so vivid that, finally, it was impossible to ignore. I walked faster as I rounded the last bend.

My street looked the same as it always did this time of year. Leaves were falling, crimson and gold under my feet, the sun already making its descent in a cool sky. Summer was gone, and the beauty of fall had been passing me by too. I wondered what else I missed. What was happening outside my Scarlett-induced haze and where might I be when it finally lifted?

I was determined. Tonight, as uncomfortable as ending my avoidance would be, I would face reality. My sneakers crunched a trail down the leaf-littered path to the house and I ignored the smell of cannabis drifting from next-door's open window. Tonight, I would open those letters and start to plan, to carve out some kind of path for myself to move forward, to live through this, here, in reality. I needed to fix things, to fix myself, and to face the music—as terrifying as it was.

The key shook in my freezing fingers, and I paused before I put it into the lock. My father... He was dead, I was almost certain he was dead now, yet his ghost still haunted me, filling me with uncertainty. The hairs on the back of my neck stood up as I forced myself to turn the key and step inside.

I stayed still for a few uneasy breaths, my back against the thin door I'd closed audibly behind me, though my grip on the handle was still firm. If he was going to come for me, I wanted my escape route ready. Nothing moved. The hallway looked exactly the same as it had when I left this morning: faded carpet and a pair of worn-out slippers I hadn't yet tossed out.

My sigh of relief was the only sound in the silent space. Letting my hand fall away from the door, I stepped into the hall. I made a beeline for the kitchen and the responsibilities that had been calling me for days now because, finally, I was ready to answer.

All my breath left me as I was propelled backward so fast I felt like I'd been hit by a car. I braced for an impact that never came. When my back landed against the front door, careful hands cushioned me from being hurt. Her body was cool against mine even through the layers of clothing between us, and her irises danced. Everything around us was still, only my slightly heavy breathing breaking the silence.

"Scarlett..."

I breathed her name, half question, half celebration.

"Rayne..."

My name sounded magical on her lips. It sounded like flying and falling, sweet and sticky and rich, and it clung to her tongue like treacle. My heartbeat started to even out after the surprise of finding her, then the realization she was really here settled, and set it racing all over again. She watched me intently as always, and suddenly, I had no idea what to say.

"Hi..."

I knew the greeting was lame, and her expression broke just barely. The faintest hint of a smile played on her red lips, this time colored by lipstick, not blood. The beginnings of a blush were starting to creep up my neck, though I tried to force it away, remembering my earlier conversation with myself, about who I wanted to be. She seemed to notice. The fingers behind my head slid down past my ear, tumbling down the column of my neck, making my breath catch, until they settled cool around my throat as if she was about to choke me.

My body belonged to her so easily and it scared me. I relaxed under her hand, which made no sense given how vulnerable it left me, given what I had seen her do to my father. Scarlett seemed pleased by my willingness to let her touch me. She flexed her fingers ever so slightly and the colors in her eyes accelerated in response. Finally, the first twinges of fear found me.

Fear was just a conditioned response. I knew she wouldn't hurt me, not now. I couldn't place her mood, but I didn't feel threatened. I swallowed audibly, and panicked, sure she heard me. Her intense questioning over my fear of her came back to haunt me. I needed her to stay. Tilting my chin ever so slightly, I steeled my nerves as, inch by inch, I let my head fall backward until it rested against the door.

For the first time since I'd gotten home, I felt her breathe. Cool air fanned over my skin, goose bumps rose over the tops of my arms, and warmth flooded through me. I should have been afraid. Last time she bit me had hurt, and not just because of the broken bones. I watched her, forcing myself not to hold my breath to wait for the moment she might lunge for me like she had my father. She wanted to.

The feeling that had been growing, swelling between us, finally broke over me, and her, and all at once, I knew we both knew she wanted to.

"You can..."

I hadn't meant to whisper the words, I hadn't meant to say them at all, but she wanted me, and she was so much to be wanted by.

"Why?"

When she spoke, I studied her mouth, trying to catch a glimpse of fangs. I saw nothing and had no answer to her question. I stayed still, my back against the door, my neck exposed to her, while I trawled my brain for an answer that wouldn't make her think I was insane.

"You saved me."

I would have given her this even if she hadn't. Somehow, I felt as if I would give her anything. I regretted not being more honest, yet the truth was embarrassing at best and ridiculously hard to explain.

"I just...want you to."

I didn't understand my own willingness to be hurt once again, but I wanted to give her my blood. She wanted it, me, and I wanted her to have me. She was conflicted, torn somehow, by my reasoning. I didn't want her to be confused. I wanted her close to me.

"I want you to have me."

It came out rushed and breathy. Tears pricked at the backs of my eyes. I wanted desperately to be acceptable for her, to explain this just right, and make her satisfied. Pearled teeth sunk into a plump bottom lip, and I was certain her irises were changing faster, the colors mixing and swirling and spilling into one another as she leaned closer.

Her teeth were cool against my neck and I fought a flinch when they touched me. I felt nothing out of the ordinary, just her cool tongue and a smooth hardness I assumed was teeth. She mouthed my neck, applying barely any pressure, let alone enough to break the skin, before the motion faded into cool, wet kisses that made me squirm on the inside.

"You want to be mine?"

Her voice was undiluted now, rich and bitter, thick as tar yet heavy with gravel. The question could mean so many things, but it didn't matter. The answer spilled up from the very deepest part of my chest, ricocheting off the inside of my ribcage until it touched every part of me.

"Yes."

The seconds after my breathy, broken answer were charged, brimming over and bursting with static. Her irises spun so fast and I sensed the profoundness of my answer to her and, growing beneath it, something that felt frenzied and frantic to me. Whatever it was, it consumed Scarlett. I didn't question how I knew this, but I did, and when she lunged for me, this time, I was ready.

Her kisses were cool but firm. The gentleness of the night before was gone, and I was her puppet. Her slim fingers tilted my chin toward her and her tongue slicked sure, certain, across my lower lip. There was no time to think or to plan. She was the driver now, but my body seemed to know what to do, and I pressed my lips back against hers, though that only seemed to deepen the frenzy.

One cool hand had slid down from the small of my back and come to rest much lower. The pads of her fingers strayed dangerously close to the seam running down the back of my jeans, following it between my thighs. Nobody had ever touched me there, and her mere proximity sent heat exploding behind my eyes, in the back of my throat, the pit of my stomach, and, to my embarrassment, between my legs.

"Not tonight, Princess."

It was almost as if she could hear my thoughts, taste my mood the same way I could feel hers. The embarrassment that she knew didn't linger long, and neither did the misplaced rejection that sprung up with her denial. I wasn't ready—it was less than a month since she'd given me my first kiss.

"Are you a virgin?"

She spilled the question into my collarbone, strong fingers still holding my chin as she kissed along the neckline of my shirt, making my head spin. I tried to nod; my head still pushed back against the door, but I knew she caught the attempt. She purred her approval against my skin. I should be scared, or at least out of my depth. Scarlett was older than me—my best guess was twenty-seven, maybe older still—she was undoubtedly more experienced with being intimate, and there was the small matter of her being a blood-drinking murderer who was enquiring about my virginity, yet I wasn't afraid.

She was all I felt. The odd feedback loop between us filled me up, branching out behind my now-closed eyes, seeping into every corner of my brain. I couldn't think about anything but her, the weight of her body against me, and those kisses, cool as summer rain on my burning skin. Pain pulled me back momentarily, and as I watched her, I realized I hadn't even noticed her raising my wrist to her lips.

She watched me again, swirling eyes on my face now her mouth was fastened to my wrist at the same lopsided angle it had been the first time. I wanted to ask her why she didn't set her mouth flush against me, but the tide moved out and the drag was uncomfortable, making my chest tingle when she reached the very end. It only let up when the pulling stopped and she swallowed. I didn't trust myself to speak.

The action felt sacred, and I was strangely quiet, reverent, as I watched her watch me while she took what she wanted. She was beautiful, like a car crash, bloody and taboo, the same kind of horrific you knew you should look away from but somehow, just couldn't. The hand not holding my wrist had slid from my chin and settled against my cheek, and I leaned into her touch, a softness seeping into our exchange that stayed until she was done.

I winced when she pulled back, catching only a second's worth of a glimpse at the blood from the spot on my wrist that had been a scar just a half hour ago. Again, she raised her finger to her mouth, and I saw a spot of crimson there too before she pressed it against the wound. It burned like a match to my skin. The burn stopped quickly, and I knew the puncture would be healed.

Before the fear she would leave again could really settle, the solid wood of the door was gone from my back, replaced for a brief second by gravity, before I was back against something that felt equally cool, but softer, as Scarlett held me against her chest. We ascended the thinly carpeted stairs of the only home I'd ever had, faster than I ever had before. I clung to her, one hand fisted in the thin fabric of her dress, the other hooked over a slender shoulder, cloaked in the same leather jacket she'd worn the night she saved my life.

"Not that one..."

The words came out so quiet I worried she hadn't heard me, but we didn't linger any longer in front of the closed door leading to my father's room. Scarlett said nothing on the matter, carrying me down the small hall and stepping into my room. I was immediately embarrassed.

The old quilt my mom had made for me sat messily over my twin bed, all gingham and flowers and six-year-old girl. My underwear drawer hung open, and the star-stenciled walls of my childhood were all there, laid out for those dazzling eyes to see. Next to her, I was so ordinary, and so was my life—my room, hardly changed over the years, half because no one cared to decorate with me after my mom died, and half because I didn't want to alter the room she had made up for me. My room was my inner sanctum, and so unexpectedly, it was host to the most fascinating person I'd ever met.

Scarlett said nothing, though the amused little smile was back on her lips, and I knew my cheeks were flaming. She set me down on the bed carefully, and as soon as she stepped away, I missed her contact. Her back was to me as she unabashedly looked around the small space. I cringed inwardly, dread rising as I tried to follow her line of sight, trying to see which personal little piece of me was being turned over by those eyes so far removed from my mundane world.

"I... I just never really... I haven't had a chance to redecorate it since—"

I was tired of tripping horribly over my words. No excuse or explanation would hide it or change it, and I felt like the little girl this room was decorated for, young, plain, and naive against the backdrop of her magnificence. My age hadn't seemed to bother her during any of our encounters, and I hoped desperately this wouldn't make it arise as a problem between us now.

"It feels like you."

She seemed amused still, but the words didn't sound mocking. Either way, I was relieved when she climbed onto the bed beside me. Not only was she finally focused back on something other than my bedroom, but it seemed she would stay, and this time, I hadn't had to ask.

I shuffled over, my back pressed against the wall beside my bed as she laid down and reached out for me, in one fluid motion.

We lay there for a while, quiet, and I bathed in her presence, drunk on the gift of being this close to her. The ease with which I existed beside her surprised me again, and I wondered when it would stop. Her body was cool next to me, her arm strong around my waist, like a shield. She was effectively holding me down, but it felt as if she was holding the rest of the world away, and I liked that without questioning or second guessing myself.

Fingers had been tracing shapes against my waist, and they caught my attention as they moved, resurrecting the wanting that had burned through my body by the door. I shivered as they dipped below the thin cotton of my shirt, touching my bare skin. She enjoyed taunting me, playing with me like this, and I let her, though this time I was determined not to completely fall apart under the bidding of the very tips of her fingers.

I had so many questions, and now seemed as good a time as any to start seeking out answers, though part of me was still cautious. Scarlett had chosen to stay, and that meant so much, yet it still felt fragile, like one wrong word could send her away.

"Last time..."

I broached the subject carefully, hating how loud my voice sounded as it broke the silence. She pressed against me, her chin resting on my shoulder as she laid half on her side, seeming perfectly content there, just looking at me. When the topic brought no negative reaction, I continued with the question that had troubled me most.

"You were hurt, did my father do that to you...? Is he...alive?"

My voice sounded flat, and I wondered for a second if she would find me cold, think me a monster for not caring more, but I just didn't. He had died a long time ago for me, and all that was left was relief the unpleasant encounters with him had come to an end. She was still relaxed beside me, her presence almost feline, and for a second, I imagined if she could, she'd be purring while I twisted my fingers through the ends of her hair.

"He's dead."

She delivered the news, her inflection as emotionless as she'd been when she murdered him. My only response was a nod. The relief was back, and wrong or right, I liked it much better than the fear of before.

"Are you sure?"

I had to ask, and she leaned in closer, her lips pressing soft against the lobe of my ear.

"Trust me. He's dead."

I turned slightly, burrowing closer to her, and she pulled me in. Testing, I let the arm that had been pressed against the wall reach out, my hand settling in the dip of her waist, the same way hers had earlier. She didn't protest, kissing the corner of my mouth, and then closing her eyes. I took it as a sign I wasn't getting any further answer, but still, I was curious.

"What happened to you?"

I let my fingers trace the curve of her hip. Her eyes opened lazily, one green, one brown, to study my face. She was uncomfortable with the subject now, which seemed strange given we'd just addressed the murderous elephant in the room with ease. Her tongue slicked across her lip, and I noticed the way her lipstick had faded, wondering momentarily if it was smeared across my mouth.

"I got into a scuffle, nothing I couldn't handle."

Her eyebrows arched, and that amusement played on her face again, only this time, it read false. She was hurt, seriously hurt, at least that's how it had looked to me.

"Who hurt you?"

The curiosity faded into concern and I stilled my fingers against the thin fabric of her dress, silently awed by my own brave persistence. When things were difficult, uncomfortable, or caused me embarrassment, I was a notorious bailer. Lying there, tangled up with a woman who could be anything from five to ten years older than me, whose eyes moved inhumanly, who had killed my father, I was suddenly committed. My long-lost conviction finally found me. Maybe up until this point, I had just never cared about anything enough?

As hard as I tried, Scarlett kept her eyes carefully away from mine, and I wondered what she was hiding, and why this subject was so sore for her.

"They're dead now, so what does it matter?"

The words came from her lips so suddenly they made me jump. Her tone was cooler than her skin, hard and unfeeling, each word clipped, tiny bullets spewed out to chase me away. What drove her to be so sore about being hurt? Pride?

"It doesn't. I just don't like the thought of anyone..."

I paused for a second, my mind automatically taking me back to the bathroom and the way my stomach had seemed to fall out of my body at the sight the blood, the way she staggered, the crack in her cheek...

"I can't think about you hurt."

It was my turn to look away. My emotions were so powerful around her, it made me feel alive, as if I'd spent the last six years dormant, sedated, and suddenly, I felt everything. Tears glazed my eyes ever so slightly, but I knew she would see them no matter how hard I tried to hide.

"So don't..."

It was a command at first, and she caught my chin in her slim fingers again and turned my head back to her easily until we were face to face and I could feel her softening.

"Don't..."

The word was a whisper and she kissed me, tenderly this time, slowly, a gesture I had no idea how to return or even decipher, so I clung to her until once again we were just lying there, facing each other on my single pillow.

She was the moon, and I was the tide; when she moved, I moved. My emotions were reactive to hers, and I could feel mine were palpable to her, though I had no idea how strongly. Silence had always been a welcome thing to me; awful things barely happened in silence, and I was grateful she seemed to enjoy it the same way. At school, there were awkward silences, pregnant silences, expectant silences, but with Scarlett, it was easy, almost as easy as it was to be silent all by myself.

My mind still worked quietly in the background, mulling over her answers, or lack of them. She was a complex puzzle. Outwardly she looked so assembled, intimidating under her heavy makeup, and her showy dark clothing, but beneath, something else simmered. I could taste her power in our kisses sometimes, when her fingers were just a little too tight around my throat. I caught glimpses of her brokenness, when she lingered half out of the door, inexplicably afraid to stay. She was a puzzle, and I sensed pieces were missing, and some were broken, bowed under whatever weight made that heaviness live deep inside her eyes.

"What are you?"

The question formed in my head and fell from my lips in perfect synchronization. It didn't matter. She was the most complex being I had ever met, her depth was like the ocean, and the mass of the entire world existed again, a hundred times over, unknown and untouched below her surface. She was beautiful, and I was fascinated. I ached to know her story, to hear it laid out for me in words, not just to taste its flavor like I did.

"What do you think I am?"

Her reply was unhurried and unfazed.

I had to choose my words carefully.

"I met a girl at school, Jade, and she reads a lot of vampire books, and I just... I'm not exactly sure, but it...made me wonder..."

There was no delicate way to phrase it, and I hoped whatever glorious, blood-drinking, murdering, unnaturally cold and strong thing she was, didn't have a strict code for political correctness that listed the word "vampire" as a no-no.

Scarlett smiled at me, a reaction I hadn't been expecting. The fondness in her eyes was hard to miss, and it felt almost as if she was proud.

"And do you think Jade is smart, or do you think she's crazy?"

She tapped enquiring fingers against my side, demanding an answer.

"You drink my blood, your skin is cool, you're strong, beautiful..."

The last word made me blush, but I pushed on.

"The only thing I ever heard of to come close to that description is a...vampire."

She seemed to consider for a moment before she nodded.

"Yet you're still not afraid?"

It was an observation and a question. My heart picked up again, my palms tingled. The edges of my consciousness were fuzzy and ridiculously clear all at once with the confirmation, with finding out something more than just plain old human beings existed. I wasn't afraid. I reached up and touched her face, proud of myself, because finally, I felt like I was getting something right—maybe I was just drunk on this strange new discovery.

Scarlett let me draw circles around her chin for only a few seconds before she swatted my hand away. I sensed her mood darkening.

"You know what I eat, but do you know anything else?"

Now I was nervous.

"I don't know how old you are..."

"Twenty-eight."

Her reply was matter-of-fact, and it was clear that being ten years my senior meant nothing to her; the news weighed a little heavier with me, but not because it was negative. It was just another facet of the sum of all this, and as I had with every other piece of our relationship, I needed time to analyze it, to weigh it in my mind and add it to the picture all these facts and encounters and feelings painted of us.

"How long have you been twenty-eight?"

She smirked, and I was relieved at some small break in the tension, a parting of the dark clouds, though the reprieve was temporary. She didn't answer, at least not in reply to my question.

"I'm not like your books and your movies here. I'm not the tortured soul who longs for humanity, I'm not meek or lost, or obsessed with my own mortality...or lack of it."

She'd lost me, switching tracks across a course I hadn't followed, and I didn't know how to reply. I felt her waiting for my understanding, but when it never came, she continued.

"I'm not...good. I don't sleep in a coffin, or turn into a bat, there's nothing romantic about what I am, the things I do, the things I'm capable of. I passed by your neighborhood at the right time, I smelled a buffet, and you were too pretty to kill... I'm nobody's hero."

A little piece of me fractured. For me, the moment was so profound, it was the collision, the beginning, and the end, and to hear her diminish it like that, to strip it down to almost nothing, hurt. Her words stung me, and I knew they would stay with me, long after she left again as she inevitably would.

"I'm different, you've never met anyone like me, but that will fade, and then me sinking my teeth into you won't feel the same, it won't be romantic, it won't make you feel extraordinary. It will just be a chore, and I'll just be a monster."

All her conviction seemed to be spent, traded in the end for what sounded like her resigning herself.

"Some things aren't yours to take away."

It rushed out of me and sounded angrier than I had meant to allow.

"You can tell me what you are, and about the things you do... But you can't tell me how I'll feel."

I pulled away from her slightly, resolved to keep staring at the same spot on her collarbone, but something forced my eyes up to meet hers.

"I'm...ordinary, and for you, this might not be the same, but you're not a monster. I've seen you do monstrous things, but you're more. You can try to convince me to see you in the way you want me to, but you can't tell me how I will feel, or how I do, because that's mine."

I paused, slightly winded from my outburst.

"You're like nothing I've ever known, for reasons far more than you're weirdly cold and like O negative more than OJ."

Finally, I caught a hold of myself. A blush threatened to color my cheeks.

Scarlett was quiet for a long time, and I lay still, refusing to bend or buckle or apologize because that would be insincere. I had meant every word and I forced myself to stand by them, even though fear she was about to get up and disappear from my life for good crawled down my spine again, making it hard not to do something to make her stay.

She kissed me without warning. Her lips were frantic at first, though they settled until they were no longer trying to mold mine or control them, but just existing alongside them. I matched her kisses, gentle, slow. Finally, I was learning to kiss her back. I could feel her smiling against my mouth.

"I've never met anyone like you either."

That was the only concession she made, the only inch she gave in what had unexpectedly become a game of push and pull between us before all my anger had died a cool death to her kisses, fire yielding to ice. She threaded her fingers through my hair and something about the motion forced me to relax. Our comfortable silence returned, and I welcomed it, content with the progress we'd made somewhere amongst her words and mine.

She kissed me from time to time, just dragging me back from the edges of sleep, yet as hard as I tried to fight, it beckoned me. I wanted to stay and live in this moment with her for as long as I could, but I was drifting.

"Go to sleep, Princess." Her voice floated to me from somewhere close yet far. "I won't be far away."

Chapter Five

LOOKING BACK, I wish I had known. Those last few moments with her were so precious, and over the days that had bled into weeks, I was devoured by the regret that I wasted even a second of them. She had lulled me into such a sense of safety, security, and her final words stayed with me, emblazoned in my mind. "I won't be far away." Once upon a time, they were a promise, glowing soft and warm, a dream to fall asleep to. Now, I didn't know if she was a liar.

It was exactly two weeks and a day since I'd last heard from Scarlett, and in that time, things had begun to fall apart. My life was spilling open at the seams, and everything, the good, the bad, the poison and the remedy, it was all pouring out, drowning me.

The knocks at the door from my father's former benefactors became bricks through the windows. The letters piled high and the list of things I couldn't explain to the rest of the world had outgrown my optimism. I was out of my depth, and worse than all that, Scarlett had left me. If she really was close by, I couldn't understand how or why she was watching me suffer.

My eyes were red as I sat in the tub again, staring at the splintered door still half hung on its hinges. It was real, something concrete that proved all of this, *she*, was more than just a dream. I could still feel her; at least I thought I could. Our connection was muffled now, like a long-distance call on a single bar of cell service, so faint that some days I questioned if we even had one at all.

I missed her. I ached for the safety of her embrace and the etherealness she brought to my life. With her, my life was elevated above the ordinary, and my everyday suffering, and the mounting problems I had no fixes for. I'd felt as if I had an answer, a reason to endure, to live through this. Without her I was alone, and I was terrified.

I fell through life. School was the same mind-numbing mundane affair it had always been. I pulled my invisibility cloak tight around me and it grew more heartbreaking each day when nobody noticed how broken I really was.

My gaze drifted to the dirty mirror above the sink and I recoiled. I didn't want to see myself. I'd watched the girl inside that mirror for so many years, seen her grow from the mere top of a pale head to the sad and sallow thing with another inexplicable black eye. I hadn't been lucky enough to catch a glimpse of her more recently, with a beautiful woman beside her and knowledge very few people possessed making her look light, all her apathy gone, the comfort of an arm around her waist letting her finally dare to feel.

I couldn't sit there any longer. Scarlett was everywhere, the spot where she had stood bloody in the doorway, the splintered wood that had caved at her demand, the place she had laid down with me, and the hallway I imagined she'd used when she walked out of my life. Yet she was nowhere.

I got up and ran. The stairs came faster than I trusted myself to take them, but I did. All thought for the unwanted visitors who might hear me or be waiting for me was gone. I stepped right through what was once a glass door but was just an empty frame since I'd fallen through and shattered it, and out the front door into the street.

Before I stopped myself, I stood on the sidewalk, trying to decide on a direction, looking for a sign, as lost in my unplanned venture to find her as I was in my entire life. Just like the answers, Scarlett eluded me.

The bottom of my lungs hurt and my heart beat against my ribcage, knocking the breath out of me from the inside. I vibrated, nervous, terrified, furious energy working its way through me. I wanted to scream and let it all out, to tear her out of me and away from me. I took a deep breath, tears in my eyes. I just wanted her to come back.

It took too long for me to feel the cold. The sun had been down for hours, but time was lost to me. It simply didn't matter—ten seconds or ten hours, they all felt the same, the dull ache in my chest didn't have a quitting time, it didn't respect bedtime or Sundays, it was constant. Part of me was grateful it never let me forget her. Shivering felt good, like some kind of release or punishment or maybe just a new way to suffer. I stood there until I was so cold it hurt.

Sirens wailed, nothing unusual for my neighborhood after dark. Just like my father, the area had decayed terribly in the years since my mother's death.

My mom. I wondered what she would think of me now, what she would think of Scarlett, and why everyone who seemed to care about me left me behind? It was a selfish thought and I knew it, but that moment of self-awareness was enough for me to force life into my frozen limbs and walk back toward the house.

Thick fog was all around me. Though I couldn't see it, or touch it with my fingertips, it hung viscous around my temples and my limbs. My every movement felt slow and forced, an uphill struggle to wade through thick tentacles that refused to let me go. I made it to my room, but before I could lie down, I saw her in my mind, lying on my bed, her swirling eyes on me and the amused little smirk on her lips. I turned and stormed away. I headed for the bathroom, too afraid to sleep downstairs and unwilling to go into my father's room.

The tears came before I made it through the door, and I let them, because what else was left to do?

I couldn't carry on, not like this, not without her. I sunk down, pathetic, my back against the tub, my head on my hands, and I spilled my guts. I cried until I couldn't breathe, couldn't cry anymore.

I cried for my mother, for her death and for her absence in my life. I cried for myself, for my sad half-life and for the lost glimpse I'd had of something more. I cried for all my fear, the letters that continued to come through the door, and the men who came after them. I cried for Scarlett, for the strange instant connection that terrified and bound me to her, for her to come back to me and for her to have never left. I cried until the tears ran out and my energy ran dry and finally, for the first time in days, I fell asleep, where I simply ceased to exist.

THE REPRIEVE WAS short lived. I woke to the sound of glass breaking downstairs, another uninvited visitor come to torment me. I knew it wasn't Scarlett, she moved too easily, and she had never been so careless, insensitive, maybe.

Pain seared in my neck, my temples, as I sat bolt upright, peering out into the darkness of the hall, my hands groping the linoleum beneath me for something, anything, to use as a weapon. The rocks through the downstairs windows had been anything but subtle, the visits had been getting more frequent, and the threats called to my father through the crack in the old front door more violent. I was sure if it was the men who were after their money, by now, they wanted more than just that.

Someone moved downstairs. The shuffle of their feet over the carpet, the occasional bump, sounds floated up, my senses hyperalert, my heart beating fast. Moving as soundlessly as I knew how, I slid across the bathroom floor. All the fog of that glorious sleep was lost on me as I shimmied back against the wall, behind what was left of the broken bathroom door.

My best hope at this point was they would take what they wanted and leave. I thought briefly of my possessions and was both relieved and saddened to realize I had nothing worth taking, not to them anyway. Cool air tickled me from the broken windows downstairs. I hadn't known how to repair them and hadn't dared to turn on the heat and add to the already growing bill pile. The hairs on my arms stood on end but not because of the cold. Footsteps were on the stairs and I leaned my head back against the wall, closing my eyes and fighting to keep my breaths even, quiet.

Fear should have been swallowing me. Maybe I should have tried to get out of the house, tried the phone to call the police if it wasn't disconnected already. I was afraid, but I was resigned, and I wasn't sure what was more frightening.

My own capacity to adjust, just to live, to breathe, through the most of dire of situations had always been high, but lately, it had grown a life of its own. The footsteps were in the hall now, just like the murderer had been in my house, and the vampire in my bed, and somehow, I existed still.

The footsteps stopped, and I waited in the dark, my eyes squeezed closed, my arms clasped around my middle, holding myself together in yet another impossible situation. Hope surprised me, rising from the pit of my stomach, a phoenix from the ashes. If Scarlett really was close, if she still cared about me at all, she had saved me before, and now would be the time to come back and save me again.

Shoes scuffling against carpet turned to soles moving sticky over the linoleum. They walked until they came to a stop, directly in front of me. I was found, and too afraid to open my eyes.

Silence. There was nothing but silence, and it took me too long to realize I was holding my breath. Scarlett wasn't coming. She had left me alone to my fate, just like my mother before her. There was nothing left. I opened my eyes.

Everything was faded in the dark, and my eyes adjusted too slowly. The legs in front of me were slender, slimmer than the burly, jean-clad ones I expected, and too long. My gaze traveled up, my blood running hot then cold as I squinted to make out the form of a decidedly feminine torso in the light, before I finally looked up to the intruder's face. It took a few more seconds of blinking and waiting for my eyes to adjust before, finally, I saw her. I was overcome with relief and uncertainty.

"Jade?"

Nerves shredded my voice, her name two octaves too high and fear-broken.

Jade Pearce stood in my bathroom, looming over me like a nightmare, not the benign and oddly persistent girl I'd met at school.

"What are you doing here?"

The words spilled out, relief took over, and everything in me relaxed too fast, though the adrenaline hangover still made me want to vomit.

"Are you okay? Are you in trouble?"

I forced myself to a shaky stand and brushed my palms over my jeans, suddenly conscious of my appearance. The violation of her appearing like this inside my house of secrets was starting to register. She barely moved, I couldn't even see her breathing, she just stood there in front of me, eerily still, framed by the dim moonlight filtering through the dirty window. Finally, she seemed to come back to the situation, or snap out of whatever thought she'd been caught in.

"I'm fine... Well, actually, I'm not, it's complicated."

I nodded, stepping closer to her so I could see her face. The same concern that was written on her features before she had disappeared from school was still there, only now it was amplified, playing heavy at the corners of her lips, in her eyes.

"You haven't been in school..."

I stopped myself before I started to pry. I'd been on the receiving end of those kinds of questions, much less than I probably should have been, but enough to know they did no good.

I wasn't ready for anyone to see this side of my life, the house where I was at the mercy of my father for so many years. Where his ghost chased me in the form of debts and unfinished business, the house where I was with Scarlett.

Jade wrung her hands and shifted her weight in a way that told me she too was hardly comfortable with the situation either.

"Do you want a drink, I have...some soda somewhere, or water?"

My hostess attempts were lame at best, but I had no idea what else to do. I hadn't had anyone over to my house since I was eight years old, and this hardly felt like a slumber party situation. Jade shook her head, a sad smile flickering to life on her previously unreadable face, though it didn't stay long.

I ached to make her feel better, to set her at ease, yet I had no idea where to start. She seemed so different than the inquisitive girl who had sat down with me at lunch. All her expensive clothes were gone, traded for dark jeans and a thin black sweater that looked too big for her lean frame.

"You must be freezing, the heat is...broken."

I automatically reached to touch her arm in apology, though she moved when I moved and my fingertips brushed over the back of her hand. Once again, her skin was the same tepid temperature that belonged only to Scarlett. The familiarity set my mind reeling, though I forced it out of my mind. I wouldn't let Jade down again for the sake of the woman who had so obviously forsaken me.

She looked at me strangely, expectantly, and I had no idea what to say to her.

"Rayne..."

She reached up and tucked her long dark hair back behind her ear, turning away from me ever so slightly, so the moon lit half of her face. That was the moment I saw it.

The pale light caught her eye, the luminescence drawing me to look, dragging me in until I took a step forward. I couldn't care that I was staring because my heart missed two beats, and I could hardly breathe. Three seconds later, I was sure. Jade's eyes were alive, the irises moving, swirling, all their lackluster dusky brown gone, replaced by twin hazel orbs exactly like Scarlett's. Her voice faltered slightly when she spoke.

"Don't...freak out..."

I took a step back and Jade took a step forward, though she stumbled over a piece of the splintered doorframe and fell right at me. I caught her taller form on instinct, all the turmoil over those inhuman eyes gone, forgotten as I continued holding her tight, even after she steadied herself.

"Are you okay?"

I scanned her for any sign of injury, relieved when I found none. I reached up and tucked the hair that had fallen in her face back behind her ear. It wasn't until the gesture was complete and I was pulling my hand away that I realized

I had acted with so much assumed familiarity, and my cheeks flamed. It was completely and utterly unlike me.

"I'm fine, I'm fine, just—"

"Clumsy."

We said the word in unison, prompting a brief smile, a momentary breath of a laugh on both sides, before we became somber again under the weight of the situation.

"You know what I am."

Jade sounded nervous, but her words were a statement, not a question.

I thought for a second before I gave my answer. Jade Pearce didn't seem like something to fear, but even in her absence, Scarlett was my most precious thing, and I would do anything to avoid betraying her. There were no signs of malice or contempt in her face. Hazel eyes were heavy on mine as she waited, and finally, I nodded.

"Do you know who I am?"

Just ten minutes ago, she'd been my unexpected lunch partner, the girl who seemed to actually like books as much as I did, the strangely ethereal and oddly beautiful new transfer student at Jaffrey High, but now, she was a stranger.

"No..."

Sadness colored my voice even though I hadn't intended to let it. Jade's expression cracked, and finally, she moved, tucking back her hair, chewing on her lip, looking just like the girl I'd met just a few weeks ago.

"Look, Rayne, I'm sorry. I didn't mean to lie. I mean, I just—"

I wondered how on earth she could be like Scarlett. The woman I remembered was so sure, her every word felt carefully chosen and perfectly delivered, made by design for its exact purpose. Scarlett was strong and sure and pure raw power, and Jade Pearce stood before me, beautiful, yes, but clumsy, struggling over her words, so flawed, in Scarlett's shadow.

"Your eyes..." I spoke the words as I thought them. "At school, they were brown...just plain old brown."

"Contacts."

Slender shoulders rose in an apologetic shrug, and I had a thousand questions, but Jade spoke again.

"You know Scarlett."

A pang of something catapulted through my chest, hot and unfamiliar to me. It took me a second to recognize it as jealousy.

Scarlett was mine, my most private and most treasured thing, and to find now that someone else knew her, spoke her name with such ease, such familiarity, it set my teeth on edge. I wanted to rip Scarlett's name away from Jade, because she was still just another girl at school, another face in the cafeteria, and nothing from that place was supposed to taint this. Scarlett was my dream, nobody else's.

I nodded stiffly, curiosity, desperation for any information on where she might be, as well as my inherent inability to be impolite, propelling me to answer.

"You haven't seen her for a while, have you?"

Jade's statement bled into a question at the last moment, almost as if she was confirming something she already knew. I shook my head, dumbstruck, and wondered who the hell she really was, and what she wanted with me or Scarlett.

Dark hair danced just past her shoulders as she nodded at my response, her eyes on the linoleum, avoiding my gaze, and I sensed she was choosing her words carefully.

Some barely conscious part of my brain wondered if my face looked as comical as I thought it might, a horror reel rewound and replayed right in front of my eyes, leaving me with a conclusion that seemed apocalyptic now. Jade Pearce had come to school the day after Scarlett first came to me, talking about vampires and tragedy and *Romeo and Juliet*. She'd disappeared shortly after Scarlett had, and now she was here having broken into my house in the middle of the night, asking me questions about the other woman.

"Is she... Is Scarlett your...your—?"

I swallowed dumbly because I couldn't find the word. I had no words for what Scarlett was to me, except one— everything. This was an answer I didn't want to find. Maybe ignorance could be bliss. Maybe if I escaped now, I could unsee this, unfinish the puzzle and go back to a world where Scarlett was still mine, at least in my head.

Jade waited for me to finish, her perfect brows bowed in confusion. I couldn't stand to look at her for another second. She was everything I would never be. With the contacts gone, she was truly stunning: high cheekbones, plump lips, shimmering hazel eyes and an air of decidedness about her I knew I would never possess. Why would Scarlett want me, choose me, over that? I was just her buffet, like she said.

Tears rushed to my eyes and all my politeness was gone, cored out of the very deepest part of me, and replaced with red-hot hurt and anger. My sneakers squeaked against the linoleum as I turned and made for the doorway.

"Rayne?"

Her voice chased me, and I just wanted her to disappear. She could say my name, scream it until she was hoarse, but I never wanted to hear her say Scarlett's again.

"Rayne..."

Something compelled me to stop, to turn and go back, to tell her everything would be fine, and I wouldn't leave her, but the fire in my chest was stronger, burning everything it touched, so I continued.

Hearing her footsteps on the stairs behind me, I worried she might fall and take me with her, sending us both tumbling down into the hall below, but I kept running.

"Rayne... Stop, just wait, I can take you to her."

I told myself it was lies. Maybe Scarlett had disappeared from Jade's life too, and that's why she was here, to steal all my memories and grind them down and sift through them for information, then leave me here, without Scarlett, without anything.

I tripped but managed not to fall, my fingers already reaching for the handle of the front door. I had no idea where I'd go. It was the middle of the night, I had school tomorrow, and town was covered by a heavy freeze, but none of that mattered. I just had to get away.

The brass was cold under my hands, but before I turned the handle cool fingers were on mine. I yelped in surprise because she had caught up the length of the hall unnaturally fast. Clumsy as she was, Jade didn't seem capable of such rapid movement.

"Please, just stop?"

Her voice was pleading, apologetic, and I had no idea why, because with her fingers closed over mine in a vise grip, her body pinning me against the door, I had no choice anyway.

"Let me explain, just let me explain."

I heard her take a deep breath and callously wondered why she bothered to breathe. Scarlett did so very intermittently.

"Scarlett... She's my sister. My big sister, she's nine years older than me. We live together with my parents, she buys me books, and it was because of me that we came here... Because I wanted to go to school."

Jade's mouth kept moving, and I realized she was pouring out facts, anything she could think of, information and truths, throwing me whatever pieces of their life together came to mind, so I might actually believe her. Somehow, I already did.

"Your sister?"

I repeated the words back in a whisper, and Jade nodded, relief evident on her face.

"Her name is Scarlett Pearce, and she's my sister. I came here to find you, for her."

"Scarlett sent you?"

The hope that riddled my voice was disgusting, and I knew it was painted all over my face too, but I couldn't make myself care enough to try to hide it. She hadn't left me. She wanted me.

Jade's face fell, and I knew all that hope was misplaced.

"Not exactly... She misses you, though... I know she does. She needs you, she needs a reason... Just... If I said I can take you to her, would you come?"

My brain scrabbled to catch up, trying to process all the information and deal with the unexpected question that sounded almost like a proposition. I felt dumb as I stood there and stared.

Seconds passed, and finally, Jade seemed to take pity on me.

"I don't have long, we don't have long."

Her tongue slicked over her lips before she spoke again. When she did, her voice was strong, though I sensed she was hiding her discomfort, maybe even fear.

"Do you love my sister?"

I continued to stare blankly at her, and finally, I nodded. Whether Scarlett cared for me at all, as far as I knew, for as much as I knew of love, I loved her for all the minutes she was here, and through every painful minute, she was gone.

"Yes."

The admission was quiet, but it rung like a gunshot, resounding, ricocheting around my head. I'd never said I loved anyone, not like this, not in my entire life.

"She needs you..."

Jade was pleading with me and I had no idea why.

"If I take you to Vires... Everything will change, you'll be in danger, and things are so... It works differently. But Scarlett is powerful, and she'll protect you."

My mind worked overtime trying to connect all the dots, to follow the trail of breadcrumbs Jade was laying out before me, but there was still so much I didn't understand.

"What do you mean, different? Where is...Vires?"

I panicked, yet relief sent hot adrenaline flooding through my limbs. I hardly knew anything about this girl, about the place she spoke of, even about Scarlett herself, yet I knew I was going with her.

Jade shook her head, making it clear we were out of time.

"You'll take me to her, tonight?"

A sense of self-assurance rang in my voice and I knew I was passing the last exit, the point of no return, because if Scarlett was the destination, I would follow Jade Pearce wherever she was going.

"Yes."

The answer was simple, and it was enough.

Finally, Jade stepped back, her cool hand falling away from mine. It was only then I realized we had been standing so close, so easily inside each other's personal space for longer than I should have been comfortable with. This was it, I'd dreamed of this day for years, and now, I was leaving this house, this town.

"All right."

I nodded, half to my company, half to myself and turned to open the door, though Jade stopped me before I could.

"Wait... Don't you want to get anything to bring with us? It can't be more than a backpack, but Rayne, where we're going... I don't know if... I don't know when you'll be able to come back."

She sounded apologetic, her voice low and careful, and it reminded me of the doctors when they told my father my mom was finally dying. Sadness crept up, unbidden, twisting around me and swallowing me up for a second. For better or for worse, this was my home; upstairs were the few possessions I valued, my books, what little remained of my mother's things. This was also the house where she was lost, along with my childhood, the forum for my living hell the last seven years.

There were no ghosts here that could hold me now because I was free. Not because I waited it out and came of age for college, not because Scarlett had saved me, but because I was making a choice. I was freeing myself, and that feeling swelled inside me, filling me up until it was the only thing I needed to take from the house.

"I don't need anything, and we're short on time."

I looked back to Jade. She was beautiful even in the dim light, and I was so glad she had come, so grateful she was there with me.

"Let's just go?"

ANOTHER HICCUP RIPPED up from my chest and I hoped against all hope that I wasn't about to puke all over Jade Pearce's expensive-looking boots. I stumbled sideways and slumped down against the closest tree. Vampires ran fast. Being held on Jade's back, while we covered what felt like an alarmingly large distance, might have been enjoyable if I didn't suffer with horrendous motion sickness.

Branches snapped under Jade's weight as she paced back and forth in front of me, and I looked up at her awestruck. She was barely even winded.

We had been in the woods for a good while, though my sense of time felt completely skewed by the velocity with which we had moved. The coyotes howling in the distance and the whisper of the slightest wind penetrating the thick wood told me we were deep in the heart of a forest, probably just outside Jaffrey.

"Where are we?"

I barely had the breath to ask. My face stung from being whipped by cold air and my eyes were still streaming.

"Vermont."

Jade was distracted and seemed unfazed by our location. Shock jolted through me at the realization that I was so far from home. I tried to ignore it, but I'd never even been out of state. I hiccupped again and hazel eyes, bright in the moonlight, turned to me.

"Are you going to be okay?"

I nodded, immediately regretting it as another wave of sickness rose and swallowed me. I leaned my head back against rough bark and tried not to think.

"When we get to Vires, we'll have to get past the wall guard. There was a place Scarlett and I had been using to come and go, but since they found it, I sort of had to improvise."

Jade spoke quicker than I had ever heard, and her nervousness unsettled me. I was tired, cold, and sick as a dog. I wanted the end of this hellacious journey, and to see Scarlett, to touch her, and know I had made the right choices. I took a deep breath and caught myself just before I nodded and sent the trees spinning again.

"Okay, just tell me what to do?"

I asked the question, and I had a thousand others all vying to be answered too. What the hell was I doing? How had my life gotten so utterly derailed? How did a city exist today and have a wall guard? I was tired, I didn't remember the last time I ate, and I had already decided to put all my faith in a girl I had known for barely three weeks, and all that was left to do was to see it through, to carry on.

"I'll carry you, but we'll have to be fast, no stopping, no talking... Fast and quiet, that's how we always managed it."

Long, slim fingers pushed back thick dark hair, and her gaze returned from whatever distraction had kept it somewhere off to our right.

"Has Scarlett bitten you? Don't lie to me, I need to know."

That feeling of invasion rose up in my chest and I wanted to tuck my wrist into my jacket and shake my head. The information felt private, like something that was just mine and Scarlett's, but Jade was my only route back to her now, and the urgency in her voice told me it was no time to lie.

I nodded sheepishly and forced myself to stiffly hold out my wrist for her to see. The single round scar shone white in the dim moonlight.

Jade stiffened as she looked at it and quickly looked away. Sensing her discomfort, I tugged the sleeve of my jacket back down and waited.

"Never show anybody that in Vires." Her voice was dark and heavier than I'd ever heard it. "If they find it, lie about where it came from, and make sure it's a good one." She paused, and I heard her inhale. "If they figure out what it is, never, ever tell them my sister was the one to drink from you. They'll kill you both."

My blood turned to ice.

"We have to go."

Jade sounded angry almost, and guilt swallowed me. Everything in me hated disappointing her or feeling as if I had let her down in some way, though it made little sense. I was also terrified; who were these people, and why were there such heavy punishments for an act I had no idea was a crime?

There was no time for me to ask any more questions, and no more moments left for me to catch my breath.

Cool fingers wrapped tight around my arm and something caught my leg, then the world moved around me and I was slung back up onto Jade's back. I clung to her slim hips with my thighs for dear life, my hands clasped so tight around her neck I knew it ought to choke her, even though I wouldn't.

We ran. Distance and time ceased to exist, and all there was left was Jade and me, and the whip of the wind around us. I buried my face in her shoulder, and strangely I enjoyed the contact, my only comfort as we sped toward the unknown. I thought of Scarlett, replaying our moments together on the never-ending reel that had started the moment she'd burst unbidden into my almost-death.

Jade continued to run, and I let my mind drift, forcing myself to embrace this, to let the fear fall away with every hyperfast step we took. I had never cared much for my old life anyway, I told myself as we hurtled forward toward Vires, toward Scarlett.

Chapter Six

THE PACE FELT almost human as Jade carried me still, the dark barely beginning to break, the promise of sun scarcely peeking over the woody horizon. I blinked to clear the tears the wind had whipped into my eyes. Up ahead a huge wall loomed. From this distance, in the dim light, with my streaming eyes, it was nothing but a shadow, taller than my house piled on top of itself ten times; it looked as tall as the buildings I'd seen in pictures of New York City—maybe even taller.

We continued to jog, and I tucked my head back down, Jade's hair soft against my cheek. I was ready for this part to be over, the uncertainty, the journey, the million questions that wouldn't let me have any peace. I just wanted to be there, to be with her, to be safe again. Emotionally, I had no sense of her mood, but I felt our proximity had increased. The knowledge we were so close to her warmed me right down to my toes as Jade plowed headlong toward the gigantic barrier.

Jade slammed to a halt so fast it knocked the breath out of me. A chorus of hissing rose up around us; it came from beneath me and off to both sides, in front and behind us.

Looking up, I commanded my watery eyes to focus. What I saw sent all the warmth plummeting out of me. Faces surrounded us. Though there were only five or six of them, we were outnumbered, and as little as I knew about Vires, I knew this couldn't be good. Jade took a step back, and a gust of cool air brushed my cheek. When I looked behind us, a tall man already blocked our exit.

"Jade Pearce?"

The hissing had subsided, though the memory was burned into my brain. The sound, the way Jade's body rose up below me, the way the faces around us were twisted, eyes narrow, lips pulled back and fangs bared, it was all so animalistic. The nerves in Jade's voice when she replied were undeniable.

"Who's asking?"

Her intended bravado fell flat, though the men kept their distance.

"Riley Richards, wall guard. You know I have to ask, Miss Pearce, what were you doing outside the wall?"

I was a powerless spectator, dumbstruck and afraid. All I could do was watch the scene play out before me, and long for Scarlett.

"I was exploring. I wanted to look one more time at the schools there, the books..."

"Liar."

The accusation came from the man behind us. Jade whipped around so fast my head spun, though her hands were raised, all her fight gone. I clung to her back like a puppet, silent.

"Trent..."

The name was a reprimand, and the gruff man appeared between Jade's accuser and us.

"*Miss Pearce* has told us where she was, and while the infraction will have to be reported, I see no need for any drastic measures tonight. After all, her sister will no doubt be looking for her..."

Something switched, a light came on. The mention of Jade's last name had altered the course of the entire interaction and speaking of her sister solidified that. I was fascinated now, as I always was by anything to do with Scarlett, and I watched too intensely, forgetting to be as afraid as I ought to be. For a second, I was lost again, seeking to decipher the puzzle, trying to drag myself just one tiny step, a single inch, closer to her.

"Scarlett is waiting for me."

Jade sounded surer now, and my heart soared at the mention of Scarlett's name. She was waiting for us, for me. I could feel she was close, closer than she had been in what felt like an eternity, and I was so ready to bridge the last of that gap. I ached to be with her.

Jade stepped forward and the men stepped back, parting, leaving the dimly lit path ahead of us clear. For the first time, I saw the city ahead, though it still looked very far away. Between the dazzling illumination of the high towers and us was a vast area of few lights, and I wondered why the wall was so far from the actual area that was inhabited. Nevertheless, we were on our way.

"Wait..."

And just like that, we were stalled, we were foiled, we were undone. Before the man even spoke, I felt it. Something rose in my chest, strong, guttural, and I knew I had to try to protect Jade.

"Miss Pearce, you are free to go home, of course. I'll escort you through the Fringe and the Midlands myself, but the human..."

"She's a tower servant. I brought her with me to tend to my needs."

The lie was smooth, and though I wasn't sure why, I was glad Jade had at least gotten that much down.

"Of course, but we'll need to verify that. She'll go to the bunker tonight, and once her name and work detail are confirmed, she'll be returned to the tower."

Work detail? I was lost, and once again, that feeling was back, boiling water swallowing me. I had no idea how to swim against the tide in this unfamiliar place.

"Scarlett won't like it. She needs the girl tonight...every night. She has a specific...importance to my sister, and I promised I'd have her back before dawn."

Jade was holding it together, though as I tried to make sense of what she was saying, I was falling apart. She made it sound almost as if I was Scarlett's lover, though it was dirty somehow, tainted. The way she spoke about me made it sound as if I was disposable to Scarlett, and I hated that, but it didn't matter. I just wanted to stay with Jade and avoid wherever they wanted to take me to check the work detail I wasn't sure I had.

The man ran his hand over his chin and continued to rub his neck, looking at me for the first time. I waited for him to lick his lips. The vision of his snarling face, those deadly fangs, still burned behind my eyes.

"I'm sorry, Miss Pearce, if the other Miss Pearce has a problem with the protocol, she'll have to take it up with the Government. I've got my orders, I'm sure you understand. The girl goes to the bunker, and you go home."

Jade was losing it. I felt her weight shifting, the soft tickle of her hair on my cheek as she glanced around looking for an exit that didn't exist.

"Call my sister. You can't do this. Call Scarlett."

She sounded frantic and I clung to her tight, my arms around her chest, my cheek pressed to her ear, half out of fright and half in a vain effort to comfort her, to protect her from the bodies that were closing around us. It was no use.

I was ripped away from her, dragged backward by hands gripping my shoulders, then wrapped around my chest with bruising force. I was silent, limp against the cold body holding me; I had learned a long time ago that sometimes, the best way to make the pain stop was to completely fail to react.

The man who had done most of the talking still stood close to Jade, speaking calmly, but hazel eyes were on me and I had never seen her look the way she did. Dark hair was windswept, blown across her face, her full lips were parted ever so slightly, falling at their corners under the weight of emotions I could only guess were regret, maybe fear. I hung slack against the man—vampire—who held me, and watched as the calm man reached out, taking hold of Jade around the arm, and beginning to guide her away. Then, I exploded.

Never in my life had I gotten into a fight. I'd never really had anything, or felt anything, worth fighting for. Watching him put his hands on Jade caused that to change. It broke me somehow, tore me down the very middle and sent something ripping out of me I had absolutely no idea I possessed. I screamed; it was a battle cry, a war howl, and it tore out of me as I twisted and turned in the stone-clad grasp that held me. I kicked and clawed, though my nails wouldn't penetrate the cool skin of his strong, bare arms. I was furious, and I had to get to Jade, to save her. It wasn't a choice anymore—it was a compulsion.

Everything I thought I knew about myself was gone, ashes on the breeze, burned up by the anger, the possession, the protectiveness in my chest. I wanted to throw myself down and die so she could go free, I wanted to tear all of them to pieces and paint their blood across my skin. I had to make sure she was safe.

I bit down on the rock that bound me, still howling furiously, stomping again and again on feet that refused to bruise, and kicking at knees that refused to buckle. I fought with everything I had, and hazel eyes watched me with a sad, confused expression, but it didn't matter. My lungs burned for more air, but I barely stopped long enough to take a full breath before I screamed again. Then, with a heavy thud, the world was black.

EVERYTHING CAME BACK slowly, but as soon as it started to make sense, memories hit me like a runaway train. I remembered it all. Jade Pearce breaking into my house, my split-second decision to come here, and the vampires at the city wall, who had incited such a rage in me. Concrete was cold under me, and looking up, it was all I saw above me too. The ceiling was so low that my muddled brain guessed I could barely stand without bumping my head, and last time I checked, I was only five feet and three inches tall.

Claustrophobia found me, seeping to touch the very edges of my skin, lapping at me gently, and the longer I spent in this space, the further it would crawl into me. I wanted Scarlett.

I couldn't feel her mood, but I knew she was close still. I rolled to my left and was met with nothing but another concrete wall that lurched as my head spun. When the dizziness stopped, I turned my head to the right, glad my stomach was empty as the world spun around me again. There was no concrete there, but there were bars, thick bars like a jail cell, though my eyes hadn't adjusted enough to see beyond them yet, not in the dim light.

The place smelled like rust and disinfectant, and I couldn't marry those things together; decay and cleanliness, they made no sense. I tried until the bleach burned my nose.

My body hurt like the morning after a beating, my ribs were bruised, and every breath sent a dull, distant ache through my chest that felt worse in the cold. The pain was crushing, and the sensation fed the claustrophobia again. I closed my eyes so I could forget about the bars, at least for now.

I knew better than to feed any kind of monster because fear would only make it grow, and my reaction to all this was the only locus of control I had left.

Carefully, I picked back through the night before, the huge looming wall in the forest, the vampires with their hissing, snarling faces, the way Scarlett seemed to be a gamechanger for that interaction between Jade and the wall guard. My mind slid unbidden to Jade, to the way she had begun to panic, the slight shifts in her weight, the subtle turn of her head as she looked for a nonexistent exit. The rage that had overcome me felt so far away. I remembered with crystal clarity the grating hardness of that cool arm under my teeth, yet the girl who had fought back felt like someone else, as if she was dead now. The first tears of self-pity wet my eyes; I had let Jade down, and though I didn't understand why, it felt unforgivable.

My head throbbed and the concrete I lay on was just a hard surface for the back of my skull to continue to pound against, even though I wasn't moving. The last of my fight, my will to stay conscious and unravel the puzzle, was leaving me, draining away with every tear that spilled warm onto my cold cheeks.

I had come here for Scarlett, yet I was alone in a concrete box and she was nowhere to be found. I had to believe she would come, that all this wasn't for nothing, but the cold fingertips of doubt had touched my spine, and they were traveling slowly upwards to wrap tight around my neck and choke me. A single sob escaped before I could shut it down. I had to believe I knew her, that what felt so far away and so long ago back in Jaffrey had been real. I had to believe she would come. The alternative was just too dire.

"Hello?"

A soft female voice came from somewhere beyond the bars. I opened my eyes, though I saw nothing at first. A jolt of hope and fear shot through me, and suddenly, I couldn't find my voice to reply.

"Joseph..."

The voice was just a whisper now.

"Joe... Are you awake? Is there... Is someone else here? I heard them bringing someone in. We're like you, we're from the Fringe. If you want to talk, we're human..."

I listened to the words carefully, but something kept me from replying. She sounded kind, maybe a little afraid, but stronger than I felt. I wanted to latch on to that strength and steal any hope it could give to me, but my mouth wouldn't move. Maybe it was the shame of someone hearing me cry, maybe I was just too tired, too cold, too hurt. I closed my eyes again and let myself drift away.

"I know you're probably afraid, but I'll be here when it's time to wake up... Hopefully. They put the lights on when the sun goes down."

Only my subconscious brain heard her. I was already lost, back in my pit of uncomfortable black.

SNAP. SUDDENLY LIGHT burst painfully behind my eyelids, and I sat bolt upright so fast the world swam. I shuffled myself backward until I hit against a cold wall and blinked hard. There was a second, just one horribly disoriented second where nothing made sense, the concrete, the bars, the body lying in a cell across a narrow corridor from me, but it passed faster this time.

The blackness had been almost welcome, the dark of last night...yesterday...I didn't know anymore. Life inside this dungeon seemed timeless, unnatural. The air didn't move, there wasn't even a whisper of wind, no warmth from the sun outside the building. The girl's words from last night came back to me—*the lights come on when the sun goes down.*

My head still hurt, and my mouth felt like it was full of sand, dry and grainy, and I wondered again about the stillness, the dryness of the air.

The space I was being held in was as small as I had feared, a low ceiling and three concrete walls; to the front were finely spaced thick bars. They looked metallic, as impenetrable as the heavy padlock holding the hinged section. I scuffed the heels of my dirty sneakers against the floor—concrete too, it wore my shoes without taking even a scratch itself.

Something moved outside my jail cell. The body I had noticed earlier rolled, stretching out against cool gray, before pulling upwards to sit, long brunette hair splayed over slim shoulders. My heart jolted painfully, but after the figure had rubbed their eyes, I already knew—the way she moved was all wrong, and when she turned her head to look at me, I was sure. She wasn't Scarlett.

Large eyes greeted me across the small space, and she offered me a careful smile. I wasn't close enough to see if her irises were swirling or still, but this was the first gesture of kindness I had received inside the city walls and it was much needed so, tentatively, I smiled back.

"Hi... Are you okay?"

This time, I was determined to reply. I nodded.

"I'm...fine, I think."

I swallowed hard, my mouth so dry that forming words was difficult.

"What is this place?"

I shuffled forward slightly, jeans scuffing the hard ground as I moved toward the bars.

"Stop!"

The girl's cry left me frozen in fear for a long moment. Pushing out a breath, I craned my neck to try to look down the corridor, to see what came next.

"The bars are electrified, don't go any closer."

She held up her hands, making sure the message had sunk in before she crawled a little closer herself and leaned against her wall, facing me.

"I'm Zara, Zara Richards, you probably know one of my siblings, maybe Silvie? You're about her age. You're in the central bunker, the Government place."

She spoke kindly, and her voice was soft. Even with the fluorescents burning down onto her dirt-streaked skin, she was pretty, big doe eyes and long straight hair, just a shade darker than milk chocolate.

"Zara?"

A male voice off to my right side made me jump, though as I watched Zara's eyes move in that direction, I realized we weren't alone in this prison.

"I'm here, Joe."

Zara leaned a little closer to her bars as she answered, and I wondered if she could see him. Carefully, I leaned forward myself, until I saw the very edge of the cell beside Zara's—as far as I could tell, it was empty.

"Someone else has joined us in hell."

Her smile turned wry, and I listened to the exchange, numb.

"I didn't get her name yet…"

"Rayne Kennedy." I filled in by force of habit.

"Hi, Rayne, I'm sorry you're here, but you're not alone, and contrary to what Zara says, you're not in hell."

The male voice, Joe, spoke to me, and I smiled.

"Well… Thank you. But where exactly am I? I mean… I'm not from here, so I don't really know what you mean by a bunker."

I felt stupid, like an inconvenience. In that moment, I was glad my fellow captors seemed so…normal; there were no odd brooding silences or carefully chosen questions.

"You're not from here? Are you from the Midlands?"

Zara sounded perplexed and I shook my head slightly, though it was enough to irritate my headache.

"I'm from Jaffrey, New Hampshire."

They probably thought I was every bit the stupid small-town girl I sounded like.

"New Hampshire? You mean…"

Zara looked dumbstruck and a low whispering struck up in the cell beside me. I must have looked alarmed because Zara smiled kindly at me for a second.

"Don't mind Joe, he's praying. He does that a lot, you just sort of learn to block it out, after a while… No offense, Joe."

"None taken. I'm praying for you, Zar, and you, Rayne."

That was all we heard from Joseph before the whispering resumed.

Those large eyes came back to mine, and I squinted slightly, determining them to be brown.

"So, you're from…outside the wall?"

I nodded.

"Is it true there's none of them out there? That they let you live in peace, that you're free?"

The words confused me, and Zara saw it on my face.

"Vampires... There's no vampires out there?"

I shook my head. "Well, there hasn't been my whole life until last month, and I don't think there is for anyone else out there. It was...just me."

Zara looked sad. I was afraid I'd offended her or said something wrong. I was about to apologize, but she spoke before I could.

"Sorry, it's... I was born here, and I'll die here, like my family has for generations. It's...strange to think just over the wall, our lives could be so different."

She seemed suddenly fascinated by the material of her threadbare, hole-riddled jeans, and guilt gnawed at me.

"They haven't brought anyone in for over five years. We're a self-proliferating food source, don't you know. The vampires don't even have to bother stocking up on blood-bags anymore, we fall in love and have families and produce them fresh food all by ourselves."

Her mock enthusiasm made me feel sick. The meaning behind her words was sinking in, and I was afraid, afraid and so angry with myself. Zara was trapped here, and me? I'd walked right into it willingly.

I had no idea what to say, and Zara was quiet. We sat there in silence for a few long minutes and I turned my head away to give her what little privacy I could. When curiosity forced me to sneak a glance back at her cell, she still sat there, motionless, staring hard at the ground.

When she spoke again, she seemed to have collected herself. I turned to look at her, my features arranged in an expression of apology.

"Well, Rayne, you're in Vires, the original vampire city. All we really know are stories, but according to those, this isn't the only one. The city is hidden; as far as we know, we're in Vermont. It's ruled by the vampires and their vampire government, and us, we're the hard labor...and the food."

Jade had warned me, things were different here, they worked differently, yet somehow, I felt like I had been played. Nothing could have prepared me for what Zara told me. I stared at her dumbly.

"How did you even get here?"

Her tone wasn't unkind and it wasn't prying, just soft and curious.

"I was brought here by..."

I stopped myself before I could say "my friend," because now, I wasn't sure.

"A vampire?"

Zara finished for me and I nodded.

"They wanted to confirm my name and my work detail before they let me go... I don't know what that means."

I confided in Zara so easily, and probably Joseph too, because although the whispered prayers continued, I had no doubt he was listening, but what choice did I have?

"Well, they have us all on a huge registry. Fingerprints, retinal scans, that's how they'll try to confirm your name. Your work detail... If they think you have one it's good, it means you're not just bloodstock, though unless it's in a tower, it won't matter."

There was nothing cruel about Zara Richards, she seemed soft and kind, nurturing almost, yet she delivered these blows with such an even tone, unflinching, that I struggled to read her. I was still lost for words, but it was only when Zara shook her head in apology that I realized— this was just her reality, her life, like nightly beatings had been mine, and sugar-coating it wouldn't change it or help it.

"Sorry... I'm not used to being around someone...new. It's all sort of common knowledge around here."

I nodded my understanding. The only thing I had learned that had given me hope was the part about the towers, that being there was somehow favorable. I knew for a fact it was where Jade had planned to take me.

"What about the towers? What happens there?"

Zara seemed patient, and I was so glad for that, as I watched her wet her lips and begin to explain.

"The vampires live in the towers at the center of the city, all around us, actually. This bunker is the very midpoint of Vires, the Government stronghold so to speak, and the towers are all around us... Didn't you see them on the way in?"

I thought about it and shook my head.

"I think they knocked me out..."

Zara laughed. "Sounds about right for them. Bastards."

"Actually, I do remember the skyscrapers. When we were at the wall, I saw them in the distance."

The words came out too fast, and I had no idea why I was so excited I'd remembered. Knowledge was power now, perhaps my only weapon, maybe that was it. Either way, I knew I had to gain as much of it as possible, if I was ever to find Scarlett, to stay alive here. Part of me wondered if Scarlett even wanted to be found, if I should even want to find her. I pushed those thoughts away, determined to make the most of all I could learn from Zara.

"Well, the vampires live in the skyscrapers, only we call them towers. The largest ones around the bunker are where the Delta families live, and around those are all the others."

"Delta families?"

I felt as if I was in kindergarten again, lost at every turn, but oh so eager to learn, to understand.

"Asshole royalty. The Pearces, the Hawthornes, the Barrows family... There's about seven or eight of them."

It took all my self-control not to grab those electric bars and press my face as close to Zara as I could get. Pearces... Pearce... Jade and Scarlett Pearce. Despite her failure thus far to come for me, to find me and protect me like Jade had said she would, I still wanted Scarlett. I wanted her so badly, so she could explain all this, and keep me safe like she had before. Zara continued to speak.

"Delta vamps aren't just impossibly strong, fast and cruel, they can walk around in the sun too—great news for us humans, as you can imagine. They're generally the richest, the meanest, and apparently, the most genetically advanced."

The air quotes she made confused me, but I followed the rest, and I nodded. That explained why Scarlett came to me that first time before the sun had properly set.

"So..."

I was piecing this together, my thought process and my questions forming slowly, so grateful for Zara and all her saintly patience.

"If the vampires are in the towers, why is going there good?"

"They don't eat where they shit." The curse sounded so harsh in Zara's soft voice. "They only drink from the Fringe, never from their own towers, they wouldn't risk that."

I had too many questions and no logical order in which to assemble them. Every piece of information felt important, absolutely vital, though I was careful not to bombard Zara too much and wear out the only welcome I had gotten here.

"The Fringe? And risk what?"

"The Fringe is the outer ring of Vires, aside from the agricultural land. That's where we live, the humans, at least those of us who don't work in the towers. They keep us there, bring us up to the city center to work on the roads, the towers, in the market and stuff, but other than that, we stay there, and they come to feed on us."

Her voice darkened, and I was afraid of what was to come next. Part of me didn't want to hear it. I didn't want to imagine Scarlett walking through a human town, picking off Zara and her siblings, their blood on her lips and their bodies strewn at her feet like my father's had been. Zara kept on talking and I couldn't find the strength to resist the urge to know more, to tell her to stop.

"If you're in a tower, they won't drink from you because then they would have no staff. Whenever they drink, they always make sure the person is dead afterward."

Her voice was heavy with disdain and I felt like a traitor. Scarlett had drunk from me, more than once, and I was very much alive. I almost told Zara as much, but then I remembered Jade's words, the seriousness in her voice when she told me the scar and the truth of where it had come from had to be kept secret, at any cost. I stayed quiet.

"It's one of their most absolute laws... If a vampire bites you, you're done. Sometimes they drain you, but often they just snap the neck once they've taken what they want. A few times they've even left the bodies on the family's doorstep for them to find."

Her voice sank, slipping out of its warm softness and into something cold and hard—angry. I sensed the conversation drawing to an end before she told me it was over.

"If you get taken to a tower, you're a lucky one. Unless you give them a reason, they won't kill you, so I hope for your sake, Rayne, that by some mistake or miracle, they find you registered to a tower work detail."

She offered me a smile, though it looked forced, before she turned away from me and leaned her head against the wall.

"I'm going to get some rest now." Her voice floated back to me. "I suggest you do the same."

I nodded, even though she couldn't see me, and turned away myself. I wrapped my arms around my knees and did my best to hold some warmth in my freezing form.

No matter how hard I tried, sleep wasn't going to come, that much was obvious, and I doubted now I could even rest. Information didn't feel like power as I'd hoped it might. I was more informed, but rather than feeling ready, I felt more unsure than I had since the night Scarlett first came to me.

She had saved me, she'd lain with me so quietly and spoken in her cryptically amused way, her words all gravel and fire in my veins, and when she had drunk my blood, it hadn't been the violent, selfish act Zara described. I had come here to find her, to find the missing piece of the puzzle, and I hadn't expected or been prepared for any of this.

From what Zara had told me, the Pearce family were Delta vampires, genetically advanced; they could walk in the sun and lived in this society where humans were raised like lambs and slaughtered unforgivingly for food. Scarlett was a part of this society. I found it so hard to believe. That information just didn't correlate with my perception of her, the way she felt, so cool and so safe, the inexplicable emotional connection that shimmered soft and bright between us and let me taste everything she was. Dark as she was, she had never felt like the indiscriminate killer Zara's version of society, and my own experience, labeled her as.

I tried to keep the lurking thoughts at bay, to keep my mind clear, but no matter how hard I willed myself just to listen to my breath and be still, the images Zara had painted for me wouldn't leave me alone. To doubt Scarlett felt like a betrayal, but the vision of her running, beautiful in one of her tight dresses, her smooth leather jacket and high heeled pumps, blood at her lips and bodies in her wake, wouldn't leave me alone.

I didn't want to imagine her as a huntress, a killer, something dangerous, deadly, though I knew that side of her existed. In my mind, she wasn't the monster in the Fringe, snapping necks without a thought; she was my Scarlett, my angel of death and my saving grace. She was something to be handled with care, but something so worth caring for, and I couldn't bend what I knew of her to fit the mold painted for me by the way Zara spoke of the vampires here, and by the horrible act I had borne witness to her performing.

Somehow, my abstract perception of her, the one I couldn't explain with words or actions, or anything solid, was stronger, but not strong enough to put me totally at ease.

I warred with myself until I couldn't stand it anymore. Zara stayed quiet, and Joseph continued to whisper. It was to the words of a whispered "Our Father" from the cell next door that I finally felt myself drift into sleep.

Chapter Seven

THE LIGHTS WERE still on when it woke me. The heavy chink of metal on metal was close to me, but before I could react, something hard dug into my back. I rolled over and jumped away as I realized it was a boot. The man hauled me to my feet. As soon as he wrapped his fingers around the back of my neck and guided me out of the door and past Zara's cell, I knew he was a vampire. He stooped to exit the small space, and I held Zara's brown eyes for as long as I could. I was half pushed, half dragged all the way down a narrow corridor I had no memory of and thrown through a doorway. My knees were skinned on the rough floor tiles, but I didn't make a sound.

Where was Scarlett? Maybe this was because she had come for me, maybe I would wait here until she came? I knew I was lying to myself. The reaction from the men at the wall told me if I was to be returned to Scarlett, the vampire who had brought me to this room would care more about the condition I was to be returned in.

"Get up."

His voice was a hard monotone, and he sounded almost bored. I struggled off my hands and knees, back onto my feet, and turned to face him.

"There is no record of your existence inside Vires. The prints and scans we took from you last night don't match any file. Who are you and where did you come from?"

It was all so matter of fact; they had taken my fingerprints, scanned my eyes, and done who knew what else to invade my privacy while I was unconscious. If I wasn't so afraid, I wondered if I would be mad. My first instinct was to lie, to keep secrets like Jade had said, but now, after talking to Zara, I wasn't so sure.

I felt cool air before the impact. I knew what was going to happen, and my arms reached up to protect my face from pure muscle memory, though they were too late. The sound of skin on skin was amplified, bouncing back and forth between concrete and tinted mirror in the empty room. I tried to catch my breath. My eye would be black tomorrow.

"I came with Jade Pearce."

That information seemed safe, something they already knew. He hit me again, and this time I fell, my backside colliding painfully with the floor. He was standing over me faster than I could blink.

"We know who you came with. I want your name, and I want to know where you came from or I'll just cut my losses."

He licked his lips and I balked. I didn't want him to bite me, to drink my blood, to have those intimate moments with me that Scarlett had. For the first time in my life, I was terrified of being violated, though I knew I should be more afraid of death.

"My name is Rayne Kennedy. I came here from New Hampshire."

He sneered.

"Outside the wall. So, you have no work detail in Vires?"

Curious eyes were watching me, twin blue swirls. There was nothing beautiful about them despite their liquid irises.

"I was brought here to be with Scarlett Pearce, in her tower."

That wasn't a lie, but it wasn't the exact truth. I was trying to hedge all my bets, cover all my bases, and I knew I was stretched too thin.

"It isn't Miss Pearce's right to bring in anyone, that right belongs solely to the Government."

I backtracked quickly.

"Well Scarlett didn't bring me, I forced Jade Pearce to bring me. I told her I knew the location of the city and would tell if she didn't. She had no choice."

I lied through my teeth, my heart hammering. I had to protect Scarlett, to protect Jade.

"You wanted to come here?"

He seemed almost curious and I felt like a fool, but I hung my head and nodded.

"Careful what you wish for..."

He was still laughing to himself as he grabbed me roughly by the arm and pulled me to my feet. His large hand swallowed my chin as he jerked my head from side to side, inspecting my neck.

"Ever been bitten, Rayne Kennedy?"

I shook my head and let just enough fear show on my face to make my silent lie believable.

"Do you have any scars? It's well within my right to check..."

The way he looked at me scared me, and the situation was spinning out of my control too fast. Pain was familiar, it came and it went, bruises faded, broken ribs healed, but violation...it was alien to me, and for the first time in a long time, I felt truly vulnerable. I wasn't numb, not to this.

"I fell through a barbed wire fence, I have scars on my side."

My father had hit me in the kitchen and I'd fallen on the glass in my hand.

"I have one on my leg, I don't remember how I got it. It's been there since I was a child, I probably fell off a bike or something."

That one was the truth; I'd had the small scar on my knee for as long as I remembered.

"And there's one on my arm. I let my school friends put out a match on me, as a dare."

Lie. Though I had seen kids at school stupid enough to do that, and I knew those scars looked close enough to the one left by Scarlett's teeth.

"Now why would you do that?"

He stepped closer and I stepped back, though I forced my voice not to falter.

"So I wouldn't be called a chicken, and I won twenty bucks."

I was a liar, and I was sure he knew it.

"Show me."

I was done for, but I swore to myself then and there that I would never tell him who did it... No matter what he did. I pulled up the sleeve of my jacket and he took my wrist in his cool grasp. I was tempted to close my eyes and pretend, for just a second, he was Scarlett. He studied the small, round scar on the inside of my left wrist. My blue eyes watched his motile ones as he scanned the space beside it, no doubt looking for its twin puncture mark. I realized for the first time why Scarlett never fastened her mouth flush onto me— how clever she had been.

"All right, Rayne Kennedy."

Just like that, it was over. He pulled my jacket sleeve back down and led me by the arm back to my cell without another word. I felt Zara's eyes on me as he threw me onto the cold floor, but I turned away. I waited in silence until I heard the clink of the bars closing, until his footsteps disappeared down the hall, and only then, did I finally let my tears spill over.

Zara had the grace not to disturb me, and Joseph just continued to pray.

AFTER THAT, THE days began to get slower, to blur together and steal all my hope. Zara was taken away a few hours after I was brought back from my interrogation. She said she was going home, but I was never sure if she was lying. Joseph stayed, he was kind, and our conversations were brief, but his soft whispering meant I never felt alone. I could have been there a week, or I could have been there three days; according to Joseph they often ran the lights on odd patterns just to torment us. I had no idea why, or what I had done to deserve such treatment, and most of all, I had no idea where Scarlett was.

Doubt was my worst enemy, and by now, it had almost swallowed me whole. She hadn't come for me yet, and that, along with my treatment in the interview room, made me wonder if she ever would. I had believed Jade, trusted her, but most of all, I had believed in Scarlett. Though I hated myself for it, every day I spent too much time lying flat on the floor, staring at the ceiling of my concrete box, and questioning my faith in her, yet I could never quite let go. I still wanted her, I still cried when the lights were out, hoping that tomorrow, today, soon, would be when she would come to find me.

THEIR WORLD MOVED around us, and Joseph and I—we stayed trapped, frozen. I wondered very little about home, though I often thought about how easily I had disconnected from my old life, then I tried not to think about it at all. It just seemed like another sad testament to the fact I'd had absolutely nothing to leave behind.

Most of my time was spent going over the information I'd learned from Zara, making sense of it and letting it consume me as my new reality. Joseph and I talked briefly. When they threw half a round loaf and a bottle of water through the bars of our cells in the morning, he'd make jokes with me about our fine dining. I liked him, even though I'd never seen him face to face; he was gentle and kind, and though I found all the praying a little strange, I almost envied him for the belief that he could do something to change this. All I could do was wait.

My life had been chronically lonely, I'd never minded it much, but down here—I had a strong hunch by now that we were being held in an underground bunker, the stillness of the air keyed me in—my own mind was my worst enemy. The only struggles I faced besides the cold and the hunger were struggles of my own making, of waking up every morning, or night, or whatever time they decided to blind us with the fluorescents, and waiting to see if I would torture myself, or let myself have some small reprieve.

The worst was the regret, the wondering if I'd made the right choice to come here, and the doubt that flooded in with it. I would fall asleep feeling like a betrayer. Scarlett was out there somewhere, I could always feel her just touching the edges of my radar, yet I didn't deserve for her to come. Close after that was the fear. I was deathly afraid Jade hadn't been taken home the night that felt so long ago, or if she had, Scarlett had gotten into trouble with the Government for her alleged involvement. I was sure by now that the night Scarlett had come to me wounded, the bite marks and gashes in her cool, copper-tinged skin were all courtesy of the vampires who guarded the wall. The thought of either Jade or Scarlett being hurt tore me to pieces; some days all I could do was lie there and let myself burn.

These thoughts haunted me the day they took Joseph away. Finally seeing him was a welcome event, though his long, lanky frame and thick dreadlocks surprised me. I had imagined him to be short and stocky with round glasses, for whatever reason. He had a kind face, and he reached carefully through the bars when the two vampires holding him were distracted, and we held hands for a moment. It was a small, strange gesture, and at one time, I would have been grossly uncomfortable with it. Here, where I felt like I had been alone for weeks, I clung to it, tears in my eyes.

After he was escorted away and I was left seemingly alone in my prison, I finally let a few of those tears fall. Without Joseph's whispered prayers beside me constantly telling me I wasn't on my own, for the first time since I got to Vires, I was sinking too low, too close to giving up. I lay down to try to sleep and quiet the part of me that wished desperately for him to come back because I didn't want to be so selfish. When he returned, I knew I would never forgive myself for that tiny unintentional plea.

Footsteps started up far away down the corridor, and I rolled over immediately, giving up my guise of sleeping to listen. There were two of them, I thought—it had become a game for me now to try to figure out how many people were coming based on the footsteps, though they rarely came down past my cell for me to see if I was right. This pair was approaching, closer than they usually did. I sat up, trying my best to move in silence.

Hope spilled unwelcome into my chest. Though neither of the visitors walked with the telltale click of someone wearing high heels, my emotions rejected this logic with a thousand what-ifs. I wondered if there would ever be a day where I didn't still hope it was her, finally coming for me.

They passed by my bars. Noticing me, the vampire holding Joseph's arm stopped, turning him to face me. All the air left my lungs.

"Brought your little friend back."

The vampire sneered, and I recognized him as the man who had questioned me in the room at the other end of the corridor, though my attention wasn't on him.

Joseph. Poor, poor Joseph who'd had only kind words and good wishes for me since my arrival was hurt, badly.

"Joseph..."

I rushed forward, stopping myself just before I grabbed on to the bars and tried to break free.

His head hung though he raised his chin to look at me. I stared back, horrified.

"Rayne..."

When he spoke, fresh blood spilled from the corner of his mouth and the word was distorted, both by the liquid and by the gaps where some of his teeth were missing. That wasn't the worst. Thick welts ran over the tips of his shoulders and I guessed they met more on his back. One of his eyes was swelled closed. His dreadlocks were gone, tiny stumps of them remaining, splaying out almost comically from his head without the weight of the rest of the braid to hold them down, but it got worse still.

"He needs a doctor!"

I was shouting at the vampire, but my eyes were still fastened to Joseph's chest, held there like two magnets. I was appalled, I was repulsed, I was terrified and everything between. Across the bare skin of his chest, in ornate lettering, were the words "Joseph Christ"; they were written without any ink. Some of the letters still wept blood, and I tried to make sense of it all. At first, I thought they were cut into his flesh, but they were so neat. I realized with sickening clarity that he had been branded.

"Still wanting to go work for Scarlett Pearce?"

The vampire holding up Joseph's ruined form still sneered at me.

"Creative, isn't she?"

That was all he said before he disappeared with Joe from my line of vision. I heard a body hitting the floor in the cell beside me. Joseph grunted, and that was when I started to fight.

It was the same sensation as when I had tried to save Jade, but less powerful, and somehow this time, it felt natural, as if a part of me had evolved, gained strength enough to do this, rather than something else having twisted its way into my head.

I stomped my feet, I screamed, calling out over and over that he needed a doctor, telling them he would die down there, spitting profanities and threats and anything else I could think of. I called to the vampires until I was hoarse and breathless, until all the anger had simmered back down to a point where I could contain it, and finally, I fell back onto the floor.

Joseph's whispered prayers were broken with sobs, and so were his words.

"Rayne, if I die, find my family, my sister, Caroline, and tell her I love her... Tell her I'm with Mom and Dad now and we're watching over her with the Lord."

"You're not going to die, Joe, you're not going to die." I dragged myself across the floor and pressed my hands against the concrete between us. "Just hold on, they won't let you die."

I didn't know if I was a liar after what I had just seen.

"I'm going to try to sleep for a while, Rayne. You'll make it out of here, I know you will, someone is watching over you."

I didn't know if I should try to stop him. My mind reeled, information about concussions and first aid warring in my head with my compassion—if I had been in that state, all I would have wanted was for sleep to take me away too. So I stayed quiet and let him rest, though I cried, harder than I remembered crying my entire life.

Someone was watching over me. Or at least someone had been. She was beautiful, and she was terrible, terrible beyond my wildest dreams, my worst nightmares; and I had followed her here. She was everything to me somehow still, yet she was so imperfect, always so mysterious, so dangerous, and now she was this… Those words branded into Joseph's skin, and I didn't know how to carry on.

The vampire could have lied, but part of me had known before he'd said the words. My eyes had stayed on those brands, not out of macabre curiosity or even concern, but because I felt her, the imprint of her, the echo, locked in that horrific act. Scarlett had done it, I was certain of that.

What scared me the most, more than any of this, was I knew I still loved her. I hated her for what she had done, for not coming for me, but I had tasted her brokenness in my mouth, every dark and ruined and beautiful thing she was, and somehow, I couldn't deny her, I couldn't even want to. It tore me into pieces just to try to turn my back on her, because I loved her so fiercely, with more valor and vigor and conviction than I loved anything else in the world; myself included.

Chapter Eight

SOMEWHERE BETWEEN THE sound of Joseph's sobbing and his prayers, I had fallen asleep, lost to the despair swallowing me, and grateful that I didn't dream. I had no idea how long I'd been out, no idea if the lights had gone off and come back on or been on this whole time. The sound of someone, or a group of people by their footsteps, moving down the corridor had woken me. Not caring about their presence, I called out softly to Joseph; he didn't answer.

"Joe... Joseph, are you sleeping?"

I kept on trying, getting louder and louder.

"He's not sleeping."

The voice that answered me was the same one that had confirmed everything I knew to be true last night, that Scarlett was the one to blame for Joseph's injuries...maybe his death.

"Where is he?"

I forced myself not to snap, because as the party came into view, I recognized Riley, another vampire dressed in similar black khakis, and a young man with slicked-back hair and wearing what looked like an expensive suit. This was different, and it felt like a change in the game.

"He was released to his family in the Fringe."

The words were barely out of Riley's mouth before the suited man spoke...or was he a boy? He looked to be in his early twenties, though he seemed to dress far too well, too formal, almost in an attempt to seem older, to give himself more gravitas than his skinny form possessed.

"Not that it will do him any good. There's no nurse in the Fringe now, we all know where she went."

His tone was simply matter-of-fact, not cruel, though his words dripped with disdain. I was clueless as to what was going on, and so, I kept my mouth shut, rising to my feet because, suddenly, the bars between me and the three of them did not seem like protection enough.

"This is the girl?"

The suited man-boy asked the question and Riley answered.

"That's right, Mr. Chase. Caught coming in over the wall, brought by Jade Pearce."

The man he'd called Mr. Chase took a step closer, studying me.

"And she said the girl was for Scarlett?"

My stomach dropped. Maybe he knew Scarlett, maybe he would take me to her.

Those hopes were already ringing false. Something in the way his thin lips wrapped around her name told me it wasn't going to be the case. Whoever he was, he didn't feel like an ally.

Riley nodded.

"What would she want with you?"

He asked me the question, and I fixed him with as blank a stare as I could muster. It was a question I'd asked myself perpetually, until some days, I could hardly cling to my belief that she did want me, or at least, she had.

"And why would she send her precious little sister out for you?"

He was talking to the guards more than me now, and I preferred it.

"Scarlett Pearce was caught crossing the wall to leave the city a few weeks ago, sir."

The other vampire spoke, and I hung on his every word. Just hearing someone, anyone talk about her, it made her real, and every scrap of information on her, any acknowledgment that she existed somewhere outside of just myself, was like gold dust to me now.

"Got into quite the altercation. Six wall guards were ripped to pieces and set on fire, though rumor has it she barely walked away herself."

This news seemed to please Mr. Chase, though only for a second.

"And yet there was no punishment. Six of our kind dead, and another Delta walking around unscathed."

He spat violently onto the floor and I jumped. The vampires beside him shared a look. Now I knew he was a vampire like them, though apparently none of them were Delta vampires, and it was obvious he had some serious distaste for the class difference. I tried to sort all this information away, to remember it in case there came a time when I needed it, but all I could think about was Scarlett. I was right about her being hurt that night by the vampires at the wall, and she had been telling the truth when she told me whoever had hurt her was dead.

"I'll take her. Have her brought to Chase Tower, now."

My blood ran cold as I realized he was talking about me.

"Evan? Are you almost done with all the macabre in here? I'd like to go home, there's a rather nice bottle of bourbon waiting for me."

The suited man, who I had deduced to be Evan Chase, looked back up the corridor, to a place I couldn't see.

"Nobody asked you to wait, brother." He snapped the words before taking one last look at me. "Make sure a group of your men bring her to me. I doubt Pearce even remembers she had any interest in her, she's obsessed with her current pet, but it doesn't hurt to take precaution."

With that, he was gone, they were all gone: the guards, Evan Chase, Joseph. I was left alone to wonder, to be tormented by the last sentence the weasel-looking boy had spoken. Had Scarlett forgotten me? The question echoed in my head, but one thing bothered me more. He had mentioned Scarlett's "current pet," and a strange discomfort in my stomach told me he wasn't talking about a dog or a cat, or anything else from the animal kingdom.

WHEN THEY ENTERED my cell, I barely had the time to look at them, to count them, to see any of their faces, before something dark and cotton feeling was pulled over my head. I was half dragged, half carried, bounced from cool body to cool body, though I heard the telltale clink of elevator doors, and I knew, for the first time in what could be days, weeks, I was being taken up.

They dragged me onward and I let them because I couldn't stand to go back, back to the bunker, my jail cell, the chlorine and rust, the echoes of Joseph's sobs, and Evan Chase's words—the place where Scarlett had deserted me.

I tasted the fresh air as it hit me, even through the fabric over my head, and not long after that, the hood was removed. Riley held my arm now; I blinked up groggily at his face, pain bursting behind my eyes from the sudden exposure to bright light, though I was determined to keep them open.

Tall buildings whose tips were almost as high as the clouds surrounded us, and behind them were smaller towers, still impressive. The city was beautiful, and it seemed oddly functional, functioning, and I had no idea what I had expected. The forest had been so bleak, so untouched, yet here, I stood on neatly laid pavement, a road was visible off to my left, and buildings rose up around me. I heard voices calling and the hustle of people talking. Craning my neck to look back through the throng of vampires behind me, I saw what looked like a string of awnings in a marketplace. It was all so surreal.

I walked slowly, drinking everything in and trying to make mental maps and other clever things. Most of all, I looked for her. Every brunette head that passed us made me stall, and each shimmering tower made my heart stop because any of them could be hers.

Evan Chase had seemed afraid she might try to steal me back on this journey, and despite my generously large escort, I desperately hoped for the same thing. We walked, and I lagged as much as I could, my only contribution to her possible rescue mission. As we left the ring of larger towers and began to walk around the ring of smaller ones, my hope was dying. We stopped outside a door too soon, and I looked back frantically, soaking up the last of it, the sun, the breeze, the sounds of some sort of civilization; the last of the chance, the opportunity, for Scarlett to come and save me.

We stepped inside the doors, and it had passed.

The first thing that struck me was the décor. The floors were smooth granite, and the place was oddly light and airy, given the people who resided inside were vampires. I was ushered toward another elevator, and I watched as we waited for it to arrive. Riley's grip was solid around my arm, and I might as well have been caught in stone. My chance to escape had passed, and I tried not to let myself mourn the fact. I was above ground, and for now, that would have to be enough. Whether or not Scarlett was coming for me, I was one step closer to finding her.

We ascended, so far up that my ears popped uncomfortably. When the doors dinged open, Evan Chase was waiting.

He seemed agitated and anxious, though it obviously wasn't for my arrival. His gray eyes grazed over my face for barely a second, before they were fixed on Riley, questions heavy in them.

"Well, anything?"

"No, sir. We got here with no problems."

Riley replied easily, though I heard the boredom in his voice. Maybe he thought Evan's game, whatever it was, was fickle. I still didn't understand what exactly was going on around me, and why Evan was so eager for us to run into Scarlett. If he had wanted me brought here, it made no sense that he hoped she would intercept and take me away.

"You didn't even see her? Or her sister, or her pet—the nurse from the Fringe?"

Evan's questioning continued, and Riley replied with the negative each time.

I stood there dumbly, my brain caught, glitching, wrapped so hard around a single piece of information that everything else was lost to me. "Her pet—the nurse from the Fringe." I didn't know what horrified me more, the fact that Scarlett had a human girl who was described as her pet, or that there was someone else close to her, someone who according to Evan, she was obsessed with.

The more I thought about it, the more it stung, the more I felt like a silly little girl who'd run off into the woods to chase a dream, only to wake up and realize it had been a nightmare. I didn't want to be Scarlett's pet, I didn't know exactly what I did want to be to her, but it wasn't that. Still, I couldn't deny I was jealous. She had always been mine, at least to me, and she was something I had never wanted to or planned on sharing with the rest of the world. Now I wondered if she was ever even mine, or if I was always just hers?

Around me, the conversation had continued, and only the tightening of a cold grip on my arm brought me back to the present.

"Take her to the staff quarters on your way out. Ask for Cece and tell her she can stop her insufferable grumbling. She has an assistant."

Though he issued demands rather than speaking, the same way Scarlett had done, somehow, he lacked the finality, the absoluteness she had possessed, and it showed. He lingered as the party of vampires and I stepped back into the elevator, watching, as if he was waiting to ensure that what he had ordered would be done.

We stepped back out into the lobby on the first floor, though it was as close to leaving the tower as I got. Riley led me to a door off to one side of the high-ceilinged space, and I went because, by now, I knew fighting would be futile. He rapped on the wood once and then flung the door open, pushing me to step inside ahead of him. The lighting was dim, and my eyes took a second to adjust.

Ahead of us was a long corridor lined with doors. A lopsided old camp table was set up at the end and standing behind it was a woman of about thirty. She looked from me to Riley before she spoke. It took me a second to realize she was checking our eyes to see who was human and who wasn't.

"Yes, sir, what can I do for you?"

"This girl is to be taken to Cece. Mr. Chase says she'll be her assistant."

With this, Riley pushed me forward, and then, with a cool gust of air, he was gone in a heartbeat, the door swinging closed behind him.

CECE TURNED OUT to be an older woman, human. She looked me over with equal parts interest and boredom when I arrived at the door on the corridor that was apparently hers.

"I asked for an assistant, and you're what he sent me? Don't suppose you've ever held a broom, have you, girl? You don't have a hidden talent for making the silverware sparkle?"

She looked old, maybe sixty, but her eyes were sharp and her words were sharper.

"Never mind that, get in here before we have the rest of them come knocking. Rare to have your own room here, you know... Where did you come from? You're too clean for the Fringe."

I looked down at my filthy jeans and my blue jacket that was torn down one arm.

"I came from the bunker, ma'am."

Politeness seemed like the best way to handle this, and immediately, I was gratified. Cece's face softened and she rose an inch in height. It was clear she appreciated the address.

"Well, I suppose you'll do. What's your name?"

"Rayne."

I rubbed my cold hands over the dirty denim on my thighs and peered past her—she was barely taller than me. The room we stood in was small, smaller than my room at home. Twin cots were inside, one pushed against each wall. The one to the left had a worn patchwork quilt, extra pillows and shams lined the space where it met the wall, and at the foot and side of it were boxes and belongings; the one to the right was bare mattress except for a cotton sheet. I already knew which one would be mine.

Cece followed my gaze.

"I know what you're thinking. Our young Master Evan is quite generous. We have real beds here, and it doesn't get too cold, not even at night."

I looked at her dumbly—it was freezing on the corridor, and the room was barely better—but I didn't detect any sarcasm in her voice.

Sharp brown eyes watched me, her gray-streaked amber-colored hair was rolled up into an elaborate twist, and she wore a white apron over her black slacks, her outfit half obscured by a floor-length thick duffel coat.

"Now..."

She wrapped her bony fingers around my arm and led me to the bare bed.

"You're quite lucky you landed with me. The others are eight to a room."

She gave me a wry smile, and I tried to return the expression, struggling to keep up, to take in my sudden change in circumstance after endless days in the bunker.

"I'm the head of the maid service...which is composed of me, me, and me... But I have the power to enlist any of the others to help me with odd jobs here and there. It's my job, and now yours too, to keep the tower looking spick-and-span, for the good Master."

Sarcasm was definitely present that time.

"I clean every floor of this tower that's in use by the Chase family, every day, and you're going to help."

I nodded stiffly, sensing she was waiting for me to say something.

"How do they...pay us?"

I had a feeling I already knew the answer.

Cece laughed, a rasping, hacking laugh. It bubbled up from her chest and hung loud in the air around us before she leaned toward me and her face became totally somber.

"They let us live."

From there, conversation died, and Cece went off to see to her errands after she informed me that I would start as her assistant tomorrow, and I ought to tidy myself up as she had a standard to uphold. I had no change of clothes, and there was no water in the room. My hair was still in its braid, though strands of it were loose and wild around my face. I reached up and flattened them down as best I could. I didn't dare to unbraid it and risk letting it tangle—I had no idea when I'd next see a hairbrush. It was funny. Until Cece mentioned it, I hadn't really worried about my appearance— there had been far more important things to worry about— but now, I felt absolutely filthy.

The room had no windows, and this kind of imprisonment was becoming a common theme in my life. Back at my house, I was a prisoner to my father, to myself. I had escaped and chosen to come here to find better, to find Scarlett. All I had found was a different kind of cage.

I thought about that for a long time. Though my body ached from spending so long on the concrete floor, it didn't feel safe to lie down on my cot, so I sat there and stared at the mismatched scraps making up Cece's quilt. Evaluating all the choices that had brought me here led me slowly, sneakily, back to the reason I had made them, and by the time I realized how far my mind had wandered, it was too late to derail it.

I remembered it all so clearly. The rust of my blood in the air and the limpness of my father's body, the way she shrugged it off with such ease when she was done. I remembered Scarlett in perfect detail, though the time between her hovering over me and my waking up days later was still lost. Her hair had hung forward, almost tickling my face as she loomed above me, her lips were still slightly parted, and the corners of her mouth were wet with bright crimson blood.

She was beautiful to me then, captivating and disturbingly fascinating, and terrifying. The second time she came to me, she was compelling beyond belief. The memory of her cool weight against me, slim fingers wrapped around my throat... I wanted to lose myself to it, to let go and lie back and live it, relive it, escape.

The door opened so fast it swung on its hinges and hit the wall with a loud thud, making me jump backward further onto the bed. Heat bled into my cheeks when I opened my eyes and saw Evan Chase standing in the doorway.

Silently, I had to reassure myself that my thoughts were my own, because somehow, standing in front of him, having him burst in while my body was just starting to burn from the memory of her, felt like an invasion, an intrusion, beyond a coincidence. I told myself I was being paranoid.

"Rayne Kennedy."

His hands were in his pockets and he stepped into the small room. I was grateful he didn't close the door behind him. I felt too vulnerable here, like this.

"I trust you like Chase Tower?"

He held up his hands now, looking around the room as if to admire it, mocking. I nodded because it seemed like the smart thing to do.

"Good, now tell me. What did Scarlett Pearce want with you?"

He waited, intently, holding on for my every word, and I struggled to find anything to say that would somehow make this all go away, make him lose interest in me, maybe even convince him to just give me to Scarlett.

"*Well*?" he yelled, his voice breaking into the closest thing to a screech I thought a man could manage. In any other situation, I would have stifled a laugh.

"What does that stuck-up bitch want with you? Is she fucking you? Drinking from you? Training you? What?"

His questions came fast, and I didn't like what any of them implied.

"Do you mean... Jade's sister?"

It was a simple question, only meant to stall him and buy me time, but just like that, it gave me my angle.

"Yes."

He hissed the word and I could tell his patience was running out.

"I don't know, I came here with Jade... We met in school, she's my best friend. She said she had to leave, but we could be together here. She's the best friend I ever had, so I came."

He studied me. His gray eyes were hard, steely, and I knew he wasn't quite convinced. I spoke again.

"You're not going to tell, are you?"

His gaze flashed with interest, and I was bluffing harder than I ever had in my life.

"When we came, I told the officers I'd forced Jade to bring me because I didn't want her to get in trouble. She told me she lived in Boston. I thought we would live in the city together, that it would be fun..."

I lowered my eyes pathetically, and his frustrated sigh told me he was buying this.

"Did she ever drink from you?"

I snapped my blue eyes up to his liquid ones.

"Drink... What do... Do you... Jade's not..." I did my best to look horrified. "Jade's a—"

"Vampire." He finished my sentence and continued, exasperated. "And stupid enough to bring you in here, but smart enough to say you're Scarlett's."

Pacing back and forth in front of me, he rubbed his temples, and I watched as all my false pieces tumbled into place, and whatever plan he'd had fell apart.

"You're not going to tell, are you?"

This time, the fear in my voice was real, though momentarily I wondered when I got so brave, brave enough to play these games with anyone, let alone vampires. I feared horribly my bravery could mean bad things for Jade.

"There would be no point."

He spat the words, with a venom that surfaced from nowhere, and stayed as he continued, turning on me, his face twisted into a mask of resentment.

"The Government will protect the Pearces, their precious punishers, just like they always do, because to them, having one stupid gene accounts for more than any other contribution, even if this entire society was built on it."

My mind held on to his words, particularly "precious punishers," though I had no time to analyze them as he continued.

"The only reason they know why some of us can walk in the sun is because of my father's work. We isolated the Delta gene, the Chases, and yet here we are, inferior, secondary to them, secondary to *her*. She's sick and superior and she thinks she lives above the law, yet the Government rewards her, they protect her and forgive her."

He had come closer, so close that his breath was cool and moist on my face. I fought not to close my eyes. I knew he was talking about Scarlett.

"She is nothing but a sick puppet and old money. My father built the very premise that flung this entire city into the twenty-first century, and he has the technology to take it further, to give all of us the Delta gene, to make us all day-walkers and rid us of this ridiculous divide... And where is he now?"

Finally, he stepped away, and I took a sharp breath, resisting the urge to wipe my face.

"Disappeared. Taken into the bunker. The man who paved the way for our great city..."

He laughed a bloodcurdling laugh, and I dug my fingers harder into the edge of the mattress. Evan Chase's intensity scared me; he reminded me of the tyrants, the radicals we had learned about at school. I knew I was unimportant to him, just a pawn in a much bigger game plan, but it was becoming increasingly obvious that Scarlett was the king, and the queen.

"And we live here, his family, kept out of the inner circle, forever in the shadow of the Delta families, the Pearces... Scarlett Pearce and her short dresses, her dead-eyed servants, and all her fancy knives."

He was frantic now, pacing again, his words building, rising to something, as he grew taller.

"But we'll take Vires back. My father will get the credit he deserves, and the Chases will take our rightful place, not below the Government, but as them. Scarlett Pearce and the other Deltas will be crushed under our feet, then we'll do what should have been done long before now and give every vampire here the power to walk in the daylight."

He stopped, though he didn't look at me, and I wondered if he even remembered I was there. My blood was ice; the thought of anyone hurting Scarlett put bile in my mouth and a sick dread in my stomach. If I thought it would do any good, I would have lunged at him, but my strength had never been physical, and it certainly wasn't going to be in Vires.

"I'll take Vires for my father, just like they took him from us, because they didn't know to take one other thing... They don't have his insurance policy. I do."

He rubbed the back of his hand over his mouth, and he seemed, oddly enough, to be catching his breath—strange, given he didn't have to breathe, unless of course that was something Scarlett could do because of this Delta gene. I didn't know.

"You're no use to my plan, but you'll stay here. Cece needs an assistant and I need this place ready. Soon, everyone will want to visit. Soon, we'll be the important ones, once we free Vires from the tyranny of the Government and the Pearces."

His eyes were glazed for a few seconds, and I sensed him imagining whatever sick victory he thought he might find before he came back to the moment.

"You'll start tomorrow. Do your work, stay on my good side, and I'll let you live."

With that, he was gone, the door slamming behind him just as hard as it had when he entered. I was left alone, to try to decipher his frenzied monologue, to decide how much stock I could place in his words, how much someone who seemed, to me, slightly unhinged might actually be capable of. Most of all, I was left alone to worry.

FROM THERE, TIME moved fast, and it moved slow. I was the property of the Chase family and Cece's housekeeping assistant for three long and painful weeks where everything remained utterly the same. I was trapped, choking on my fear of what Evan Chase was planning for Scarlett, of why Scarlett had never come to save me, and of what she might have had planned for me if I'd made it to Pearce Tower with

Jade. The more I heard about her in hushed whispers and hateful rants, the harder I questioned what I knew of her. Ultimately, my faith in her would bend, but never quite break. She stayed beautiful to me, despite the copious descriptions of her as a bloodthirsty Government punisher, who enforced the laws of Vires with torturous consequences worse than death—and reveled in it.

Life inside Chase Tower felt archaic, medieval. I learned quickly to address Evan Chase and his siblings as "sir" and "ma'am" after a backhand to the face one monotonous morning. The pain was almost welcome, because just for a second, I felt as if my head had been lifted from the stagnant water that drowned me slowly, and for the first time in weeks I took a breath. It was over too fast.

Cece and I cleaned every inch of the tower floors that were inhabited by the family—surprisingly, there were only five of them, out of the ten, maybe fifteen I thought might exist up the tall structure. The fifth floor was the only one totally off-limits to us, and according to Cece, it contained Evan's father's old laboratory.

Though I was nothing more than a ghost, resuming my old role and slipping back into my invisibility cloak, this time, I had a purpose. Though I hadn't seen the sun for weeks, and my heart fell further every day I heard nothing from Scarlett and felt so little down the emotional line I once believed tied us, I watched and listened and devoted myself to gathering information because that was all I could do.

Evan Chase had some kind of weapon, something that could hurt vampires, something unprecedented, and something he and he alone had the cure for. That was as much as I could glean from a snippet of a conversation here, a scrap of handwritten paper there. As much as I spied on him, he never seemed to notice, he was so absorbed in whatever plot he was cultivating, and that was fine with me. The one time I had walked into his room when he was replacing a painting on the wall, he had been particularly angry, though he underestimated me so chronically that when I asked if he wanted help dusting his paintings, he let me go without a beating. Those were commonplace around here, and at least once a week someone returned to the corridor crying.

Life in Chase Tower was no cakewalk, but somehow, it felt like a decent alternative to the bunker. It was as though I lived in a bubble keeping me in and keeping the city out, the place where Scarlett beat and branded people, and others starved in the Fringe while the vampires took life as if it was meaningless and exploited humans in every way. I had learned a lot, about the brothel in the city's core, the personal slaves some of the vampires took and trained, and some days, my life inside Evan Chase's home felt safe; dull and bland and colorless, but safe.

Of course, it was only a matter of time until that bubble would break, rupture, and bleed out in the most glorious rush of color and adrenaline I knew I had been craving. After almost two months of being totally absent, finally, Scarlett reappeared in my life.

Chapter Nine

CECE WOKE ME up in a frenzy, and I had no idea what time it was. The alarm that usually sounded down the corridor at 06:00 a.m. hadn't yet, or at least I thought it hadn't. Either way, Cece was standing over my bare bed.

"Girl... Get up. Master sent a message, he's hosting a dinner, tonight, and he wants the tower pristine."

I nodded groggily, wishing only to stay under the relative warmth of my thin sheet and in the darkness of my dreamless sleep.

"Come on!"

Cece raised her hands and beckoned for me to get out of bed.

"Scarlett Pearce is coming to the tower tonight, girl. Everything has to be just so, the Master is going to be in a foul mood no matter what, but we might as well cover our bases."

Just like that, I was wide awake. Lightning had struck me; every nerve, every synapse, every sinew of muscle was awake, alive, ready. All my hope was as justified as my snap decision to come here. Today was the day, and, finally, Scarlett was coming.

MY PALMS WERE slick with sweat turned pink, though my fingers had stopped bleeding. Cece and I scrubbed and swept and polished until our hands were raw. A message had come before noon, telling me the Master had decided I would be present for the dinner, and I should come to the dining floor by six o'clock that night. I'd had all day to go over his motive for this, to consider it inside out and back to front. All I could come up with was that this was some sort of test to see if I had lied and had any real affinity for Scarlett. Or perhaps he hoped to see that she somehow cared for me.

The way she was described in this world made me doubt it. I'd heard enough to know she was considered brutal and bloodthirsty, dangerous and power hungry, but I'd also seen enough of Evan Chase to know he hated her, resented her for her genetics, or maybe something else. If she wanted me even in the slightest, he wouldn't pass up the opportunity to dangle me in front of her face—I was eternally grateful for that. I just had to see her, to stand in the same room as her and wait for everything to fall back into place, just like things had fallen perfectly out of it when she first found me.

I waited with my back against the smooth wall, as I'd been instructed to. Cece had been clear that I wasn't to move off the wall, I shouldn't speak unless spoken to, and I should keep my eyes off the dinner table for the most part. I was basically commissioned to be a statue, though I didn't mind. Somewhere along the way, I'd grown fond of Cece, and perhaps she liked having me around too, though whether it was because she made me clean the toilets, or because she liked the company, I had no idea.

My mouth had been dry all day, and it was dry still. Evan Chase hadn't said a word when he entered the room, and he continued to act as if I didn't exist. Other staff hurried around the long table silently, fixing the silverware, laying out dinner rolls and appetizers that made my stomach twist painfully—it had been weeks, maybe even a month since I had eaten anything other than stale white bread and kidney beans. The master of the tower hovered by the window, the glass in his hand meant to profess his nonchalance, though he seemed nervous. He shoved one hand in his pocket, then pulled it out again to run over his hair, then lowered it to fiddle with the hem of his jacket. Once again, Evan Chase looked like a boy in a grown man's suit, and somehow, I knew he was a child playing with fire.

For a second, I pitied him, though I regretted it instantly. He had only hit me once and compared to the stories filtering through the servants' corridor, life inside Chase Tower almost seemed like a reprieve, yet he was the enemy. The memory of his gray eyes, hard as nails and set like steel as he spoke about Scarlett, came back to me, and just like that, it was so easy to hate him.

Scarlett was coming. The inside of my head felt like a broken shortwave radio; I'd go off down one track of thought, but then the conversation would falter, the frequency would grow faint and blur and something else would cut through, an urgent message, as impossible to ignore as an SOS. Scarlett Pearce was coming for me.

Just to keep from holding my breath was a battle, because I had waited for her, I had served my time, lived through my trial, and repented for my doubt, and I was so ready to be with her. It had been so long the memories felt worn now, faded in my head, a photograph touched too many times.

I ached for the real thing, to feel her cool skin through her minimal clothing, to feel the aura of complete safety and absolute danger she inherently came with. I wanted her ice-cold lips on mine to tell me I was vindicated, and those galaxy eyes, and some sort of promise that it all wasn't for nothing, that somehow, this would turn out right. I wanted Scarlett to set me on fire again and burn me out of my cage. And after all that, I needed a hundred answers.

Most of all, I just wanted her.

My heart dropped, tumbling into my stomach and churning there, tossing and turning as the clack of heels rang on the corridor outside the door. I could feel her, she was coming. Her emotions were untouchable, a smooth stone wall, but her presence was a wildfire, burning closer and closer, ready to destroy everything standing in its path. The door opened and I wanted to scream, to throw my head back and fall to my knees and cry. After weeks of living on hope, I was justified. After a drought that almost killed me, I was drenched in pouring crimson rain, saved.

She stepped into the room and I was frozen, feeling everything all at once, while my feet bound me to my spot, and what little strategy I had left managed to hold me still and silent.

I had lived for this moment, fallen asleep to it in the evening, and woken up crying for it in the middle of the night. The ways she might greet me had been numerous; her slim arms around me, maybe her cold body against mine, or maybe just my name on her lips, as magical as she always made it. In my dreams I was always brave, always daring, but now, looking at her in her magnificence, I was less, nervousness making a meal of all my carefully built confidence, until it was uncertainty as much as strategy keeping me by the wall.

Eyes swept the room, but I was too far away to relive their colors. I watched, holding my breath until they were on me, and even after they were gone. The ease with which her gaze passed over me made me ache, sent the first slivers of devastation spilling into my stomach. Fireworks were exploding all around me because she was back, she was here, we were together, yet she was silent down our emotional connection, ice cold and razor sharp, and when she had looked at me, the flashback I had felt from her wasn't enough.

I couldn't exist in a world where she didn't want me, a world where all of this, my trading of my ruined but familiar old life for a new but equally ruined one, would be for nothing.

Evan Chase interrupted my staring. He moved toward her faster than humanly possible, and I choked. In the time it took for me to blink he was standing in front of her, and the fear his sudden proximity to her brought with it was enough to get my body to move.

I was barely half an inch off the wall before I felt it.

Stop.

For the first time in weeks, whatever lived between us roared back to life, and I could hear her voice in my head, feel her pushing, holding me against the wall with a single command that was totally absolute and unbreakable. It knocked the breath right out of me, because just for a split second, I felt everything. All her anger, her despair, the sleepless nights of planning and her hours spent by the window looking out over the city that held me away from her. The shards that pierced her skin when she broke the mirror the night she found out Evan had taken me, and the anticipation as she walked through the lobby just seconds before the present, her trepidation at seeing me. I saw flashes of myself through her eyes, bloodied and dying, cold and scared on a bathroom floor, peaceful on the bed, and somehow, I was always beautiful, at least to her.

The tsunami rushed in, and I let it swallow me. Long after Scarlett had thrown the dam back up, I still basked in the life it had drenched me with, after weeks alone in a desert of uncertainty.

"Evan..."

Her voice was low and dangerous, and the scene before me was going to unfold with or without me. The command in my head was still heavy, it seeped into my being, and for better or for worse, I knew I wouldn't leave the wall. I didn't question if I physically could; the interaction happening between the vampires was too important.

"Scarlett..."

He sneered her name. It only made her smile that amused smile I knew so well, twisted slightly now, dangerous on her painted crimson lips.

She looked different to me, yet she was exactly the same. Her makeup was dark, smoky lids and thick mascara, smooth olive skin and blood-red lips. A deep green dress hugged her body below her leather jacket, and her shoes were her standard black patent pumps, tall and shiny. She looked as deadly as I knew she was. Her outfit was familiar, but her expression was harder, more unreadable than I had ever known it to be. The hints of softness I knew could touch her features were long gone, and what was left behind reminded me of the night she had killed my father.

Somebody else entered the room behind her. I only noticed when the door clicked as the woman who trailed Scarlett closed it. She was taller than me, and a little taller than Scarlett. A crimson satin dress hung on her slim form and golden hair fell halfway down her back. When the woman turned, I didn't recognize her. She kept her eyes to the carpet underfoot, but it was impossible to ignore her beauty. Her features were finely set and perfectly proportioned; though she was slender, she filled the dress in a way I never would, and there was an air of something about her, something I feared I would never possess. For the second time in my life, I was jealous to my bones over someone being close to Scarlett.

"You brought your pet..."

Evan looked past Scarlett, and despite the terseness of the greeting, the room seemed to relax. I stayed frozen, wound tight with jealousy and anxiety, my old friend doubt tickling the back of my neck. Scarlett had waited for me, she had wanted me, been furious about my capture and suffered guilt about my coming to Vires. I had felt it all first hand, yet I was unsettled by the blonde woman's presence, and by the very fact that Scarlett kept a human being as a pet, like an animal.

Scarlett stepped around Evan, seemingly ignoring him as she proceeded to seat herself at one end of the table, taking the head without invitation nor question. Evan's wineglass trembled when he turned and saw her sitting there, leaning back against the chair, relaxed for everything he was on edge, but he said nothing.

"Aria. Sit."

Scarlett spoke, and I watched the woman as she sank down to the carpet, her hands in her lap, her head bowed like a child. She obeyed the command like a dog. It was grotesque, repulsive, yet it fascinated me. Scarlett radiated power, she was magnificent, and part of me was aware that she was dark, twisted, and utterly malignant. I pressed my palms against the wall and, for the first time around her, I tried to censor my emotions. Part of me was scared by the display, but the awe I felt, the jealousy still pummeling my insides—that scared me more.

Evan moved slowly to sit beside Scarlett. Without a word, he waved his hand, and staff poured in from a door on the wall opposite me. I had no idea why I was expecting them to eat a four-course meal for dinner.

I recognized a few of the men who dragged them in; they sometimes said hello on the corridor downstairs, but now, they were strangers. Their faces were masks, some of disgust, some of anger and hatred, but none of them stopped. They dragged a girl who looked around my age and a boy, slightly older, into the room.

"Just what you like, no? Eighteen, pretty girl, virgin too I'm told... Though if you want to play with your dinner, someone will escort you to a room. I'd prefer not to watch."

"Have you been stalking me, Evan... Should I be worried, or flattered? Who knew you paid me so much attention?"

Scarlett's voice was sickly sweet when she replied, though it was laced with bitter mocking.

"I drank before I came. I like to catch my own kill."

I wasn't sure if I was relieved to hear that or even more mortified. Either way, my stomach rolled uncomfortably. The girl looked so normal, so much like me, or Zara, or someone from school. She was just a teenager, brought here to live or die by Scarlett's choosing. The parallel that sprang unbidden into my mind made my heart beat faster. I closed my eyes when she screamed. When I opened them, both the boy and the girl were dead in my fellow servants' arms, their heads hanging loose, necks twisted to an unnatural angle, and being carried away. Evan Chase was wiping his mouth.

"You don't want to drink, you've barely said a word, why did you come, Scarlett?"

Evan's frustration was growing, along with his obvious discomfort.

"You invited me, Ev-an." The way her lips and teeth wrapped around his name made it sound comical.

"To drink and...chat. You're a well-connected woman, who better to discuss the politics and prosperity of our great city with?"

They were playing games, dangerous games I didn't fully understand, though I knew he had invited Scarlett here so she would see me, and so he could see her reaction. So far, she hadn't even looked at me. I told myself it was because she was smart enough to know better.

"You want to know if Daddy dear is still alive?"

Evan stiffened, curling his fingers into the seat of his chair so hard that when, finally, he caught himself and relaxed, I saw clean imprints of each one.

"You know something about my father?"

Scarlett nodded nonchalantly, then plucked the man's wine glass from his hand and raised it to her lips for a long swig, before she made a face and threw it across the room. The glass smashed against the wall and I jumped at the sudden sound, cringing as she spat the dark liquid unapologetically onto the beige shag carpet beside her chair.

"He's alive."

She made no attempt to explain or apologize for her actions, reclining again, those eyes I missed so much fixed on Evan's face. She was baiting him, and it seemed like such a bad idea. Vampire politics were lost on me, but something about the way I had come to work at Chase Tower told me Scarlett couldn't just take me away at her whim. I belonged to Evan Chase, according to the laws of the city of Vires, and so far, Scarlett's efforts to take me back had consisted of amping up her usual abrasiveness and spitting red wine on his carpet.

"He's deep in the bunker, but last I heard, he was as alive as you can be when you're dead."

Evan leaned forward, and for the first time he looked his age, he looked vulnerable.

"Are they torturing him for information, what?"

Scarlett had already lost interest.

"I don't know, Evan, I told you all I know, and that's only what I heard. I haven't had reason to go to the core lately. I do my work, keep my hands dirty."

She shrugged before she looked directly at me.

"Get me a drink, something stronger than this. Bring the whiskey."

She looked away.

There was nothing, no flicker of recognition, no spark down our connection. I felt nothing, and it scared me more than anything had since my arrival in Vires. What I had sensed from her earlier when she had told me to stay back paled, shimmering out of view as if I was looking at it from above the water and it was too deep below the surface for me to retrieve. It slipped between my fingers just like all my other memories of her had over the past weeks, and again, doubt's cold kisses nipped at my temples.

Scarlett was still speaking to Evan, her tone flat, all the spark of the game diminished. Her words seemed almost comforting.

"You need a drink." She was still playing. "Are you deaf?"

She spat the words, and only when she looked at me again did I realize I hadn't moved. I turned quickly and made a beeline for the door, stumbling in the same dirty sneakers I had worn the night she saved my life. Outside the dining room, I could breathe, yet I was suffocating. Moving away from her was unnatural, it was anti-gravity, and every piece of me strained, screamed to go back to her. Luckily Cece was waiting. I guessed she had been listening, and a bottle topped by two glasses was thrust into my hands before she ushered me back into the room. I had no time to think or plan.

Nobody looked up when I entered, and I almost tripped over the woman who had accompanied Scarlett, having totally forgotten she was there. I whispered an apology and she turned her head ever so slightly, offering me the ghost of a smile. She was human; her eyes were a brilliant but natural green. Not knowing what else to do, I set the bottle on the edge of the table and stepped back against the wall.

The room was quiet, devoid of sound but brimming over with tension, and the static charge against Scarlett's emotional radio silence was killing me. She poured two generous glasses of the liquor I had retrieved, and they both drank in silence. I watched them watch each other over the rim of their respective tumblers, and I wondered how this would all end.

"You need to cheer up, Evan. Perhaps you'll accompany me at the punishment center tomorrow."

Scarlett swirled her drink and I wondered why she was volunteering to spend time with the man who was keeping us apart, whether he knew it or not. Evan shook his head, and something in both their faces told me he was never going to say yes. That and the way he ran Chase Tower—there was no branding and no real beatings here.

"Well, what about a game? We both know I'll beat you at every variety of poker, so what?"

She drummed her lacquered nails against the hardwood table top as if awaiting an answer, though everyone in the room knew the question had been rhetorical.

"I brought my pet... How about a little test? She's been doing well lately; I'm almost bored with how good she's been."

Scarlett paused for just a second and then she laughed. The sound was soft, yet it sent goose bumps over my skin.

"Sometimes, I miss all the fire, all our little struggles, but then I remember, there's no greater pleasure than winning on a horse you broke yourself."

"What are you getting at, Scarlett?"

Evan spoke curtly, and I sensed he was tiring of this. He had sent orders to us so early he must have been keyed up since before dawn, and the emphasis that had been put on everything being just so for Scarlett's visit told me he cared deeply about her perception of him.

"A bet."

She explained herself easily, unperturbed by his shortness.

"We'll see who has the more loyal pet. Winner keeps the loser's."

Just like that, she had won his interest.

"You'd give her up? You've been training her for weeks, all those displays and punishments in the market, the big show about taking the only nurse in the Fringe... Why?"

"Call me confident."

She took another large mouthful of whiskey, and I wondered if she was drunk.

"Or cocky."

Evan was getting braver by the minute. It was obvious by the way he had spoken about Scarlett he found her arrogant, and maybe he thought this was his chance to exploit that... I worried he was right. Scarlett seemed totally at ease.

"The nurse for..."

She waited, and Evan glanced around the room. His gray eyes settled on me.

"You want the girl. Of course, it all makes sense now."

Scarlett shrugged.

"You caught me. My sister can be quite persistent, and she seems to really like this one."

I didn't know how she knew about my story, or even if she did, but I was grateful our accounts of my arrival in Vires seemed to correlate.

Everyone was quiet, and I knew he was considering. The weight of the decision hung in the room, and I wondered if Scarlett was holding her metaphorical breath, as I held mine.

"If you don't want to risk it, I understand, Evan. Your family never was much for risk...for winning."

She looked totally at ease, running her fingers over the grains in the wooden table top, her slim form reclined, her gaze lazy as it lingered on his face. She was a black panther, playing with her prey, and he squirmed in her grasp.

"And yours were always all for arrogance."

He tried to deliver his reply smoothly, but his voice was frayed, and it occurred to me for the first time that vampires mustn't sweat—if they did, I was sure Evan Chase would be drenched by now.

"Fine."

His cards were down, and just like that, the game was on.

"Your pet against mine, the owner of the most obedient keeps both."

Scarlett's expression cracked ever so slightly, and I knew Evan was playing right into her hands.

"You've been training the nurse for weeks, I've had the girl for barely two."

Evan protested like a child, but she simply waved him quiet.

"That just means Aria has had weeks to grow to resent me, hate me even. She loses this challenge and she's yours. If I was you, I'd like those odds... Of course, I'm me, and I know how well I've trained her. I believe she won't act against me, even if it is in her own best interest."

For a sliver of a second, I could see why Evan found her to be so grating. I knew Scarlett was pushing his buttons, but she pulled off egotistical and arrogant so very well. Part of me didn't doubt she had every reason to be. The girl she called Aria had barely moved since she had sat on the carpet, and she stayed quiet now, a passive observer in a discussion that would alter the course of her future in a way I guessed would be drastic. Of course, it could also alter mine, and all I had to do was lose.

He turned, and the cold, quiet anger simmering in his steely eyes scared me. His victory rode on me, his chance to win, and I knew from his outbursts, from observing the hatred he felt for the Delta vampires in his daily life, that letting him down would not be forgiven. Once again, all I could do was count on Scarlett to protect me and ignore all the times she hadn't.

"Sit down, now."

He pulled out a chair for me and I forced my leaden legs to move. I crossed the room and sank down beside him. Scarlett's eyes were on me, the corners of her lips were turned up, and she studied me carefully. I looked back at her, forcing myself to hold her gaze. The display of courage would have been gargantuan a month ago, yet it came so easily to me now. I almost felt as if she owed me the eye contact.

"Aria."

Those odd-colored eyes never left me as she spoke, even as she threw back the chair beside her and the girl moved to stand beside it.

"Mistress..."

It was the first time she had spoken, though her voice was little more than a whisper. As much as I wanted to continue to look at Scarlett, to watch her irises gravitate around her pupils, I couldn't help but turn my attention to Aria. Somehow, she too was a piece of what Scarlett was.

"On...the chair?"

My heart fell. She seemed somehow disbelieving and I wondered what Scarlett had done to her, how she had broken Aria down so thoroughly that she could barely believe she was being invited to sit in a seat. My eyes lingered on the slender collar around Aria's neck. It was studded with sparkling crimson stones...scarlet stones. The ownership it displayed put bile in my mouth, and again, I questioned my own desires—was whatever game I was entering into one I really wanted to lose?

I knew Scarlett from the inside out; I felt her more than I had any hard facts or concrete statistics about who or what she was. To lose the game would be to lay myself at her mercy; by the end of the week, I too could be wearing her collar and be enthralled with the possibility of being allowed to sit at a table like a human being. I stopped myself. I had come here for her, to save her or whatever Jade had said, and I had come here for me, to be with her, because my life had been so devoid of color without her. Now, even if her colors were bloody reds and faded black, I would take them, anything over the nothingness.

Scarlett had dragged her down, and Aria was in the chair, and I was out of time to decide. I knew what I would do, against my better judgment or not.

The game had begun.

"Let's cut to the chase, shall we?"

Scarlett smiled, a wicked smile. I could sense something terrible was coming, something cataclysmic, something that would send me spinning back into her blood-tinged world, set me back on the rollercoaster after weeks of waiting in line under the blistering sun. I was terrified, but I ached to feel the wind whip my face.

"Give me your gun, Chase. I know you're packing, probably silver bullets... You do know that's just a myth, don't you?"

She was goading him, and he stiffened beside me.

"I'm going to enjoy beating you."

His tone betrayed his words, as from somewhere on his person he produced a gun and slid it with a long metallic scraping noise across the table.

I choked. I didn't know what I was going to be asked to do, but I knew I couldn't kill someone. Panic gripped me, icy and hot. I looked to Scarlett, but she was busy playing with the barrel, wrapping her long slim fingers around it with too much familiarity for my liking. With a series of clicks, she manipulated the weapon in ways that were unfamiliar but reminded me of the gang movies my father had sometimes watched on TV.

Hands wrapping around my thigh made me jump. My knees hit the underside of the table and a soft noise of fright escaped me. I looked sideways and Evan's face was an inch from mine, his eyes boring into me.

"You do exactly as I say, or I will make your life a living hell and you'll wish they killed you coming in over the wall. I will make you suffer."

He dug the pads of his fingers into the soft flesh at the top of my leg, and I nodded, resisting the urge to reach down and pluck his digits away, one by one. He was a madman in that moment, his eyes were so intense and so wild as they held mine. I could feel the rage broiling below the surface, all his resentment and, I suspected, the grief he felt at the loss of his father. I was now his ticket to some sort of retribution, and I was about to fail him horrifically. He held on for a few more seconds, and I continued to nod, biting my lip to keep quiet, until finally, he let go.

Scarlett watched the whole exchange, unmoving, apparently unconcerned with it, though from the corner of my eye, I thought I had seen her flinch when he had first put his hands on me. Perhaps it was just my mind being kind, letting me imagine she cared—I didn't know. She was all I had now, I had placed my bet and set my allegiance long before this point, and I was bound to see it through. No matter what she did, or what I discovered, she was still the one who haunted my dreams, she had still saved my life, and I still craved her, unbearably.

Her every move was liquid, smooth and measured. She dangled the gun carelessly from her index finger and waved it a little while she smiled wryly at Evan. She basked in his discomfort, and I wondered if this was really as important to her as it had felt when I'd experienced her emotions while she'd looked for me. She seemed to be in her element now, because although it was a game, she had all the power, and she knew it.

She placed the gun in the very center of the table and leaned back, studying it for a long moment, before she tapped it, pushing it slightly further toward my side of the table.

"We each give them a command, winner is the first to follow. Loser loses their pet to the other."

"What's the command, Scarlett?"

Evan's question set her gaze on fire. Something I didn't recognize burned across her features and lit up her eyes. She looked elated, excited, and I suddenly doubted it was because she was about to win me back.

She didn't answer his question; instead she turned to Aria.

"Look at me."

The words were soft, quiet in a way that felt deadly intimate. The woman raised her chin to comply.

"When I tell you to, you're going to pick up the gun, quickly..."

She was going to tell her to shoot me. Scarlett was going to tell Aria to kill me, and I was supposed to lose...to let her. Air caught in my throat and choked me.

"You'll pick it up, and you'll put it to your head, and pull the trigger."

The room was silent, and I wanted to vomit. None of this felt real, nothing ever had with Scarlett, but this was different. Nothing was magical now. Her presence didn't shimmer softly around me; she didn't make me feel safe and loved, and like I wasn't alone. She was a dark shadow looming on the horizon, and for some reason, I continued to run headlong toward the point where she eclipsed the sun.

"You took out the rounds?"

Evan interrupted, but Scarlett's eyes stayed on Aria. I watched the intense, silent exchange between them until it was over.

"Yes, Mistress."

The words were all Aria said, but when she lowered her eyes again, tears tracked down her cheeks, and I knew she would do it. Evan had to be right, Scarlett must have removed the bullets... She must have.

He grabbed me roughly by the neck of my shirt and yanked my face close to his, my ribs colliding with the arm of my chair, the force bruising.

"She's taken out the bullets, so you do it, do you hear? You do exactly as she said, when I tell you. You pick up that gun, put it to your head, and pull the trigger. If you don't, you'll wish you had...even if it kills you."

I nodded, numb.

"Do you understand?"

I nodded faster and he shook me once, jerking my body hard, making my chest batter against the chair again. I wanted to vomit.

"Yes...sir."

I was glad I remembered the title. By now, Aria wasn't the only one with tears in her eyes. This had gone too far, too far for me to stop, to turn around, and honestly, sickeningly, I was too close to being with Scarlett again to be sure I wanted to.

"So we're ready?"

Scarlett didn't wait for an answer.

"On three, then. One, two, three... Now, Aria, do it now."

She gave her command just as Evan barked his at me.

"Pick it up... Pick it up or I swear to God your life won't be worth living."

He continued, his face close to the side of mine, his voice ringing loud in my ear, while across the table Scarlett sat silent, her command issued.

"Pick it up, or I'll make them all suffer. Cece will go first, and they'll all watch while she's beaten to death... Pick up the gun."

For the first time, I considered that I might have to win. Cece had been kind to me, she had accepted me into her room and into her life. Though she kept to herself, she had made me welcome, she had let me belong in a way so few people had. My face must have fallen, because just as I thought it, I felt Scarlett push back.

No.

Her command was silent, but it rang in my head, heavy, and it paralyzed me. I couldn't pick up the gun if I tried, and now, all doubt that I didn't want to was gone.

In one swift move, the gun was off the table, and I couldn't stifle the scream that erupted at the sight before me.

"Don't do it... Don't—"

Evan hit me hard across the face, the force sending my body spilling over the opposite side of the chair. I stayed there for a few seconds, my hand over my bloody mouth. The shot rang before I sat up, and when I did, Aria was dead.

I looked from her body—her head lolled over the back of the chair, her golden hair splayed over her shoulders, the perfectly round hole in the middle of her forehead just beginning to bleed—to Scarlett.

Scarlett was still as a statue, and she was looking straight at me. I trembled, and I reached out for her emotionally, because now, I was terrified. This had been more than a game, it was real, and somehow the death I had just witnessed affected me more than my father's ever had.

Everything was quiet in the wake of the shot. I heard muffled footsteps outside the door, but no one dared to disturb us. My breathing was off-kilter, ragged and broken, and I stared at Scarlett, screaming a thousand silent questions, and as always getting absolutely nothing in return. We stayed like that until, finally, Evan Chase exploded.

He grabbed me by the shoulders, and pivoted out of his seat beside me, to land on top of me, an unrecognizable snarling, spitting mess. My voice was lost, I couldn't scream, it happened so fast, and now, all I could see was his fangs, the fangs that would pierce my throat, maybe tear it out, though it wouldn't matter. Once I was bitten, by Vires law, I was as good as dead anyway. He leaned down toward me and I closed my eyes.

The bite never came. His nails tore open my arms when he was dragged off me, and his body colliding with the wall sounded like bricks falling on concrete. Scarlett hovered over me now, perched on the table, looking down at me, her eyes wild and feral, her fingers twisted into claws.

I gazed up at her, speechless, breathless, and tried not to burst into tears. She looked so different like that, terrifying, terrible, but wild and powerful and beautiful. Once again, she was my savior.

She leaped away, jumping clean from the table to land on her feet and kicking Evan Chase back to the ground before he could get up.

"You don't touch what's mine."

She spat the words and the man pinned under her thin stiletto heel hissed back, though he made no attempt to rise.

"You set me up, Pearce, you set me up, again!"

Scarlett turned and walked away, wordless, but Evan wasn't finished.

"Why did you leave it loaded?"

He shouted the words louder than was necessary in a quiet space and, as terrified as I was of him, my mind echoed the question.

"You must have been sure you'd win. Why kill your own pet?"

Scarlett whirled around.

"Insurance policy. If by some miracle I had lost, I'd rather die than give you an uncontested victory."

He didn't believe her, and part of me didn't either, but it didn't matter.

"You're all the same... You, your father, the Government. So superior, and why? Because my father identified that gene, because he realized you'd evolved to walk in the sun... Without him, without me, you'd be nothing more than a nightwalker too, ignorant and stuck in the dark... We'd all still be equals."

He was livid, back on his feet and ranting uncontrollably. Scarlett moved closer to me. I longed for her just to come, to take me away from here, back to a quiet place, a place where she could be familiar, soft and still and mysterious, not the cool and calculating killer she was hailed as in this world. Of course, she stopped before she reached me and moved back across the room and right into Evan's personal space in barely the blink of an eye.

They stood like statues. Evan was almost a full head taller than Scarlett, but it didn't matter. She stared him down, a sick smile twisting its way onto her beautiful face before she uttered a single word.

"Thanks..."

She was daring him, and I remembered what I had heard about her killing the guards by the wall... I was sure Evan Chase had heard about that night too, because though he shook with rage, he stayed frozen. Still she waited, baiting him, testing him. Her face was in his now, more than his was in hers, and she wanted him to try, to strike her, to make any kind of stand against her. Even without really knowing their respective physical strengths, it was obvious if he tried she would tear him apart.

She laughed, a singular little noise that was barely more than a hum passing her lips before she turned and, finally, came back to me. She wrapped her arms around me and I wanted to cry. I clung to her shoulders like a child, trying to cling to all the safety I used to find in her, though it had already come back. Her slim arms were tight around my waist and she led me easily toward the door.

"Goodnight, Evan."

She called the words over her shoulder, her tone dripping with amusement, and I had a horrible feeling we hadn't seen the last of Evan Chase.

Chapter Ten

OUR DEPARTURE FROM Chase Tower passed in a blur. I didn't hear the words Cece called after us as Scarlett dragged me to the elevator; I didn't think to say goodbye or thank-you.

She smelled just as I remembered, rust and hard liquor—whiskey, and her body was cool against me, strong. I closed my eyes and clung to her, breathed her in and held on to her for dear life, because without her, my life had been so barren I almost didn't want to live. When I didn't step out of the elevator as it dinged open, Scarlett didn't seem to care. She lifted me easily, and we were moving again. My new position left me free to bury my face in her neck, in her hair, and I did so unapologetically, tears of relief soaking her. She said absolutely nothing to me in return or protest.

I sensed we were nearing the door before we reached it, the air was thinner, colder, and when she carried me out of the tower, for the first time in weeks, the wind nipped at my cheeks. I didn't lift my head, more starved for her than I was for natural light and clean air. Heels continued to click, counting out our journey, and I stayed frozen, content just to live in that moment, the one where she had found me, and for better or for worse, I was with her, I had done what I came here to do.

I heard the car door as it opened, and when she leaned down to slip me into a leather seat as cool as her skin, it took me a few seconds to unclasp my fingers and let go of her. As she slid down beside me, I caught a glimpse of her face through my watery eyes; it was made of stone, cold and smooth, expressionless. I felt like a tennis ball, beat back and forth over the barren ground between two sides, one where I was overwhelmingly safe, and the other where I was suddenly and heartbreakingly unwanted.

She sat beside me, so close, her bare leg cool against mine, even through the denim of my worn and filthy jeans. Tired of staring into the nothingness of her face, I looked down at our limbs, my scrawny dirty-jean-clad legs against her perfectly muscled, olive-toned bare ones. Her trademark heels finished off the stark comparison, and suddenly it was more than just our legs, it was a metaphor for everything she was, and all the things I wasn't. Tears welled in my eyes as I wondered how I had ever deluded myself into thinking she wanted me.

Scarlett spoke quietly to the driver, a single hushed command to take us home followed by a long pause where she seemed to reconsider. "Take us around the outside of the Midlands a few times first, and put the divider up, I don't want you staring at me for the rest of the drive."

A soft motorized humming immediately followed, and an opaque partition rose between the driver and the front seats of what I assumed was a very fancy car, and we were alone.

My eyes drifted out of the window. I gazed out through the thick tinted glass, and suddenly, I was tired, numb after everything. Every choice I had made, coming here, waiting for her, not picking up the gun, hung around my neck like leaden weights, stealing all the elation I had felt at her walking back into my life. Moisture dried, cracking against my arms, catching on my shirt, then I remembered Evan Chase's claw-like fingers as he'd hovered over me, and realized I was bleeding.

She came from nowhere. There was no soft swish of her body against the leather, no inhale or exhale as she decided to move. Without warning, Scarlett wasn't just beside me, she was all around me. Cool air tickled my cheek from her breath and the swiftness with which I had somehow ended up, barely jostled, in her lap.

I looked up at her, a million words caught on the tip of my tongue, a thousand questions burning behind my eyes. She gazed down at me, and her irises were liquid silk, green and brown and brilliant, dancing for me. She was unsure somehow, testing, and I realized it had been weeks since she had held me like this, weeks since we were alone together. My heart was already racing. I wanted her. My lips parted to breathe her name, but as soon as I decided to give that concession, she was already there.

She kissed me, carefully, softly, her lips just as cool and smooth against mine as I remembered them, and then everything seemed to give way. The temperature difference was so welcome as her tongue pressed against my teeth. She kissed me with a savage hunger, tepid arms wrapped tight around my waist, soft pressure on the back of my head telling me her fingers were threaded in my hair.

She kissed me like there was everything, and like there was nothing, like the past month hadn't existed, and like there was no tomorrow to come. She burned all my regret for coming to Vires, all the doubt that had haunted me when I had thought I was forgotten. She kissed me so hard that my aching body, tired from too much hard labor and sore from Evan Chase's rough treatment, was liberated from feeling anything but her consuming burn. Scarlett held me to her like I was a life preserver. Between those consuming kisses, she looked at me like I was the sun, the stars and every vital thing in the world.

I had lost all the pieces of myself that could hold on to the fact she was a murderer, the patron of the words branded on Joseph's chest, the mistress to the broken dead thing Aria had been. She was perfect to me, as she always was. All the facts that might taint her dissolved away and, with a bravery that surprised me, I kissed her back.

Her hands roamed over me, but all my modesty was momentarily stripped bare. Living without her, staring into a future where she no longer wanted me, had broken the barriers between us down. When her palm rolled flat over my breasts I didn't balk; when her fingertips brushed my bare skin above the waist of my jeans, I only shuddered at the pleasure ripping foreign through my stomach.

Everything was righted again, so easily repaired, and I felt the frenzy between us, something mutual, one singular emotion swallowing us both. Scarlett drew back from my lips, and she looked at me, her eyes on mine, dark with want. Though I was breathless, between my thighs burning, I followed the transition from one desire to another with absolute ease. I lifted my wrist in the same second she reached for it, and as she fastened her mouth to me in that calculatedly lopsided way, our eyes never left each other.

An alert flickered at the edges of my consciousness. This was dangerous in Vires and being caught would mean trouble for us both. The familiar tide of Scarlett drinking from me, the uncomfortable pull and the smooth release as she swallowed, washed any concerns away.

I lost myself to her completely, as I always did when we were together like this. Contentment filled me up, and I felt her growing sated too, saw it in her eyes. I could tell my pride at it pleased her. My apparent devotion seemed to make her hold me impossibly closer.

The cool air around us stung the reopened scar as she pulled her mouth away. I watched her with lazy eyes as again she raised her fingertip to her lips and pressed it bloody to the wound. She set my healed arm back in my lap, pulling my parka tight around me. My head lolled onto her shoulder, and her lips tickled my temple. All my questions were gone, all the desperate words I had wanted to say vanished, because now, feeling her, knowing her through our connection, it was enough.

"You shouldn't have come here." The words were low, broken as they were dragged over the gravel that had always lived in her voice, but they were undeniably tender, untouched by any real displeasure.

My answer was equally quiet, murmured against the soft skin of her neck as my eyes slid closed, warm and sweet.

"I know."

My words held not a sliver of regret.

I WOKE TO something cold against my temple. Cold, not cool. I opened my eyes to find it was no longer Scarlett's shoulder I rested on and her arms were no longer wrapped around my body. The tinted glass of the window stuck slightly to my skin as I sat upright. The space inside the car was dimly lit, the dark of evening having sunk around us while I slept.

Across from me, Scarlett was motionless, a living statue, her head turned away as she looked out of her own window. Looking past her, I saw twin lights outside tall glass doors, though nothing was visible within.

I missed her already, her tepid touch and the kisses that felt like an anesthetic. While she held me, it was so easy to forget about the rest of Vires, about my father, Joseph and Aria, about all the indecision and the pain that bore such weak opposition to how utterly devoted I knew I was to her. When she was separated from me, even by the small space between us now, doubt instantly found me again—I wondered if that would ever stop? I had only ever experienced her as something fleeting, here today and gone when I awoke, but she was here now. I let the thought comfort me, breathe life back until me until I could finally take a breath.

"Scarlett?"

Her name fell from my lips quietly, broken and imperfect, a pale comparison for the woman it belonged to.

Oddly colored eyes found me, a hardness in them I hadn't thought to anticipate. Immediately, I wondered how long I'd slept. Usually after drinking from me, she was warm, soft, almost pliable against my side, but the silence was enough to confirm that this time, things were different.

"You don't call me that here." Her voice spilled like treacle, thick and dark around the demands that were so natural to her. I didn't know how to respond. Again, I felt empty.

Her fingers twitched where they lay against the smooth black leather, and just for a second, I thought I saw softness in her eyes and hoped she might reach for my hand. She didn't move, her fluctuating irises fixed on my face.

"There are things more dangerous than me in Vires, Rayne." Hearing her say my name, as foreboding as her tone was, still made me dizzy. "Things even I can't save or protect you from, which is why Jade should never have brought you here." There was nothing cruel in the phrase, but each syllable struck me like a physical blow, and suddenly, I was waiting for her to leave me again. When I failed to respond, her eyebrows pulled together ever so slightly, but she seemed to dismiss my lack of reaction and continued to speak.

"The worst of which is knowledge. More specifically, the knowledge that I..." She paused for barely a second, but I caught it. "That you hold some interest for me." Her tone was so flat and matter-of-fact, and I wondered how hard she had worked, how long it had taken for her to perfect and conjure a mask that engulfed her face, her voice, her entire being.

"If anybody finds out, you become a weapon, one that will be used against me until it destroys us both. For that reason, unless we are alone, and I specifically ask otherwise, you're to stay away from me, and treat me with respect."

I opened my mouth to reply, but I had no words, my brain churning over this new information too slowly. I wondered if all the day's events had finally caught up with me, if perhaps I was in some sort of delayed shock. I nodded.

"That starts with addressing me properly, as Mistress."

I could tell she had delivered the demand before, though the faintest glimmer of her discomfort with it was palpable in the unexplained way her feelings sometimes were. As quick as the discomfort had arrived, it was gone.

I nodded again, fear finally breaking through the numbness. My thoughts immediately fell back to Aria, broken, sitting obediently on the ground and wearing Scarlet's collar like a dog. Was that what I was to her now? What I had come here for?

She was already opening the car door, the smell of wet pavement finding me, cold air making me shudder, even under my filthy jacket. I watched her as she rose from the car, shapely and muscled—perfect. I scrambled across the seats and stumbled out after her, tripping over one untied sneaker on my way up. Fingers caught me around the arm just a little too tight, making me wince before she set me back on my feet and yanked her hand away.

Scarlett said nothing as we made our way down a short path and through the glass doors, the lobby inside similar to the one in Chase Tower but much more elaborate. Something in the high ceiling and the expensive dark stone made the place feel familiar at least.

Her heels rung against the floor as we walked, and I followed her into the elevator unspeaking. Her crimson-nailed finger pushed the illuminated number fifteen.

After the doors slid shut, they opened again too quickly, and as they did, I realized my time alone with her was over. I shrunk behind her instinctively, and the fingers that twisted in the back of my jacket and flung me out of the metal box ahead of her stung. Some part of me knew this must be part of her demand that I stay away, that we keep whatever I meant to her hidden, but fear was stronger, and I dug in my heels, the unexpected movement forcing her to stop close to me.

"This is where you'll stay." Her voice was too loud to be just for me, and as at least twenty pairs of eyes settled on us while she gestured grandly around the space, I knew she was putting on a show.

Men and women stared back at me, their ages ranging from around the same as myself, to fifty, maybe sixty. This entire floor of the tower seemed to be open plan, with no real furnishing, all bathed in a fluorescent-blue light from the tubes lining the ceiling. Cardboard boxes, old pillows and tattered blankets lay in odd formations here and there, and as I looked closer, I noticed how they formed little living areas, a vain attempt at privacy and possession in a space that allowed for none.

I couldn't stay here, but Scarlett was already leaving. I balked and tried to follow her, but she stepped back into the elevator, the hush that had settled over the room making the pounding of my heart in my ears even louder.

"As you can see, at Pearce Tower, we're quite generous with our accommodations. There's a shower and toilet behind the curtain up back." She winked at me, and I wanted to throw up all over her stupid shiny shoes. A sick smile played on her face, and in front of her audience. She was shining, so much that I suddenly doubted it was an act at all.

Desperately, I watched the steel doors close, taking her away, though she didn't once look up at me. And then I was alone with the crowd.

Seconds passed, and the murmurs behind me grew and evolved, switching into urgent conversation and spilling into a sea of noise, voices. I stared at the doors still, because turning away meant it was over, she was gone, and I was alone to face...this.

Something touched my hair and I spun around, my hand clamped over my mouth to stifle a scream. I jumped back from the man with the limp and floppy blond bangs who stood too close to me. I hadn't heard him approach.

"Welcome, Princess." The endearment only compounded my sudden urge to vomit. Sidestepping him, I walked away as quickly as I was able, tripping over bodies and twisting between them, the floor too small for the number of lives it held. I could hear him following me, feel his filthy breath on the back of my neck, or maybe that was just the fear.

"She's pretty..."

"Yeah, she's pretty..."

He spoke and the group who seemed to have joined him replied, echoing each other's thoughts like a pack of hunting animals.

"Come back here, pretty..." They called out, but I didn't turn around. Panic mixed with claustrophobia until I could hear my own breaths. Where would I go when I ran out of space to run? I walked faster.

"Did Scarlett Pearce fuck you? I heard she's good."

"She's just her type... Pretty little girls..."

"Maybe she fucked Scarlett too..."

The drone continued, and the men following me jeered, though really, they were more like boys, my age, maybe a few years older. Tears spilled onto my cheeks. I stumbled over a leg, jumping sideways at the angry hiss that surprised me in response. I hated Scarlett for leaving me here, but I wanted her, I wanted her so badly to save me. The thought sent more hot tears of anger, fear, and panic tumbling down my cheeks.

The smell of people, sweat, and confined living was stifling, and the dark blue drapes at the back of the room were coming up too fast. I had no idea where I would go when I had no place else to run, and nowhere to hide. My brain couldn't comprehend that they lived like this. The more makeshift cardboard privacy screens I passed, the dirty torn blankets for beds, the more the panic swallowed me. I wanted to go back to my father's house, I'd even go back and live there with him, because that pain was familiar, predictable, but this... I wouldn't survive here, and Scarlett had deserted me.

"Are you her new pet?" The blond man spoke again, closer to me now. His fingers closed around the top of my arm, and without stopping or turning, I yanked it out of his grasp and broke into a run. I tripped and stumbled more than I took steps, though I heard the pack giving up, disappearing, for now.

"If she was Scarlett's pet, she wouldn't be here, slumming it with us."

"I'd like to make her my pet."

"Yeah, and mine."

"No way, she's mine..."

I kept on moving until my palms were pressed against a white wall, turned blue under the odd lights. I couldn't feel the smooth surface, my hands numb with panic, the stillness of the wall alerting me that my body was shaking, hard.

I glanced around, a door to my left appearing like a light in the darkness. I bolted toward it, already aware the hope in my chest was dangerous.

I half fell into the hallway, the banging of the door back against the wall ringing out like a gunshot in the blue-tinged space. It was quieter out here, and though eyes were trained on me from the stairs going up, and down, and the small landing area around my feet, they returned to whatever they were doing much faster, and no one spoke to me. Out here on the stairwell, I had found a reprieve, however brief.

Not trusting my legs to go down, I wound my way up the stairs before me, careful not to bump or knock anybody. Somehow the atmosphere out here with all its hushed conversations felt less forgiving. The stairs twisted around on themselves. I passed two older men smoking something that smelled like burning plastic; a girl seemed to be drawing an intricate design on the inside of her thin arm with something small and sharp. I didn't stop to look.

I climbed until I reached the next hallway, two locked doors forbidding me from exiting onto the next floor or climbing any higher, though the sight of the empty little landing space was enough. Sinking down, I pressed my face into the quilted sleeve of my jacket, the one thing familiar in all of this, knowing I couldn't hold back the coming hysteria. And I cried.

Tears soaked through to my arm, and I cried until my throat was sore from my stifled sobs, my head throbbed, and my eyes burned. I cried until I had no tears left, and I had cursed Scarlett Pearce for leaving me here a hundred times, and begged, screaming down whatever connection I had believed we had, for her to help me. I cried until I was empty, kicking and thrashing and screaming, pounding up against the four walls inside the confines of my head, while I sat there motionless.

By the time I could breathe again, I was resigned to my new fate. Self-preservation arose from somewhere within me, surprising me. My ability to carry on should be shot to hell just like everything else, yet I knew I would. The plan had already formed that I would stay awake, alert, and I was thankful for my small sleep in the car, what felt like a lifetime ago now.

Staring at the blue-tinted walls, shivering with nervous energy, for the first time in my life I realized perhaps my carrying on wasn't an achievement or an ability at all. Perhaps it was just another sad testament to the fact I'd never had a choice.

SOMEWHERE OVER THE course of the night, the adrenaline had turned to dust in my blood, and all my anger had evaporated into cold. My eyes hadn't closed, and my mind had refused to stop turning everything over and over, unable to let it lie.

I knew she would come for me eventually. Somewhere between all the tears and the brokenness, a strange self-assuredness had found me. Scarlett had saved me. She'd kissed me, touched me, lied for me, and left me here. I had tasted her feelings for me through the tenuous connection we sometimes shared. Shivering against the wall, as the cold and exhaustion replaced the terror and the regret, finally, I had convinced myself that for reasons unknown, I meant something to her.

I held the knowledge tight around myself as a girl a few years older than me summoned me from my place atop the stairs, leading me wordlessly back through the room I had run through the night before. I held some appeal for Scarlett. Her performance in front of the elevator, her callousness as she placed the gun on the table, the brands on Joseph's chest—they had taught me to be careful, wary, not to trust exactly how much. But she had saved me, and she was making an effort to keep me, and with nothing else left, I was determined to use that advantage. I couldn't bear another night on the fifteenth floor. If she cared about me at all, she wouldn't force me to. There had to be another way.

The thoughts broiled below the surface as I followed the girl's dark head out of the elevator, hardly noticing the subtle change in décor that transitioned from business to home, just barely. The floor was still granite, large square tiles of the stuff, smooth below my dirty sneakers, though the walls were a rich shade of cream, windows at either end of the long hall pouring light into the space. As we walked, I caught flashes of a life: a large kitchen through one door, a glossy black grand piano through another, a bedroom with a worn tribal rug and a high bookcase. This was where she lived.

We stopped abruptly outside a door, where the nameless girl knocked twice and then spoke for the first time since she had found me on the stairs. "You're to go inside and wait in the bedroom, Mistress will see you when she's ready."

She arched one eyebrow as she gave Scarlett the title it seemed she demanded from everyone here, disdain heavy in her dark eyes. She turned to leave, changing her mind at the last minute. "Want some advice, kid?"

I could only have been a few years younger than her by my estimation, though my eyebrows rose automatically in response, questioning.

"Don't fight her, the sick bitch likes it."

I watched as she walked away, numb. All the resolve I had built up through the night splintered. How many more were there? Aria, this new angry girl, me... Scarlett's pets, her playthings. Maybe she cared for me, maybe she didn't, but the seed of doubt was planted now, and suddenly all my grand plans were turned to dust at my feet, their fatal flaw exposed. To Scarlett Pearce, I was nothing if not replaceable.

I pushed open the door. The realization still lingered, bitter in my mouth, as my eyes scanned the bedroom. I closed it softly behind me out of habit and took only a step further forward before I stopped.

The bedsheets were smooth black satin. The drapes framing the glass balcony doors matched their shade, tumbling down thick and opaque—the kind I knew would easily block out the sun. The entire room was finished with rich, almost red mahogany and black. Even down to the faintly lingering smell of whiskey, it was Scarlett.

Through the door that hung half open at the other side of the room, I could hear the artificial rain of a shower, feel the faintest caress of the steam against my cold skin. My heart dropped into my stomach as it occurred to me that Scarlett might be in there. Automatically, I took a step forward, curiosity and the impossible magnetism she had drawing me in, further into the lioness's den.

My sneakers were silent against the carpet. I remembered before, before all this, on the floor in the bathroom of my father's house, in my old bedroom, by the front door. All the times she was still relatively untainted to me, the times she had asked me if I was afraid of her and somehow, my answer was always no.

Here, in this place where everything was so out of control, where there were monsters worse than a beating before bed, I realized my answer was changing, inch by painful inch, though I resisted all the way.

One more step forward, and I peered around the door, the steam hot on my face, moist against my dry lips, making me feel just as filthy as I knew I was.

The bathroom was glorious, all dark natural stone and stainless steel, though my eyes had barely grazed the walls, the furnishings, before they had found her. Dark hair tumbled down her back, slick with flowing water, and she looked small, as small as me, slim and breakable. I watched pale hands run over dark hair, though my attention always strayed back to the same place. Below the dark strands, across her smooth back, thick ropey scars crossed each other, seemingly unending.

I knew I should look away, go back and wait by the door, cease this invasion before it became something I couldn't take back, but I was bound. These were pieces of her, rare, hidden glimmers, genuine and beautiful and telling, things I knew were never meant for my eyes, for anyone's eyes. Scarlett was exposed, and I didn't want to pry, to take advantage, but I just couldn't look away.

All my self-built gusto was gone, my idea to bargain with her crushed. She was perfection, the first kiss of morning dew on a blood-red rose, and beside her, I was a wilting wildflower, damaged and flimsy, broken. Without thinking, I reached for her down the invisible tie that had bound me to her since the first night; aching to taste this moment inside her head, as well as see it.

She snapped her head around, and the earth shattered around me. For one glorious, terrible second, I saw her vulnerability, her shock, the invasion painted all over her face before the mask slipped into place and it was gone.

My back hit the wall with a heavy thud, knocking all the breath out of me, setting a dull ache in my head that spread like wildfire as I looked up into swirling eyes. Her fingers were tight around my throat, though her lips were crafted into an almost perfect smirk. She had crossed the space before I could blink.

"Like what you see?" She sneered the words. Her question barely reached me. I struggled to breathe in and out and wondered who had put those lines there, who had taken the girl I had seen for that split-second, and made her into this, such a grand pretender, the woman with the guns and the brands and the breaking.

"You're beautiful..." I didn't even mean to say it aloud, but it was an inadmissible truth; she was beautiful and impossible and terrible. I watched through hazy eyes, surprised I felt it when the words touched her stone skin, permeating, until without warning, Scarlett cracked.

Her lips were rough against mine; her tongue was cool and slick when it forced its way into my mouth. As soon as my sleep-deprived brain caught up with her, there wasn't a piece of me left that would resist. Scarlett's fingers were rough in my hair, but gentle as they stroked my cheek. I tried to lift my head away from the wall, to kiss her harder, but it only seemed to tighten the vise in my hair and make her press into me more, holding me in even tighter control, one hand around my throat again.

Pinned against the wall, I let her devour me. By the time she pulled away, my lips throbbed in time with parts of me I hadn't known were capable. She held my head back still, and for a long moment, all we did was stare at each other, both breathless even though I knew she had no need for oxygen.

Rich browns and woody greens spilled into and over each other in her eyes. As I took her in, heat filled my cheeks, her nakedness suddenly painstakingly apparent.

She laughed. The sound was like gravel against the strings of a cello, and it rang within me long after it was over. I smiled.

"You should never have come here, Rayne." She echoed her words from the previous night.

"I know," I replied automatically, both our smiles pulling up just a little further. It was so easy to believe I was the only person in the world when she looked at me like that. Even if I wasn't, suddenly, I didn't think pretending would be so bad.

Her grip around my throat loosened, but I didn't move. I wondered why she'd held me back? How the scars across her pale back correlated with her need to control everything, always?

"Don't make me go back down there." The plea spilled out my mouth, a whisper, and I was as surprised by it as she was, her perfectly sculpted eyebrows knitting together as she watched me lick my swollen lips. I didn't know now if I was asking out of fear, or pure desire to stay with her.

She looked away, and I already knew the answer. I let myself linger over every detail of her face, how she looked without all the dark makeup, her rich, olive-toned skin overshadowed by the pallor I guessed accompanied being what she was.

"It's safer, for us both." I could feel her searching for my understanding. I tried to keep my mouth shut, but I was already growing compliant. "I can't afford to let you become another weakness for them to exploit."

She sounded almost sad as she spoke, the pads of her fingers grazed my cheek, and without breaking from her gaze, I nodded. "Okay..."

The word was a whisper, but it was loud enough to hear, and without warning, she pressed up against me again, her naked body on my dirty clothes, her eyes intent on mine, demanding. It took me a second to realize what she wanted.

"Yes...Mistress." She nodded her approval, though the tiniest hint of a smile kissed the edge of her mouth, her eyes soft.

"Clean yourself up, I'll leave clothes on the bed for you." She gestured to the open bathroom door, the shower that was still running, and I moved forward, passing her on leaden legs. There was no denying I felt dirty, hot in unfamiliar places, and absolutely frigid in others, the memory of Aria in her collar tickling at the edges of the haze of safety, of belonging she always induced in me.

I took one last look at her face, not daring to let my eyes fall any lower, before I walked into the shower and closed the screen. I knew when I came back out, Scarlett would be gone.

VOICES HUMMED AROUND me, a quiet babbling background that somewhere over the past three days had become my norm.

The wall was cool behind my head, my jacket wrapped around me tight, the too-large, black sweats Scarlett had left for me after my shower, concealed below it. The whisper of the memory made me lick my lips. The ghost of her rough mouth on mine wasn't enough to sate whatever thirst she had left inside me.

A brief uproar erupted on the landing below mine. Cards fluttered into the air, before they were gathered and dealt again. I'd heard enough by now to know they were playing for raisins today. Yesterday, it had been a ragged old winter hat.

My idle pastime was so different than any of my thirty or so roommates, and I closed my eyes again, reaching down the silvery, elusive connection, and waiting, for either sleep or some glimpse of Scarlett to find me.

As much as I hated the fifteenth floor, it was becoming familiar, a constant source of anxiety and danger I was slowly learning to regulate. Up on my landing, I was usually left alone, though the catcalls that escorted me from the elevator and out to my hallway showed no signs of letting up. Of course, the knife helped with that.

My hands had shaken when I'd lifted up the thick sweatpants on Scarlett's black satin sheets and it was there, waiting for me. She changed me. I could feel the cool weight of the metal now, where it pressed against my ankle inside the too-large socks I wore under my familiar sneakers. Every time Scarlett touched me, every time she had come to me in my old life, and each time she interacted with me here, she changed me, molded me, empowered me to evolve, and forced me beyond the limits of what I thought I was able to tolerate.

I was at home now with the knife; the power in it that had scared me previously comforted me. For the last two nights, I had managed to get some sleep, propped against the wall.

She was quiet tonight, or at least, my line to her was. I dug my hands deeper into my pockets, ignoring the slight shiver threatening to leak out of my stomach and into my limbs. The cold rice and beans we'd gotten for dinner hadn't been enough, mostly because I never finished with the vampire guards standing over us while they distributed us each a little foil container and bottle of water, then watched us eat.

Part of me was glad I hadn't felt anything from Scarlett. Around this time the past two nights, she'd surprised me with violent flashes of anger, and pain, and red, always red. I didn't know if they were feelings or visions, but they were more vivid than any of my dreams. They woke me from sleep, took me away from anything else I was doing, and left me uneasy, for many hours after the connection fizzled out again. I had a feeling those flashes weren't meant for me, and I wondered where Scarlett Pearce went at night.

Of course, I could ask her, though she had been doing an exceptionally good job of keeping her distance the last few days. We were never alone together, never in the same room for long, and her eyes never met mine, no matter how hard I sought them out. I missed her, and I wondered if this was all there would ever be, if I had traded my messy, mundane and familiar existence in New Hampshire for this. I fell asleep at night wondering if living in the periphery of the sun, close enough for these longing glances and fleeting hopes, was any better than having never known it existed, to begin with.

The opening of the door on the hall below vaguely piqued my interest, though my eyes remained closed. When I heard a familiar voice, they flew open.

"Here, pretty... Where are you hiding?"

The muffled steps of boots on the stairs told me that he wasn't alone, and worst of all, with him coming up, I realized I had trapped myself in the hall. I jumped to my feet and tried the door behind me that led out onto the sixteenth floor, then the one leading to the next set of stairs—both locked.

"There you are..." My blood ran cold and I turned to greet him, them. The card players looked up at me from the stairs below, worried eyes on mine as they were stepped over and around. I watched with desperate eyes as they got up and disappeared back the way the men had come. My palms were slick with cold sweat and I wiped them on my coat, taking a deep breath, ready to conjure a good, loud, scream—the only defense I had left.

The knife.

It burned me now, as if the blade was hot against my ankle. He was on the last step, and I was running out of time. I reached down with fumbling fingers. I yanked up the leg of my sweats, pulled it from my sock, and held it straight out in front of me. My hand shook.

"Leave me alone." As panicked as I felt, my voice was surprisingly strong.

Laughter rose up around me, and I took a step back, bumping into the hard plaster of the wall behind me. They hadn't even faltered. The blond man stepped closer, so close that his chest was only a few inches from the tip of the blade. It wasn't the first time in my life I'd debated whether I was capable of killing another human being, but Scarlett had taken care of my father before I'd decided. My hand shook harder.

"Are you going to stab me, pretty?" He was sneering now, and aside from his voice, the stairwell was silent. I was alone with them.

I sucked in a big gulp of air, though my mouth was barely open, the scream dying in my burning throat when my arm was twisted painfully in his grasp and his hand covered my mouth, suffocating me. His fingers smelled like soil and sweat. I thought about biting him if I could, though the idea made me gag.

"No need for that..." His voice was soothing, though I didn't miss the edge on the words. Of all the things I'd feared in my life, this kind of violation wasn't one of them. I wanted to crawl out of my skin and run away, but my instinct to play dead when caught was taking over so fast. The knife was ripped out of my hands, and for one sickening second, I wondered if Scarlett would still want me once they had stolen me from her, and from myself. There were tears in my eyes and I hung my head.

A rough hand found my hip, squeezing the delicate flesh over my hip bone too tight, already below my jacket.

Fight.

It came from nowhere, from the same place as the command that had held me against the wall at Evan Chase's tower, and it was impossible to ignore. I slammed my head forward, my forehead colliding with the floppy-haired man's nose with a satisfying crunch. Pain blistered across my awareness, but I pushed him away from me, and for a second the room stood still. He clutched his broken nose, blood pouring between his fingers. All three of them, and me, were equally shocked I had managed that.

The other two lunged for me together, and I screamed. Whether it was fear or determination ringing up from my chest was impossible to tell. I screamed and swung my legs, hitting one in the kneecap, catching the other with the back of my hand. I writhed in their grip until I was exhausted. It had taken all three of them to pin me against the wall and I struggled still.

Victory already shone in his eyes as the leader approached me. I thrashed against them, ignoring the knife, my knife that was pressed to my throat. My brain rang with a single word. *Fight, fight, fight.* His hand burned me through my shirt, crushed against my breast, and there was silence for two long seconds while I sucked in another breath and let another ear-splitting scream rip out of me.

A gunshot rang out, louder even than my frantic, furious wailing. When Scarlett appeared behind them, I realized the door in the hall below had shattered into a thousand pieces under the force she had used to fling it back against the wall.

"Hello, boys."

She delivered the two words perfectly, and then, she was a blur. I felt them being ripped away from me, heard their strangled screams, the snap of a leg, a wrist, a spine in her crushing embrace. She was a tornado of ruin, and she destroyed them mercilessly. Her mismatched eyes were alight, fervent as she ripped the blond boy's head off his shoulders and tossed it into the air before letting it roll down the stairs.

Only when Scarlett had killed all three of them and she looked up at me did I realize I was still screaming. She looked alive. Her perfect porcelain cheek was splattered with crimson, her neck, her dress soaked dark with blood. Slim fingers were twisted into claws and her lips were parted around her heavy breaths. She stared at me, and I stared back at her, at this raw piece of her, once again my angel of death. In that moment, even I couldn't deny she had reveled in it, in their blood, in all her breaking, in the death.

"Rayne."

It was barely a whisper, but immediately I could stop the screaming and scramble forward to reach for her. I wrapped my arms around her neck and let my tear-soaked face rest against the soft leather covering her shoulder.

Scarlett was still breathing hard, and it took her a few seconds to fold her arms around me, before she lifted me easily off the floor. Somewhere far removed from my consciousness, I wondered again if she simply breathed out of habit.

She bent easily, even with my weight, and retrieved the knife, before she ran her fingers over the keypad on the door leading up to the next set of stairs, and we were climbing.

"You'll be safe now..." She murmured the words, though her voice was tight, uneven, and her breathing seemed to be slowing, the higher we climbed.

I clung to her hard and let her carry me away, letting the familiar tickle of her cool breath on my cheek soothe me, chase away the thoughts of the blond-haired man and his friends—they were all dead now. Dead like my father, dead like Aria... People died around me, around me and Scarlett. Selfishly, I pushed the realization away. She was my drug, and each escalating incident only proved to some still conscious piece of me that for her, I would pay any price.

When she put me down, we were in her bathroom, the one where I had taken a shower only a few days before. I clung to her as she started the water running, not letting her fully pull away from me. Without her, I didn't trust myself not to fall apart.

My breath left me in a surprised little gust when she swept me off the ground again and set me down close to her, the hot water pouring over both of our heads. For the first time since that glorious moment in the hallway, I got to look at her face, just inches from mine. Dark eyes studied me, fingers that were oddly cool under the hot water traced over my cheekbones, under the curve of my chin. Scarlett looked murderous.

Instinctively, I held still, letting her inspect me, fighting the urge to close my eyes and give myself over to her touch. Something in her face unsettled me, and her expression seemed to darken as she touched a spot over my left eyebrow, making me wince in pain. With a startling hiss, Scarlett was gone.

Noise assaulted my ears, glass smashing, plastic rebounding off the tiles, the grating as the sink was ripped out of its place and the earth-shattering, splintering as it was tossed against the wall. I watched her through the thin glass that acted as a shower screen, the hot water pouring over me and my soaked clothes, though I didn't feel it anymore.

She turned back to me, standing amidst her destruction, and her eyes were twin pyres, blazing.

"I should have protected you." She watched me so intently I struggled to reply.

"It's... You came, it's okay." My response was feeble, and I took a breath, ready to force a more compelling consolation out of my mouth, but it was already too late.

"No." She growled the word, and then she was in front of me again, and I noticed she was shaking. I fought the urge to move back.

"No..." She repeated the word softer this time, her hands cupping my face gently. Grief and guilt were palpable for the split second the connection between us held fast. Emotion was heavy in her eyes, and I felt the echo of all her panic, all her hatred for herself as she'd sprinted to save me before it splintered too and fell away.

"You're mine," Scarlett snapped again. She grabbed me roughly by the collar of my drenched jacket. The ends of my hair, soaked from gold to caramel now, were caught between her slim fingers. I winced when she slammed me back against the shower wall, but I was compelled again, unable to look away as her eyes roamed desperately over my face, searching.

"You are mine..." It was aggressive, assertive, and heavy with a dominance I knew I could never possess. Though it twisted her face, curling her lips and tightening her hold on me, the declaration didn't scare me. Instead, it filled me up, it gave me the purpose I'd never had. In some way, her claim on me gave me one on her, and I let the thought swallow me.

Her lips attacked mine, and I was ready, pliable beneath her when she kissed me, pushing her tongue into my mouth, pulling my coat off my shoulders. The wall was as cold against my back as Scarlett against my front. As she slipped further into a frenzy, tugging at my clothes and kissing her way across my cheek and down past my ear. The connection between us drained of all interference, and I knew I could speak to her with no words, know what she needed without request. Her mouth wrapped around my throat, though nothing in me was afraid. My own certainty, my self-confidence was growing.

I pushed her away just slightly, hard enough that I knew she'd feel it, though I had no doubt she was strong enough to resist. Odd colored eyes searched mine, and I tasted her uncertainty, the vulnerability, the question she wouldn't ask, and she was beautiful, whole, human.

My voice was quiet but sincere, as I told her everything I knew she needed to hear in just two words.

"I'm yours."

LYING IN BED beside her, my body still burned for her. After my admission that I belonged to her, all her desperate energy had dissipated. The soft contentment with which she'd washed my hair and kissed my cheeks reminded me of the way she'd always behaved after she had drunk my blood.

Part of me was grossly aware that I ought to be something... Scarred, terrified, traumatized, after the men had tried to...hurt me, but I wasn't. Scarlett did that to me, she always had. Nothing could touch me when her arms were around me like they were now, keeping me from overheating below the thick down quilt and her satin sheets.

Her breaths were even, and I wondered if she was sleeping. I still felt her mood, that same contentment hanging heavy and safe around us both like a blanket. A smile touched my lips at the memory of her hungry kisses, the way she had pulled my jacket from my shoulders—the way she had wanted me.

Though she had been nothing but proper from then on—handing me the towel and leaving me standing on the bathroom floor, my clothes dripping, so I could change into the large T-shirt and shorts she had given me for bed privately—the memory of her need for me, the way I had felt it from her, was burned into my mind.

"What are you thinking about?"

Her voice was soft, raspy, tickling my ear as she pressed herself closer, her front to my back. Blood heated my cheeks, and I thought I heard her stifle a laugh.

"Go to sleep, Princess." She answered before I could, the familiarity in her words not lost on me. For the first time on hearing them, I was hopeful she would still be here when I woke up. I closed my eyes and let her easy contentment settle over me.

I was hers.

Chapter Eleven

DIM LIGHT FILTERED through the window when I woke, the thick black satin drapes left open the night before. Blinking slowly, I didn't need to turn my head to see her, to know she was beside me. I felt her there.

Scarlet's cool embrace was welcome under the thick duvet she had wrapped around us the night before. Her eyes were closed, her face expressionless, unschooled in a way I'd never seen it, at least not around anyone but me. The thought made me warm.

I worried my lip, letting my mind drift, my eyes lingering too long on a blood-soaked pile of gray fabric in the corner of the room. Again, I wondered where Scarlett Pearce spent her evenings, where she had been before she came to my rescue last night. Thinking of the encounter in the staircase made my chest tight. She had promised I would be safe now, but what did that mean? Leaning into her hold, I hoped desperately it meant this, her proximity, because from the start, she had been my security.

Questions flitted in and out of my mind as I marveled at Scarlett's unmoving form. Even the brush of thick dark eyelashes on high cheekbones couldn't keep the multitude of questions at bay. Even as I wondered awestruck at myself, lying in the arms of someone as beautiful, as strong, as extraordinary as her, I couldn't shake the hundreds of things I wanted—no, needed—to know. Part of me questioned how the woman holding me like no one else had, the woman who had touched me so gently the night before, was a vampire, and more than that, a murderer and sadistic torturer if rumors were to be believed.

It wasn't mismatched eyes on my skin that alerted me to her being awake, if she had even been sleeping—did vampires sleep? It was the emotion. I felt all her soft fascination as she studied my face, and it floored me that anyone, much less someone like her, could feel that for...me.

"How come I know what you're feeling sometimes?"

Of all the many questions I had, about Vires, about the Chases, about Scarlett herself and the rumors, this wasn't the one I had planned to ask, yet it was the one that came tumbling out, my voice still scratchy from sleep.

The response I received was non-verbal and intense, and the minute the words left my lips, it jolted me wide-awake. Panic, white-hot, thumped me square in the chest, and I knew it was Scarlett's. No sooner had it flashed through me, it was gone, the connection slammed down tight as a tanned hand whipped the duvet back, already disentangling herself from me.

"Wait..."

I sounded bold, even to my own ears, while I grabbed her wrist. Dark eyes looked down at my offending hand like it had burned, and suddenly I had no idea what to say.

"I don't mind it, you know." The words came out soft now, reassuring. "I like being able to feel you. When we're apart it reminds me—"

Scarlett seemed to repent and tugged her wrist out of my grip and cupped my face. She lifted my chin that I had just lowered, embarrassed by my own admissions. I steeled myself, determined to finish.

"I want to know you, and feeling what you feel... When you found me at Chase Tower, I didn't know if you wanted me, and then... Don't you feel mine too? I just, it's beautiful, whatever connects us, and I like it. I want to be close to you."

Mismatched eyes studied me for a long moment, heavy with something that looked almost like hope, and I was certain she was going to lean in and kiss me. But only the ghost of cool breath kissed my lips, and I watched her deflate.

"That's what you think you want, Princess."

Her words were barely a whisper into the stillness of the morning, my question unanswered, yet they were heavy with sadness. My body acted without my consent, and suddenly my fingers were brushing her cheeks, pulling her closer. Until for the first time, I was kissing her, initiating. Nerves and inexperience didn't matter. The need to let her know consumed me. How could she ever doubt how much I cared for her, loved her? Though I wasn't ready to say it yet. I tried to let it flow through our connection, pushing it outwards, pouring it into her, screaming it into the silence until I felt her lips pull into a smile against mine.

"You don't have to yell..."

The words were breathy as she whispered them into my mouth, her fingers twisting into my hair.

"Tell me what you want, Princess?"

The question felt like a trap, and though she was trying to hide it, the trepidation lurked just beyond where our lips were still grazing over each other.

"I want to be yours." The words came as easy as breathing. "And I want you to have me."

The noise she made at my bold admission blocked out the mortified ringing of my own brazen words in my ears and was borderline pornographic. I needed her, I ached for her, to be with her, to love her and show her I knew exactly what I wanted, and she was it. For good and for bad, she was everything.

Her eyes darkened, swirling irises turning molten in the light of the rising sun, as she pushed me down onto her mattress.

I WOKE TO the sound of voices, one deep, decidedly male, and totally unknown to me. Scarlett was gone from beside me, and I realized with a start I was still naked.

By the time I'd pulled on clothes from the night before and headed down the hall, the voices were growing louder. The conversation came to me in pieces. I thought about turning back, returning to the bedroom, to safety, but Scarlett was afraid.

The soles of my bare feet padded softly over the cool wood, until I lingered outside the doorway to what looked like a sitting room, barely daring to breathe.

"And how does it look when you disappear in the middle of multiple punishments, leaving them unfinished, running off to hell knows where?"

The male voice was demanding and relentless. I tried to get my breathing under control, quiet enough to inch forward and peek around the door, when I heard Scarlett's reply.

"You are not my keeper, Father. Do I not go every night? Am I not the best, the bloodiest..." She spat the words, and I pressed my back against the wall, unsure if I wanted to see the sick smile I heard in her voice painted on her beautiful face.

"Do I not punish more than any other vampire in the city, is my name not enough to send them running?"

There was no trace of doubt in her voice.

"Oh, my girl." Scarlett's father's voice dropped low and thick with adoration that sounded false even to my ears, and I didn't even know him.

"You are everything I dreamed of and more, but isn't that all you are? What I made you?" The last sentence was spat out with a viciousness that made me jump.

"You will not betray us now, Scarlett. You will not."

The ensuing silence made me nervous to breathe.

"Though I suppose I do have another daughter, if you were to fail to keep up with your duties—"

"No!"

The wave of protectiveness, disgust, and fierce raw emotion Scarlett felt at this taunt almost bowled me over, suddenly ready to rush into the room and tear the man's heart out. I could only imagine how it felt first hand.

"And how is your precious little sister? Have we made any progress on making her a Pearce, or are you still keeping her like her pet? Perhaps you have found another use for her now your last plaything expired."

Scarlett's response was a hissed, "Fuck you," and at that moment I dared to lean forward just slightly and peer into the room.

All I was able to make out of the man was a thick head of salt-and-pepper hair, as he towered over Scarlett, leaning heavily to his left on a cane.

"Leave her out of this and leave her alone. She doesn't need to be involved with any of this, you know I have things in hand. Why are you really here?"

Mismatched eyes caught me as she reached up to smooth her hands over the dress she had no doubt hurriedly thrown on this morning after our activities. For a second, shock and vulnerability flashed across her face before the mask was back in place, yet I felt the unease radiating off her.

"Your deal with Evan Chase, or whatever silly game it was. How many times must I tell you to stop antagonizing him? Those who are beneath us—"

"Are not worth the time. I know, Wilfred." Scarlett finished the sentence before he could. It happened in a flash; one minute she stood before him, the next she was on the floor. The sound that filled the air was like metal on stone. I watched, sickened, adrenaline coursing through me as his cane returned to the ground by his feet after striking her, a bruise already blooming across her porcelain cheek.

"But don't they deserve to be reminded of their place?" Her voice slipped into the dark, rich, siren song of a predator. I could almost see the man she addressed rise taller and fill back up with pride. Despite the blood staining her teeth red, she rose gracefully to her feet.

"You are a force of nature, Scarlett. Poised at the helm of our great city, where as a Pearce you should rightfully be." He reached up and I watched as he stroked her neck, feeling her revulsion, the fight not to flinch, like it was my own.

The command came, her voice in my head unexpected, making me jump, as it told me to leave. Somehow, my legs refused to move, to leave her alone with him.

"But never forget, I built you, and I can break you, starting with having our dear little Jade take your place. You haven't forgotten basic training, have you?" His fingers closed around her throat and all I managed was a single step forward before her voice in my head froze me, even as I fought to go to her.

It was too little too late, the scuffing of my feet against the hardwood floor was apparently enough. The man turned, cold charcoal eyes finding me, and Scarlett's stomach turned with dread, sending mine sinking along with it.

"Right on time. Join us. Scarlett, don't you teach your playthings not to eavesdrop?"

"Father, she's just my maid..." The waiver in her voice betrayed her, yet it was strong in my mind, as absolute as ever, when it commanded me down to my knees before her father. My chin on my chest without me even giving my body the cue.

"Is this what all the trouble with Evan was for?"

Rough fingers twisted in my hair and hauled my head back until pale eyes bored into mine. The intensity reminded me of my father, and all the drunken nights he would punish me for my mother's sins.

"Pretty, yes, but don't you tire of playing with your food?"

Scarlett was vibrating with rage, yet she remained silent, scared, though her body would never have shown it if I wasn't privy to her mind.

"If you're going to take another pet, Scarlett, and especially from another tower, at least keep it publicly. You just had to have her, and like you said, the Chases needed a reminder of where they stood. Show them. You'll take her to the punishment center with you tonight. Perhaps the girl can learn to be useful, or at least learn some manners by seeing what happens to those who fail to please our Government, and you, of course, my black diamond."

I dared to drag my eyes away from his to look at her, and wondered how she got her response out, her jaw was locked so tight.

"Yes, Father."

The room was quiet, humming with a tension I couldn't name. I watched Scarlett run her tongue over her teeth, presumably to clean them of her blood.

"Very well." Wilfred Pearce threw me, yanking my hair at the roots, sending me crashing back onto my elbows as he stepped away. I lay there, too stunned to move, as he left the room.

Dark eyes, stormy in a way that made my stomach lurch, studied me. We listened in tandem to the sharp tap of the cane as he walked away down the hall, the ding of the elevator as it arrived, and the metallic clink as the doors closed.

It took two long strides before Scarlett was over to me and hauling me up by my shoulders. I almost opened my arms to embrace her, still reeling from the encounter, my body aching from her father's rough dismissal, when she caught me by surprise. Cool fingers wrapped tight around my throat. She slammed me back against the wall, our noses barely an inch apart.

"What the fuck were you thinking?" She spat the words at my lips, and I tasted her rage against them.

"Did I tell you to leave the room? Didn't I tell you to go back just now? You will obey me." Her fingers tightened in a vise until she began to choke me, and my eyes filled with tears. The minute one spilled over, running quick down my cheek to land on her finger, she pushed away from me as if it had burned her. I momentarily wondered if it had.

She flitted three strides from me, and for the first time, I wished she was further away. Nothing but static hung between us, and I was numb.

"He could have killed you." Her eyes were heavier when she turned back to me, her anger seemed wilted and she almost looked sad. What she really felt was a mystery, for now. Her gaze held mine for a few long seconds before she was gone, faster than was humanly possible, nothing but a soft breeze on my damp cheeks, no elevator ding, no heels on the hall floor, yet I knew she had left the tower.

SHE CAME BACK after the sun had sunk below the cityscape outside the large double windows in her room, where I had waited. Any softening I had felt when the girl who had brought me to her the night before came, leaving a paper bag with two different kinds of sandwiches, water, orange juice, and a copy of *Romeo and Juliet* that Scarlett had sent, was long gone now, vanished in the wake of her continued absence.

Three soft knocks preceded her arrival, and I let the worn book fall into my lap as she stepped around the door and closed it behind her.

"Your face is better."

It was an accusation I hadn't planned on making. I hadn't planned on talking to her at all, yet the realization crashed over me, forcing my voice back to life. She ignored my eyes as she moved to the large closet, her back to me as she dragged her fingers through thick dark hair. The silence was suffocating, and suffocating I was.

I flashed back to the night she had come to me outside the wall, hurt, how my blood had helped her heal. I was disgusted with myself for not knowing if I felt so stricken by the thought she had drunk because she was worried she had killed someone, or because she had let them feel her like I did, if she'd let them live long enough.

The world was closing in around me, reality crashing over me, and for the first time, I was able to hold on to something less than the perfect vision I kept of her.

"Did you kill someone?" I moved toward her without meaning to, the sensation of her surprise at the action spurring me on.

"Do you care that you hurt me earlier? That you choked me? That you've broken my bones and forced me down to my knees? Is this all I am to you?"

My voice rose in pitch and in volume, and part of me wanted to stop, while part of me reveled in the catharsis of finally embracing all of her, finally feeling the bad, the part of her that terrified me somewhere I could never quite reach.

"Is that why Aria killed herself? Your voice in her head, like it's in mine? Did you force her to pull the trigger?"

I sucked in another deep breath to let more words fly, to pour every insecurity and doubt I'd ever had across her back that still faced me, when the air didn't come.

"Be still."

Her slim fingers were at my throat again, but this time they stayed for a second, just enough to give me pause, before they were almost tender in the way they held me.

"Now you see me." Scarlett gave me a sickening smile, and my heart dropped. Oddly colored eyes darkened as I watched her work herself into a frenzy, hiding whatever emotion might have been growing beneath.

"This is who I am, Princess, who I've always been. I warned you."

She leaned in so close that my eyes closed out of habit. I was surprised to find I still wanted her to kiss me.

"Isn't this what you wanted?" Her voice was soft and sing-song now, mocking, taunting. "Aren't I beautiful anymore? Didn't you want to know me?"

I was gathering my courage to push her away when she let me go first, the passion-tinged rage in her eyes dying, going cold.

"This is who I am." She delivered the words with such conviction that I wondered which of us she was trying to convince. "Did I kill someone? Did I drink them dry then snap their neck? Yes. You wanted to know me? Let me show you who I am."

And just like that, Scarlett Pearce had me spinning once more.

THE SMELL OF the place reminded me of my time spent below ground in the bunker, and the sight of Scarlett when she walked into the bare concrete hall filled me with a familiar sense of dread.

She was perfect, her eye makeup dark and heavy, tight black material clinging to her torso and cutting off across the smooth lines of her thighs. Her heels clacked as she strutted to the center of the room, dragging a heavy-looking wooden trunk behind her. She didn't even glance my way as she shed the soft leather jacket she wore like a second skin, and in that moment, she was more unreadable than she had ever been.

My gaze snapped away from her. The same men who had appeared seconds after she had picked up her phone, and dragged me down to this punishment center, had entered the room, only this time, they were dragging four people between them.

Bile rose in my throat as I watched them secure their captives to the wooden poles anchored across the midline of the room, their significance suddenly dawning on me. Scarlett continued with what looked to be her routine. The trunk was open now, drawers removed and the implements inside unfolded.

When she turned to address the bound and helpless humans, I could feel her eyes boring into me, her words tearing into someplace deep inside me that I knew would never be the same after what I was about to see. I tried to ignore the thought of Joseph, the brands across his chest, the blood staining the floor at his feet, the stubs where his dreadlocks used to be. I tried not to look at their faces, as some hung limp and some struggled against their restraints, all awaiting the judge, jury, and executioner contained in the form of Scarlett Pearce. My angel of death.

"We all know why we're here..."

Her voice was rich and smooth, and God it was dark and heavy. It sang to me in a way I was ashamed to realize haunted me as much as it made me burn.

"Let's get started."

Her eyes grazed over mine for barely a second, and I thought I felt the faintest of falters, the slightest pause, but no sooner had it registered, it was gone, lost to the thick crack of a long leather whip in the air.

Her nails were painted crimson, fingers wrapped tight around the handle, around the butt of a knife, the stock of a gun. She was merciless, cruel and specific in her torture of each and every individual thrust at her feet. Tears were already falling from my eyes by the third lash of the whip. Tears for the pain of those before me, for the brutality of the situation, and for myself because the only person I had ever loved reveled in it all. There was no way to deny it, no way to lie to myself anymore. Any hesitance, real or imagined, was gone, and the blood, the breaking, the screams, they inflated Scarlett, raised her high until I tasted her excitement in my mouth, and the release she found with every blow ricocheted in my chest. Blood splattered her cheeks, and she threw back her head, embracing it like warm summer rain.

Like this, she was alive, and she was free. I was sickened by how beautiful it was, how raw, how powerful. She was a predator, and she was unstoppable. This was her game and she made every rule and governed every move.

Blood stained her lips, the lips that had kissed me just this morning, though it felt like a lifetime ago. The hands that had broken me and fixed me were made only for destruction now, and she destroyed indiscriminately. The rumors were confirmed, compounded into my head, blow by blow, and they warred with the image I had of her, with the girl cowering before her father, with the sister who seemed to love her so much.

Black patent heels were glossed red as she moved on to the final body on her roster, the smallest. Somehow the sight finally woke up whatever had kept me dormant, docile, a passive spectator as I sat, bound to the hard-backed chair.

"Stop."

I screamed the word at her, trying to stand, though the rope bit into my wrists and ankles and kept me in place. Still I screamed at her, over and over, until I wasn't sure if our connection or my voice was frayed with use. She stalked toward me, and I felt her high. I knew she was lost to it, to all of this. For the first time since the night she'd come to my father's house, I seriously wondered if she was going to kill me.

The knife was cold, and I flinched as it was shoved, rough between my skin and the binds, and sawed until I was free. I stayed frozen in the chair, her hands on the hard seat either side of my thighs as she leaned into my space.

She studied me for a long second, and I stared right back, watching the colors in her eyes dance, a sick twisted waltz, brown and green dark and thick, like the blood staining her clothes.

Without warning, she leaned forward and kissed me, hard. There was no love in the gesture, no tenderness, just teeth and tongue and taking. She bit my lip so fiercely I tasted my blood as her tongue ran over the wounds, soothing for a second before she pushed forward for more. It was a kiss of ownership, dominance and something else, something darker and white-hot that I couldn't identify.

She kissed me until I was stupid, until the sting of disinfectant and the coppery tang of rust in the air around us didn't register anymore. She kissed me, and I let her, my lips parted, my tongue pushing back against hers with equal vigor I only noticed when she pulled away.

Bloody fingertips trailed down my cheek, and fire burned in dark galaxy eyes. She was going to say something, I felt the words building, forming on her lips, before at the last second, she jerked them back and whipped her head up to the waiting guards who had brought me here.

"Take her back to the tower. Put her in my room. Leave a hair out of place on her, and you die."

And again, I ceased to exist to her, as she turned back to her bloodbath.

AFTER CAREFUL HANDS pushed me back inside the room at Pearce Tower where I had spent my day, I barely waited a minute before I banged on it with my fists. My knuckles ached, but I was loath to stop, to sit down and accept this. I thought of Aria, her empty green eyes when she picked up the gun, and my efforts redoubled. I would not be Scarlett Pearce's next pet. A piece of me whispered that I wanted to be something more to her entirely. I ignored the thought, avoided dealing with the hideous implications which came with it, in favor of banging on the door.

I didn't hear the click of the lock and almost fell out into the hallway when the door opened. The lean form of Jade Pearce greeted me. Without thinking twice, I yanked her inside the room.

"Why did you bring me here?" My demand was harsh, and any camaraderie I had felt with her so long ago as we shared a lunch period or ran across the country on our adventure to Scarlett, was long gone. Jade's jaw was slack, caught off-guard, her eyes soft and apologetic on mine as she sought out the words.

"Rayne... I'm so sorry, I had no idea they would keep you and Evan—"

I cut her off without a thought.

"She's a monster!" I took another step forward, and for a second, I felt it, the strange seductive call of power I was sure lived in Scarlett's veins, when Jade, unsure, took a step back.

"Do you know what she does to people? Human beings, like me... Do you know where she goes at night? What her *job* is?" I sneered the word.

She opened her mouth to reply, but I was on a roll now, and finally I had found a target I was able to hit my mark with, something solid to blame. Someone who didn't slip through my fingers or into my head like Scarlett did every time I thought I could hate her.

"Why the hell did you bring me here?" I was a hypocrite, I knew it even as the words came tumbling out. I had wanted to find Scarlett long before Jade Pearce's appearance in my life, and I had come of my own free will. Right now, I didn't want to remember that.

"Why the hell offer to bring me here to your crazy, murdering, torturer sister?"

Jade was quiet for a long moment, her eyes glazed in a way that hurt me, physically, deep in my chest, halting me in my tracks.

"Is that really what you think of her?" The question was soft, and some of the wind started to leave the sails of my anger, my resentment and my utter confusion over all of this and how I came to be here.

Jade moved past me to sit down on the end of Scarlett's bed, her gaze finding a picture on the dresser I hadn't noticed before, a sad smile on her face. I studied the picture of the two of them as she spoke, Jade and Scarlett, the latter wearing an adoring smile as she looked sideways at the little sister whose arms were loose around her neck.

"I owe you an apology, I know that." Her voice was so quiet, almost inaudible, yet I was compelled to listen in a way even the loudest of screams had never made me.

"Do you really think she became this all by herself? Do you think she was always like this? Do you think this is her choice?"

My mind flashed back to Scarlett's eyes at the punishment center, dark and vital, her tongue running across her bloody lips to taste the devastation she'd created.

"You're the first thing in my whole life I've ever known my sister to care about, apart from me."

She wrung her pale fingers together as she made the admission. I could tell she felt it wasn't her own to make.

"After Scarlett found you, she was different... She wanted to try. Father beat her so bad I thought she was—"

Jade's eyes filled with tears and I looked down as my fingers squeezed their way between hers, her hand in mine. A million questions came and went, but I remained quiet, determined to listen, as finally, the mystery of Scarlett Pearce, of my life these last few months, began to slowly unfold before me.

"This is all she has ever known. I know how it looks and I know... She enjoys it." The words seemed as hard for her to say as they were for me to hear. "But could you believe me if I told you she's so much more than that? When I came to find you, she was losing herself, losing her humanity."

A fat tear rolled down Jade's cheek, and I watched her wipe it away. All my anger was gone, dissipated.

"It's all my fault. She does this to protect me, or she thinks she does. Father just uses me to manipulate her, he has for as long as I can remember, all I have ever been able to do is watch her suffer."

The confessions were spilling out now, and once again the picture twisted. I squeezed Jade's cold hand in mine and let her talk.

"He did things to her. She never told me, I just— When we were younger. My father thinks our family is some superior clan, that the Pearce family name is the most important thing in the world, and he wants the rest of the city to feel that way. He was terrible in his time, but he made Scarlett even worse. He broke her down until she was...this. His perfect punisher."

She reached up to tuck a lock of long dark hair behind her ear, her tongue darting out to wet dry lips.

"And the reason he succeeded is because of me, because that's the thing about Scarlett, she will endure hell, but threaten something she cares about, and she's a puppet... Can you understand the rest?"

I wanted to tell her no, to shake my head, but I just wrapped my other hand around hers and looked down at our connected fingers, waiting to hear the words right from her lips.

"This isn't all that she is, Rayne, this is just who he wants her to be, and I know, sometimes she loses herself to it, but she loves you."

The remark shot me in the chest, white-hot. Even though the words came second hand, and I wasn't even sure if they were Jade's assumptions or the truth, they lit me up, leaving me terrified of what that meant.

"She thinks you'll leave, because everybody always leaves. She's too dark, too dirty, too bloodstained, but underneath, she's so much more, and I know you've seen it too or you would never have agreed to come here. She would rather push you out the door than have you slam it in her face... I can only imagine what she did."

"She whipped four people, got covered in their blood, cut them with knives and burned them with hot metal and acted like it was all some sort of divine experience for her."

I regretted my callousness before the words had died on my lips. Jade looked as if I had punched her.

"She's pushing you away," she whispered as her tears fell on our joined hands, and it was in that moment I realized they were an odd clear pink color.

"Scarlett practically raised me, you know." Her voice lightened with new determination as we moved away from the subject of my outburst. "Mother and Father were always busy with city politics, dinner parties. Even with what Father was doing to her... Scarlett taught me to read, she taught me to write. Every night she'd come back from wherever he took her. Some nights she was bleeding, and some she just climbed into my bed and cried."

Finally Jade let go of my hand and smoothed her fingers down her cheeks, wiping away the tears that had fallen anew. "Daddy wanted his perfect family, cold and calculating, vampires who would stop at nothing to gain the social high ground and keep it. He wanted master manipulators and callous killers. I'm almost certain he would have disposed of me years ago if not for Scarlett. I don't have the stomach for it. Do you know how it feels that I'm the reason he could do this to her? One little threat against me and she'll do whatever he says, and the few times he's followed through and actually hurt me, she's almost killed herself trying to put it right. When I brought you here, I just wanted to give her something back... You see her as a monster, but to me, she's my hero. Can't she be both? Can't you love her for who she is, despite what she does?"

My eyes were glassy because Jade's words were my own struggle incarnate. But could I love her, because at this point I knew I did love her, despite what she had done, what she would likely continue to do?

"She saved me, I was in a bad situation, my dad..." I choked on the words. I had never admitted it to anyone, and I wasn't ready to start. It all felt so long ago now, a different life, a different Rayne Kennedy than this one who stood up to vampires and boldly demanded they make love to her.

"The scars on her back?"

I didn't have to specify for Jade to nod in answer to my question.

"How do you teach someone to break people? How do you put that kind of callousness, that penchant for cruelty into a child? You break them, of course, and Daddy did. He broke her so badly that some days I don't know if she can ever be fixed. But doesn't she deserve something that's just hers?"

I assumed she was talking about me.

"My father wields her like a weapon, and all the punishing helps the family stay in the Government's good graces, pushing their agenda that humans are less, chattels to be used by us as we see fit."

Abruptly, Jade stood and took a step toward the door before she turned back to face me.

"I'm sorry I brought you here, if you truly regret coming. I'm sorry I lost track of you and my plan was...a mess. I understand if you hate me, but please, just listen. She will push you away, show you the absolute worst of her, and try to chase you off before you leave of your own accord. If you ever cared for her at all, don't let her. Stay and make her show you who she really is when she thinks no one's looking. Once Scarlett loves you, and once she believes you could love her, she will do anything for you. My sister is so many things, but she's loyal, and she's so capable of love, and I think she fell in love with you a little bit the night she met you."

I had to interject because that piece of the puzzle my brain just couldn't place.

"I was half dead... Maybe more than that. I barely said a word to her."

I wondered if Scarlett could really be so superficial my looks alone were enough. The idea boggled my mind because although I realized I could be pretty if viewed just right, I had never seen myself as anything special.

"You thanked her." A sad smile played on Jade's lips now. "You saw the darkest piece of her when she killed your father, and rather than screaming, rather than wondering what monster she could be, you saw past it all in that moment, even if it was just to see the end of your own suffering, and you thanked her. She cried when she told me, because somehow you, some sickly little human girl—" She gave a watery laugh. "Scarlett's words not mine. You saw her, and that's where it started."

Jade left the room with one more pleading look. My head full to bursting with this new and unexpected perspective, I lay down on black sheets and buried my face in Scarlett's pillow. There was too much to sort, too much to make sense of. My mind lingered on the image forever burned there, of the thick scars across a tanned back, as I fell into a dreamless sleep.

RAIN PELTED THE thick glass windows when I woke. Cold hands released me as though they had been burned as I opened my eyes. Scarlett's dark gaze was on mine, I could feel it as much as see it. Half lit by the light filtering in from the bathroom, I looked down over myself to see my shoes had been removed and I had been moved under the covers. The action warmed me, but the chill of the Scarlett I had seen last at the punishment center still left me cold.

Carefully, I stood. I pulled my shirt over my head, unfastened my jeans and dropped them to the floor without the bashfulness that once plagued me. I had grown since I met Scarlett; it was impossible not to realize that. Her hair was still damp from the shower, and it brushed my arm as she returned to her own side of the bed. A large T-shirt hung off her slim frame as she slipped under the covers.

Silence was heavy between us. The few inches separating us felt like miles, further than it had ever been when I was back in New Hampshire and she was here, in Vires. I risked a look over at her, only to find her looking back. Her face clean of the makeup and the blood, her dark eyes searching mine, her full lips pulled down ever so slightly in the corners.

Jade's words rung in my head as I reached up to touch her cool cheek. She was still as stone beneath my fingers, yet her eyes tracked me with a tenderness that melted my resolve not to be swayed by all I had learned about her after I got back to the tower last night.

When she reached up to lay her fingers over mine, I realized she was scared. The emotion crept, barely breaking the surface, whispering softly to me, but I felt it all the same. She looked at me like I was the sun, like I was now her judge and jury. She was quiet, so still, and I felt her again, beautiful and dark and broken beside me, and wondered if I had ever had a chance.

"Don't push me away."

I whispered the words as I rolled, hovering over her, searching her eyes for any trace of repentance. Her lips parted just slightly, and I heard the soft catch in her breath. I leaned down and kissed her despite myself. Her kisses tasted like an apology.

Chapter Twelve

MISMATCHED EYES FOLLOWED me for days. Slowly, somewhere between the dreams of Scarlett with a whip in her hand, and her absence at night, we hit a comfortable rhythm. She became something I knew again, back from the death she'd died to me at the punishment center, though the truth still hung fragile between us, just out of view for the moment.

She had been soft, tentative with me since that night, and part of me wanted to crush her lips against mine and taste her in her entirety, uncensored. Yet another part of me was grateful she was keeping her darker side away from me.

Cold lips at my ear broke me from my silent observation. She was the closest to playful I had ever seen her, and it warmed my heart.

"Did I send Cook away so we could make breakfast, only to have you sit and watch?"

I turned my head to leave our faces just inches apart and was caught off guard momentarily by how comfortable I had somehow become with another being.

"What do vampires eat for breakfast?"

Her dark eyes danced in delight at my question. She leaned around me, letting her nose brush up the column of my neck, finding my ear again and leaving goose bumps in her wake. Her whisper was slow and seductive.

"Well...pancakes, waffles, and I personally do enjoy bacon."

I shoved her away, fighting a laugh. I rose from my barstool and moved to the mixing bowl she had left out. Seeing the basic ingredients for pancakes, I started on the batter, trying to ignore the way my insides had melted while she listed off breakfast foods. I heard her snickering behind me before the kitchen was silent, save for the breaking of the eggshell on the side of the mixing bowl. Then something cool was pressed against my back.

Long fingers settled around my waist and I couldn't help leaning into her as I added the ingredients to the bowl on rote. Light pressure on my hip drew my eyes down to her hands, reminding me of the night before when I'd sat on the plush living room sofa, listening to her play the piano.

Scarlett's music was deep and dark, haunting and twisting and as beautiful as the woman herself. Once again, I was overwhelmed with the urge to pinch myself, because somehow, she wanted me. I played no instruments, was average looking at best...

"You're thinking too hard."

She slid away from me, took the mixing bowl and whisk from my hands, and leaned back against the counter, her slender form only covered by a large black T-shirt that hung loose from it. Her dark eyes found mine, the whisk moving at an inhuman speed as she whipped the batter like a mixer machine. I forced myself not to stare.

"Will we ever get to..." I struggled for the words to describe what was tentatively growing between us. "Be like this, outside?"

Her eyes narrowed in response and I kicked myself internally for ruining what was shaping up to be another perfect morning with the woman who, for better or worse, had become the center of my world.

"Actually, I was hoping you would accompany me to an outing tomorrow night."

Her words were slow and careful, and I could hear the thought behind them, the moments spent selecting the exact phrasing. My blood ran cold.

"Scarlett..." Her name was a whisper though I had meant it to come out stronger. My face suddenly went cool, and I knew the blood had left my cheeks.

For a second, I was weightless and then the bowl was on the counter, batter still settling, and I was perched on the cool surface beside it. Scarlett stood in front of me, arms around my waist, her gaze searching mine.

"I didn't mean...there." She reached up to touch my cheek. I felt how deeply my reaction hurt her in the microsecond of feedback I got before she locked our connection down tight, turning it into a stonewall on her side. Though her eyes still held mine, the distance grew steadily in them.

"There's a party, you actually have to attend, but I wanted to ask."

She sounded defeated. She appeared small like this, looking up at me with a faraway hopefulness, turned steely at the edges by my earlier reaction to what I thought was another invitation to the punishment center.

"I'm sorry..."

She stepped away from me and raked her fingers over the skin of my bare thighs where her borrowed sleep shirt ended, taking the sting out of the action.

"So, the party, you'll come?"

She avoided my eyes as the stove top was turned on and the oil in the pan began to spit. Perhaps it would be easier, better to go along and let the issue slip back into the periphery, but the taste of her hurt still lingered in my head.

"Can't we just keep it separate?" I kept my voice careful, unsure of myself now as I pressed forward down a road both of us had been studiously avoiding since that night.

"If you attend the party without me the experience will be extremely unpleasant, for both of us." She didn't look up from ladling batter into the pan.

"That's not what I mean, and you know it." I slid off the counter and crossed the space to her, my feet cold on the granite below them. I turned off the stove and reached for her, mentally preparing myself to traipse back down this dark path, to once again acknowledge what she had done, and continued to do. I didn't know yet if I could live with it, but maybe if she would agree to this, we could try. I did know beyond all reason that I didn't want to, and probably couldn't, live without her.

I let my fingers rest on her pale cheeks until, finally, she looked at me.

"Can we try to keep it separate, what you do and...this, just for now?"

The words barely formed on my lips and I reached in desperation for the reaction I couldn't see, loath to hurt her but loath to let this hang between us any longer. Maybe like this, out of sight, out of mind, we could make progress that didn't feel as if it was built on a paper-thin foundation.

She was lifeless under my hands for a long moment as she studied me, and I wondered again why I couldn't have just been happy with my blissful ignorance, or at least the pretense of it.

"It's not possible..." She moved to pull away from me, but I held on, threading my fingers through the hair behind her ears, holding the sides of her skull while my thumbs stayed gentle on her cheeks.

"Scarlett."

She hissed in response, making me start, but I didn't let go. Her arms wrapped around me again, and suddenly the cool metal surface of the fridge was against my back, pulling a gasp up from my chest.

"Silly girl..." She whispered the words, her eyes boring into mine, gentle and sad, "You want to pretend, you want to try..." She sounded disbelieving, and Jade's words echoed in my head.

Was she right? Was I just another name in the long list of those who Scarlett was too dark for, too dirty? She brushed her thumb gently over my lower lip and set my body on a slow burn for her, because this conflict, this guilt I felt for loving her, didn't compare to the agony of a world without her in it.

"And what when we can't pretend anymore?" Her voice was still low and breathy, crashing over me, lulling me so easily that my response, my request, tumbled out with ease.

"Stop."

She laughed. The air from her mouth tickled my lips, yet she still held my gaze with an intensity in stark contrast to the humor she seemed to find in all this.

"And when I can't, either because my hands are tied, or because I don't want to, because this is who I am, then what?"

Her question laid bare my worst fears, and the one that had haunted me since my talk with Jade.

"You can't live with this." Her voice slipped, losing its seductive edge and turning raspy with sadness. Finally, she looked away from me, releasing me from the slow burn that caused my heart to hammer against my ribs. I opened my mouth to protest, but she beat me to it.

"You don't dream quietly, Princess, you can't love a murderer."

A sad smile tugged at her lips as she stepped out of my grasp. I wondered briefly if she enjoyed this kind of emotional devastation the way she did the physical.

"But I do love you..." I was thinking out loud, tears starting to fill my eyes as she walked away from me, the pancakes, the playfulness ruined. My cheeks burned with the conviction of my words, and the humiliating idea that somehow, she had been privy to my dreams, too many of which featured her.

"I do love you, Scarlett, I do..." All my worries, all the guilt, the conflict and the fear of rejection were washed out in the face of her leaving me, of her thinking I was incapable of loving her when I'd been in love with her long before I knew her well enough to understand why.

Scarlett lingered in the doorway, frozen, and for the first time since I had arrived at Pearce Tower, I let go of what I thought I was supposed to feel in accordance with moral code. I stopped applying consequences, and finally let myself embrace it. I was in love with her.

The fire that lit inside her at my words, at what I could only guess she heard silently, warmed me through as she turned back to me. She crossed the space between us slowly, at a human pace. I already felt her response crashing through my veins; she loved me, softly and gently, and with the fire of a thousand suns burning hot with her possessiveness, protectiveness. It almost swallowed me whole, and I barely had time to wonder how I'd never known it earlier, before she pulled me back to her and kissed me, gentle and tender at first, then hard.

We were stars colliding, rivers bursting through their dams to meet at the sea. It consumed me, and I let it. Scarlett's mouth was cool against my neck, the refrigerator cold against my bare backside when she shoved my panties down just enough to push her hand beneath.

Her fingers were deep inside me, my head thrown back, eyes closed. I was softly panting out my ascent to orgasm, my body tight, hot, completely at her mercy, when a dull thud from down the hall startled me. I forced my eyes open to look at her, a low growl erupting in her throat as she pulled her slick fingers out of my underwear. The whine that escaped my lips as I pressed my thighs together, mourning her absence, made my cheeks blush red. The way Scarlett looked me dead in the eye as she slid her fingers between her lips and sucked brashly on them for a few seconds only made me flush harder. I was left to fix my underwear and she was gone.

She returned from the hallway a moment later with Jade on her heels.

"I swear that end table wasn't there last night, I was just... Oh God."

Jade's eyes snapped to my beet red-face and Scarlett looked like the cat that had caught the canary.

"Were you guys... I mean... I can just—" Jade pointed awkwardly to the door. Scarlett caught her with a chuckle before she could leave.

"We're making pancakes. Isn't that right, Princess?" She was playing with me, and I had to force myself to move from where I was still crumpled against the refrigerator and take the spatula from her. I was limp, all the wrong bits of me jelly, but Scarlett's eyes shone with such glee, albeit at my expense, I couldn't bring myself to be mad.

Ignoring her, I managed to shuffle my way over to a barstool and plopped down beside Jade without ceremony.

"So, we were just discussing the party." Scarlett's voice was full of tension I knew was obvious to both me and her sister, and I immediately wondered what had caused the shift.

"You know I don't want to talk about it." Jade's reply was quiet, her gaze fixed firmly on her long fingers as she wrung them on the countertop.

"And you know you have to go, and you have to choose a...date."

I tried not to wonder about the pause.

"I have...someone to accompany me, Scarlett, her name is Caroline. Could we just drop this, please?"

Jade's puppy dog eyes had as much of an effect on me as they did Scarlett, and I shifted uncomfortably on my stool as I decided to try to take the attention away from her.

"So, what exactly is this party celebrating?"

Scarlett's emotional reaction sent little shards of ice into my veins. I tried to ignore the palpable temperature drop in the room, and both vampires seemed to be avoiding my eyes. Jade was the one to finally speak, Scarlett suddenly engrossed in stacking pancakes onto one large plate she had pulled from a cupboard somewhere to the side of the stove.

"It's a kind of history thing, a celebration of this dumb city's heritage." Jade's grumbling was cut off before she could finish, a low warning growl erupting from Scarlett's throat.

"Nobody's around to hear me." Jade shrugged. I tried not to read too far into all the weird, and all the conversation and plans that seemed to be going on with or without me. Part of me was excited for the party, to get out of the tower. A larger part of me was apprehensive, still caught on the memory of my last field trip with Scarlett.

Mismatched eyes watched me across the counter as I cut into my pancake, and I knew she could taste my curiosity. A fat chocolate chip exploded on my tongue with the first bite, and I couldn't help but moan in surprise.

In my periphery, I knew Jade was rolling her eyes, but Scarlett's were boring into me, her lips pulled up into a killer smile.

MY HEELS BUMPED nervously against the thick carpet in the back of one of the Pearce family cars. Scarlett was beautiful beside me, dark hair gently curled, piled high on her head, her collarbones exposed by the low-cut figure-hugging dress she wore, deep red just like her name. Though our day had been the usual avoidance of her homecoming as the sun hit the horizon and an afternoon of reading in the study. When the sun set again behind the smaller towers visible from her window, Scarlett had grown colder.

The distance hurt like a physical wound and, coupled with the anxiety over the event we were headed to, I ached to reach for her and force her to close it.

The tires screeched as we came to a sudden stop, and from the tug on my hand as the door whipped open, I guessed we had arrived.

My bare feet hit the cool and oddly clean concrete of the sidewalk. I barely had time to take in the illuminated city skyline, remembering the Midlands Zara had told me about so long ago, a cluster of tiny close lights just visible beyond the towers, before Scarlett tugged me along.

The building we entered was dome-shaped, jutting up behind what I recognized to be the central bunker. I stiffened on reflex, but Scarlett barely seemed to notice.

Self-conscious in my clingy deep blue dress, I kept walking. The concrete under my feet turned to carpet, and then to wood, and I stood at the mouth of what looked to be a very large ballroom.

"Follow me."

The first words she had spoken to me in over half an hour, though it felt like an eternity, were emotionless, as dead as our connection. I did so mindlessly, trying not to feel the humiliation of the lack of shoes Scarlett had unapologetically insisted on, as well as the fine platinum band she had clasped like a choker around my neck, embedded with tiny scarlet rubies. I was almost certain it was a collar.

Peering out from behind Scarlett's slim form, I immediately felt selfish for my internal grumbling about my own outfit, before a fresh wave of fear drowned it out.

The room was a complete juxtaposition. Extravagant dresses and exquisite beauty, expensive suits and cigars, against a backdrop of tattered and torn rags. It was easy to pick out those from the Fringe.

Someone grabbed my arm and I jumped back, a yelp of surprise escaping my lips. Scarlett hissed, though the sound was cut short, and I turned to her, helplessly.

"So predictable, my love..." The voice was rich and softly accented, and I looked up into the eyes of the tall, gorgeous glamazon who currently held my arm in her stone-cold vise grip.

"Camilla, you know how I get about people touching my things."

Scarlett sounded bored, but her eyes said otherwise.

"Darling, what's a little peasant girl between friends?" Camilla reached up and trailed the pads of her slim fingers down my cheek. My skin heated under her touch, her scrutiny. I ached to pull away, but somehow, I couldn't find it in myself to be so impolite, as uncomfortable as I was. Those long fingers stopped at the choker around my neck and fell away as her dark eyes flashed back to Scarlett who stood protectively, perhaps possessively, at my back.

"I trust I will see you tonight, once the public celebrations are over. Perhaps we can continue in private?" Camilla's question caught me totally off guard, as I was confronted with the jealousy I hadn't felt since Aria. Scarlett's answer was a long intense gaze and a subtle smirk.

"Summoning me like a dog?" She purred the words. "Not tonight, I'm busy with my own pet."

She took my arm and we were walking again. It took about four steps before my brain caught up and I dug in my heels. The element of surprise allowed me to yank my arm from her grasp, and the sting of being called her pet threw aside my insecurity over Camilla long enough for me to be furious.

"I am not your—"

I didn't get to finish. The air left my lungs with the weight of her body crashing into mine as she half pushed, half threw me into the closest wall. Then she was on me. One minute I was furious, fuming, the next Scarlett's tongue was running slick and demanding over my lips, parting them effortlessly, before they were replaced by her hand. Her mouth was still hot against my ear, her words almost inaudible.

"Tonight, for them, you are my pet. I am your Mistress. You belong to me, because that way you are safe with me. Make a spectacle and this will be extremely dangerous, do you understand?"

The discreet kiss of apology just under my ear didn't stop the angry tears from springing into my eyes. I nodded anyway, still wary enough of the vampires after Evan Chase had struck me, and the horrible stories circulating the tower, to argue.

"Good girl."

She led me onward without any further interruption, and behind her, I quietly seethed. When Scarlett sunk down into a high-backed chair, I moved to sit in the one beside her out of habit. A soft yank on my arm dragged me to the opposite side of her and then continued to pull. Confused, I went along, not realizing where I was headed until my knees hit the hard wood. Scarlett proceeded to push me back onto my bottom and gave me a withering look that I assumed meant I was to stay. I glared back at her, my cheeks hot with embarrassment, until she looked away.

As the night went on, Scarlett entertained multiple guests from her chair. Some noticed me, some even commented on me, like I was a new necklace or a pair of shoes. Nobody except Camilla dared to touch me. I had a feeling Scarlett wouldn't take it too well if they had, though I wasn't sure if that was because she cared for me or simply because I was hers. Watching her like this, cold and hard and as beautiful as the rubies glittering around my neck, it was easier to distance myself from her in return, to be angry about her actions, and humiliated by the way she was treating me.

While Scarlett met her guests, I was left alone, beside her yet so far away, to watch the party as it progressed. From my seat on the floor, finally, the walls of Pearce Tower were removed, and I saw Vires for all it was, in all its terrifying glory.

The vampires were easy to spot. Well dressed, for the most part, drinks in hand, and what could only be described as slaves, humans, trailing behind them. My beautiful night-sky blue dress put to shame the old, worn beige-colored slacks and polos most of my fellow humans wore. I couldn't stop myself from actively looking for Zara, the girl I had met in the bunker, and Joseph, as I watched the crowds. I could feel Scarlett beside me, though I had stopped bothering to look up, knowing she would appear to be engrossed in whoever currently attempted to converse with her. Her replies were always carefully chosen, swinging between taunting, playful, and plain bored. Her awareness tickled at mine sometimes, and I knew she was trying to gauge my reaction to all this.

Many of the vampires had humans bringing them drinks, deep red liquids, too thin to be blood, in margarita glasses. Others had their accompanying humans lined up against the wall, waiting for their call. My stomach churned at the sight of Evan Chase and plummeted to the floor beneath me as I saw who seemed to be occupying his attention.

Jade looked every inch the model I had thought her to be when she had first appeared in my high school, her dark hair loose and poker straight, an emerald-green floor-length gown sweeping the carpet as she shifted uncomfortably under Evan's gaze.

I debated reaching up to discreetly nudge Scarlett, but she seemed to be thoroughly engaged in a pissing match with an older male vampire who had a much younger human man perched precariously on one of his knees, clad in nothing but tight black underpants.

Even from across the room, I spotted the color of discomfort in Jade's cheeks, her smile clearly forced. A human girl with dark hair lingered at her back, and I briefly remembered that she too had brought a "date" tonight.

Evan seemed to be in his element, and I remembered all his attempts to be commanding, his obvious jealousy of Scarlett's natural dominance. The realization that Jade probably seemed like an easy target for him to overpower made me feel ill. Besides striking me once, and a few outbursts of temper, Evan had never been particularly cruel or terrifying, not compared to some of the other vampires, not compared to Scarlett, yet he set me on edge. His vendetta against the Delta vampires was obvious. I stewed over his slip about wanting Scarlett to pay, as I watched him leave Jade momentarily, only to catch a human girl by the arm and snatch the two drinks she had presumably been taking back to her partner for the evening.

Bodies ebbed and swayed, conversations carrying on, a polite façade on a sinister society, blocking my line of sight as Evan moved back across the grand space. He was heading toward Jade, who was engaged in hushed conversation with the human beside her. Something silver flashed bright under the crystal chandeliers, before it was gone again as Evan passed behind a large group of vampires crowded around a cluster of humans.

Jade seemed to accept the drink with grace, and the pair continued to talk, though her dark eyes were combing the room, and I knew she was looking for Scarlett. A surge of bravery came with the realization, and I politely patted Scarlett's bare calf which hung beside me. Mismatched eyes glanced down at me for just a second, before they were pulled back to her current sparring partner.

Stuck on the shiny object I had caught just a glimpse of, and somehow recognized, I continued to watch until I was rewarded. A sliver of the small flask-like canister was visible just outside of my old captor's pants pocket, as he twisted it in his fist, impatient. Jade held her drink in long fingers and I watched her laugh in a way I was pretty sure was fake, as it all crashed together for me.

I got up without thinking. Crazed rantings about insurance policies and the downfall of superior Delta vampires rang in my ears, alongside the memory of the day Evan had hit me. The day I had walked in to find his safe behind the painting open.

Bodies blocked my path, and I weaved between them, my gaze always returning to Jade. Some leered, one called to me, and most didn't even notice my passage. I wasn't sure what had inspired this sense of urgency in me. I didn't know exactly what Evan was hiding, or if he even had the ability to follow through on his vengeful plans, but I couldn't escape the warning bells causing my heart to pound against my ribcage, screaming that Jade wasn't safe.

I reached for the glass without thinking as soon as I was close enough and sent it spilling out of Jade's grasp. It broke as it hit the floor. The thin crimson liquid spilled all over Evan Chase's overpriced shoes. Anger and protectiveness beat hot in my chest, fear for Jade, for Scarlett, and frustration at myself for not talking to Scarlett sooner about what I had learned at Chase Tower. Evan had always seemed so pale against her, an imitator, not dangerous enough to be any real threat to all her bloody reds and violent black. Shards of glass glittered in the soft lighting, and for the first time, I began to wonder if I had underestimated my former master.

Thin features twisted into a familiar mask of rage, Jade's eyes were wide as she stared at me, horrified. Pain split my vision and my head whipped around, the floor coming up to catch me as the side of my face exploded into fire. I looked up to see Evan boring down on me, and instantly I was vindicated in stopping Jade from drinking whatever he had offered her.

An old, forgotten reflex took over, and I was still, waiting, playing dead as I had for years in the face of violence I wasn't strong enough to avoid. For all I had grown and changed, in the seconds that ticked to minutes in my mind as Evan advanced on me in slow motion, I wondered if I was really so different after all.

Scarlett answered for me. A breeze at my back and a blur of red and she was in front of me, snarling and spitting, hands twisted into claws.

They danced a dance my mind was too numb to follow, some nonverbal communication I couldn't understand but could feel rising in a horrible crescendo. Right before they

202 - | L.E. Royal

blew, a tanned arm hooked into Scarlett's elbow and hauled her back. Camilla stepped between them, chin held high.

"Now, now... Let's not make a scene."

Scarlett scoffed, the burning fury in her eyes chilling me to my bones, but she stayed in place behind the woman I was coming to assume was some sort of friend, and hopefully nothing more.

"You little bitch."

Evan spat the words at me, his weaselly features twisted with disdain as he looked down to where I still sat on the floor. Scarlett lunged again. Camilla barely caught her in time, positioning herself squarely between the two of them.

"Accidents happen, Evan. Best we leave it at that, don't you think?"

Her words only set him seething harder, though he seemed to become more aware of the attention we were garnering from onlookers. Finally, after a few terse seconds of intense eye contact, he deflated.

"Deltas." He spat the word, though he wasn't brave enough to finish the thought. Many of the eyes around the room zeroed in on him at the remark, forcing him to blanch, and eventually walk away, disappearing into the party which quickly resumed around us once it was clear there was nothing more to be seen.

Jade reached me first. She crouched down beside me, her cool hand in mine as she winced apologetically at the black eye I was sure must be coming along nicely. I looked up to the person I truly wanted comfort from, to find her still glued to the spot, vibrating with rage. Camilla was blocking her path to follow Evan and talking to Scarlett so quietly and quickly I couldn't hear her.

"Caroline, could you help me get Rayne up, please?"

Jade's companion appeared beside her, and as they took my hands and helped me to my feet, I was suddenly struck by the name.

"Caroline, do you know Joseph?" My vision swam, and I was grateful they held on until I was steady on my feet.

"You've met my brother?"

I nodded and instantly regretted it.

"We were in the bunker together when I first arrived. Is he...? I mean..." I hoped beyond hope I had not just put my foot in it.

"Did he survive after that bitch mutilated him? Barely, but from what I hear it shouldn't matter much to you."

I was taken back by the sudden venom in her voice as she continued.

"Are you a masochist or just so lacking morally that you hide behind the biggest bad to save your own skin?"

"Caroline... Please." Jade laid her hand on the shorter girl's arm, her eyes beseeching, and for the first time, I wondered what they were to each other.

"Right, Scarlett is misunderstood and perfect, blah blah. I'm going to get you another drink, Miss." She spat the title and Jade's expression sunk. Hurt radiated off her as the girl walked away.

"You okay?" It was a stupid question, but as I reached up to examine my bruised face, it was the best I could manage.

"She's just... It's fine. Are you? I mean I know you're not, your face..." I caught her glance behind me to her sister who finally seemed to be coming out of her rage and was nodding almost imperceptibly along with whatever Camilla was saying to her. Her gaze was fixed on the two of us.

I stared back at her, unashamed. Our eyes connected for too long and I tasted her blinding hot anger, her possessiveness, territoriality. The call for Evan's blood rallied higher and higher until my hands were clenched into fists at my sides.

"We should get you some ice." I let Jade pull me away, wanting nothing more than to go to Scarlett and to run away from her all in the same breath. I was unsure how she could feel so dark, so consumed by murderousness and destruction, and still be the woman whose fingers covered mine over the ivory keys of the piano, so gentle as she taught me simple melodies.

By the time we returned from the bar, neither Scarlett nor Caroline was anywhere to be found. Jade sat me in the chairs where Scarlett and I had begun our night and handed me a glass of water before she sat down beside me looking utterly miserable. I opened my mouth to ask but was interrupted by a soft chime over the sound system in the hall.

"Greetings, citizens of Vires. The Government welcomes you to this seventy-fifth annual founding celebration and extends a special welcome to the Delta vampires here representing their families tonight. In celebration of the values on which our great city was built, in addition to tonight's festivities, there will also be a commemorative event—a tribute to the power of our species, an homage to the chattels who nourish us."

My stomach twisted uncomfortably, and I looked around for Scarlett. Dread whispered softly in my ear, supposing she would perhaps be a part of whatever was coming.

"The Government thanks all who volunteered. A Delta vampire will be given the honor of displaying their prowess with a punishment of their choice to be performed on their accompanying human, for the entertainment and enjoyment of their fellow predators."

It was going to be me. The spectacle, the chattel, the thing with their back flayed open and words branded across their chest. I was going to be it, and Scarlett was going to be the one to do it. I wanted to stand, to get up and run, to get some kind of head start, because I knew Scarlett. I had tasted the essence of her, felt it rich and heady and dark in my own veins, and I knew she would struggle to refuse this.

Her father flashed before my eyes, bearing down on her, all Jade's stories of her youth, the many eyes that had been on us earlier. Her pedestal was high, and I had no idea if she had a way down, or if she was even willing to fall. When the occasion came, I couldn't predict if her love for me trumped her love of the dark, the blood, the breaking, and in the face of finding out, I was terrified.

The speaker fizzed back to life and the well-placed pause to let excitement buzz through the crowd expired.

"Jade Pearce, you have been chosen for this honor, please report to the stage by midnight and begin at your leisure. Request for implements can be made through the guards."

The announcement continued, but I didn't hear it. My world burst back into color, the black spots blown out from my eyes, my heart beating fast, soaring with relief and then plummeting again with dread. Could Jade do this? Would she? Once glance at her ashen face answered my question. She looked as horrified as I felt.

Guilt at my relief clawed at me. Though the party roared back to life around us, we were silent, staring at each other. Scarlett blew in like a tornado. Her fingers grazed the back of my hand softly as she passed me over and stooped beside Jade.

"You have to, I'm so sorry, but you have to... There's nothing I can do, I've tried. I can't do it for you."

The dam seemed to break. Perhaps Jade had been shell-shocked, perhaps she had been expecting Scarlett to be able to do something to change fate. In the face of her sister's words, her silence broke and tears filled her eyes.

"I can't, I won't, Scarlett. I won't hurt Caroline."

"You will." Scarlett's voice was ice cold and it chilled me to my core. Scarlett around Jade was warm and loving, nurturing and protective. Fat tears spilled down Jade's cheeks as she stared up at her sibling.

"It will be worse long-term, just know that. If I could stop this or change it I would, I've tried. The entire city is here, Jade. Father is in the back with the Hawthorne parents. Everyone is here, if you disobey them so publicly."

I wanted to be selfless, to tell Jade she could take me instead of Caroline, who she clearly cared deeply for, but a selfish part of me kept my mouth closed. Pain had been my life, my body knew what it was to bend and break and bleed, and I couldn't bring myself to go back there again. Even as my face still smarted from Evan's fist, my suffering was less inevitable now. My father was dead, and although I was unsure whether Scarlett wouldn't hurt me herself if commanded to, I knew nobody else would be able to, not seriously.

Her fingers were wrapped softly around Jade's. They were silent for a long time, and I thought I saw a thin sheen of tears cover Scarlett's eyes too, though when she blinked her mask returned.

"You need to go now. Ask them for the short whip with the knotted lash. It will be a bloody show without too much damage or pain, okay?" She searched Jade's face for a reaction, shaking her lightly, though the girl seemed to have shut down in her grasp.

"Twenty lashes, okay? Count them. Bluff, put on a show, keep their eyes on you and off her so you can limit how much you have to hurt her. Listen to me..." Scarlett hissed, her desperation beginning to crack her voice.

Across the room, I recognized the man from the bunker, along with several similarly dressed vampires, some of whom were familiar, probably from the night I'd arrived at the city wall. They were watching us, waiting. Noticing me, the man who had searched me at the start of my prison stay gave me a predatory smile. My heart pounded harder, yet more adrenaline spilled into my already hormone-addled veins as I turned my attention back to the sisters.

"Jade, you have to do this. You need to get up now and go. Switch it off. Keep everyone's attention, and you hit her hard, do you understand me? Twenty, as hard as you can. There will be a lot of blood, but it's the best you can do. Count them, laugh, crack the whip. Nobody expects you to be like me, but you can't ruin their celebration. You have to go..."

Scarlett's nervousness set me on edge. I clenched my jaw, uncomfortable in the face of my constant, my strength, being so utterly out of control. To me, she was almost untouchable, despite what I had learned about her father's controlling nature, Evan's vendetta, and her own brokenness. Seeing her so scared terrified me.

"Get up and go." She practically lifted Jade to her feet and began to lead her away, seeming to stem her frantic flow of words at last. Dark eyes looked back to find me, and the soft glow of her love, tainted black by the still-simmering anger that I had been hurt, enveloped me. It warmed me in the cold abyss of what was coming, breathing life back into me just enough for me to nod my response. As she turned her head to continue escorting Jade to the front of the room,

I caught the slightest flash of her fear, her desperation to avert what was about to unfold. The clock above the stage read ten minutes until midnight.

THE COLD METAL frame of the chair below me became a lifeline, and I clung to it in disbelief at what was unfolding. Caroline yelled profanities, fought and screamed as she was tied to one of the steel roof beams above the stage, naked.

The sight shocked me to my core, thoroughly cleansing me of the illusion of safety our bubble in Pearce Tower had created. This world was unlike anything I had ever experienced, and it wasn't something I would have ever wanted to, yet I had wanted Scarlett so desperately.

Jade stepped onto the stairs, and I watched her ascent. Even in her beautiful gown, she looked small, broken, a thin black whip dragging the floor behind her heels. The sight was jarring. Jade—sweet, clumsy, naive Jade. Jade with the best intentions and the crazy plan that had brought me here to this blood-tainted world, to the woman I loved, despite all of this.

I ached to save her, to stop this. I reached out, searching the room for any traces of Scarlett, and found nothing. She had either left or was shut down to me completely. The room fell silent as Jade stepped forward, holding its collective breath. I was taken back to the night at the punishment center, the swing in Scarlett's step, the showy cracks of the whip, and the blood spattering her face like rain. Were they expecting that here, from Jade? The thought made me sick to my core.

I couldn't tear my eyes away from the stage, from Caroline, head bowed low, almost in acceptance, while Jade stood still as a statue behind her. The crowd began to stir as the silence stretched on, slowing down while the beating of my heart, loud in my ears, counted out each passing second. Panic clawed at my throat. I wasn't ready to see another round of violence like the one Scarlett had shown me at the center. I wasn't ready to see Jade painted in that same sick red.

"I can't... I'm sorry."

Jade's words were quiet, but they were audible in the large room. The first sob pierced the air like a gunshot, and although relief washed over me, fear of what was to come nipped at its heels. Surely it wasn't that easy? She couldn't just refuse, and we would all go home, Caroline would return to Joseph to live another day in the Fringe?

The whispers whipped into a storm around me. Everything came to life, soft conversation turning to loud chatter. I sat as frozen as Jade stood on the stage, both of us waiting for what would come next. Time stretched on and twisted around itself until I wasn't sure how long we had waited. The sound system cracked back to life, and in my desperation, I wondered where Scarlett was, why she wasn't here to help Jade, help me, weather whatever storm I sensed was coming from the excited hush that fell over the crowd.

"Jade Pearce has disgraced her family and her kind. Her refusal to honor the tradition of a ceremonial punishment at this gala, and her disobedience, has been noted by the Government. We hope Miss Pearce's behavior will serve as a reminder of the principals Vires was built upon, and those which it was not. Tomorrow at noon, both Jade Pearce and her designated human will be punished at the town square. A lash for every year our great city has stood will be distributed between them."

With another crack, the message ended.

Chapter Thirteen

THE THIN STRAPS of my dress were still wet, soaked with the tears Jade had cried all the way home, when we began our ascent of the tower. She was wordless beside me, eyes red and unseeing, her hand cold in mine. A thick fog had settled over me, making it hard to see a path forward, onward, through this. My brain wondered for the hundredth time since the announcement where the hell Scarlett was?

The elevator doors opened on the thirteenth floor, the soft scent of vanilla and Scarlett's perfume telling me we were home. Just as the comfort came, it was whipped away. Waiting for us under the soft lighting of the lobby was the man who had become a frequent feature in my dreams, the one who had broken or trained or twisted Scarlett into a bloodthirsty torturer.

Wilfred Pearce's gray eyes barely grazed me before they were on the girl beside me as she shrunk back, almost stumbling into the elevator as the doors began to close.

"Daddy?"

My blood ran cold. This man wielded Scarlett, my powerful, passionate, Scarlett like a weapon. What the hell was he going to do to Jade? I took half a step between them.

"Where's Scarlett?" His words were ice cold.

"I don't know..." Jade's were barely audible.

The way he looked at her cut me to the bone and my chest ached for her. There were goose bumps on her skin where the top of her bare arm grazed mine. Wilfred Pearce looked at her as if she was a huge inconvenience, and a dirty one at that. His face dripped disdain, and I wondered if not for Scarlett, what would have become of her good-hearted sister.

"Is this what you wanted? To humiliate us? To undermine and embarrass us? To paint us as weak?" He spat the last word like a curse.

From the side of my view, I saw Jade shake her head, her eyes wide and caught on his.

"Do you know what it means to be a Delta, Jade? How about a vampire? Does Scarlett teach you anything when she's not braiding your hair and catering to your pathetic needs? Does she keep you here as we keep the humans, a pet, something to pretend to love her on the days she fools herself into thinking she needs anything of the sort?"

He took a step closer. I reached behind me on reflex, pushing Jade half a step backward, suddenly brave in the face of a situation that had undone me so many times over the years. Perhaps it was what made me so unwilling to let Jade go through the same with her father as I had with my own.

Gray eyes snapped to me and a displeased snarl curled his upper lip at the action. I forced myself to look back into those steely eyes, my heart beating hard but steady, defiant in the face of my fear. He managed a single step toward me before a sharp *ding* echoed in the open space, announcing the arrival of the elevator behind us.

Jade brushed against me as she whipped around, presumably to run to Scarlett. I couldn't bring myself to turn my back on the man who both she and her sister seemed to fear and serve.

"Mr. Pearce, how are you?"

At the sound of a voice I recognized but did not expect, I turned around to see Camilla's lean form framed in the steel doorway.

"My father wanted me to come and personally send our condolences for this evening." Her voice was silky smooth and so sincere, but I still wondered why she was really here. Her earlier interaction with Scarlett made it difficult for me to believe she had any allegiance with her father.

"Thank you, Camilla. You look lovely tonight, as always."

All the venom of just a moment before was gone, slicked back under the surface, and the shift was terrifying. This man was dangerous, nothing like my own bumbling drunk of a father who had lived in his emotions entirely. Wilfred Pearce was cool and calculating, and it scared me beyond belief. I hoped beyond hope Camilla would not leave now her message had been relayed.

"Is Scarlett home?" She slipped off her long coat and slid it onto the rack with a familiarity that chafed. I couldn't help but be grateful for her presence, no matter how much I questioned her role in Scarlett's life.

"She's not." Wilfred looked approving at the request.

"Do you mind if I wait? Perhaps I can talk some sense into this one's head while I do?" She inclined her head at Jade, a soft playful smile tugging at her full lips.

Wilfred nodded his concession. With a sharp look to his youngest daughter, he stepped around us and punched the elevator button with one crooked index finger.

"Goodnight, Miss Hawthorne."

When the elevator doors finally closed, I felt the breath of relief Jade breathed on the back of my neck, as Camilla's bright-eyed smile fell away.

"Thank you, Cami, I know your father didn't—"

"Hush." Camilla cut Jade off entirely and turned to make her way down the corridor, leaving us with nothing to do but follow. She led us to Scarlett's bedroom door and slipped inside without hesitation. She waited for us to join her before she turned and locked the door behind us.

I let myself drop to sit on the bed, the cool breeze from the open window making the fine hairs on my arms stand on end. Camilla pulled Jade into a tight embrace, though her eyes stayed on mine over her shoulder.

"What's done is done, but goodness, darling, couldn't you have just given them what they wanted? Do you have any idea what all this has caused?"

When Jade pulled away her eyes were wet again. "You mean me being publicly whipped in the square tomorrow?"

Camilla pushed her down on the bed beside me.

"No, silly girl. Do you really think your sister would let that happen? And of course, my father didn't send me over. As much as our families are united, he's drinking scotch and laughing his stupid bald head off at yours right now. Scarlett asked me to come and keep you out of harm's way until she gets back."

"Where is she?" I spoke without meaning to. Possessiveness emboldened me, making my tone a shade more demanding than I intended.

Camilla's chocolate eyes studied me.

"She's saving her sister from being hurt, as she would save you. Do you have any idea what you could cost her?" Her tone was free of accusation, gentler, and her eyes narrowed in genuine concern. I had an idea, based on what I knew about the law in Vires and her father. When I didn't answer Camilla continued, "Everything, this could cost her everything. But of course, she just has to have the pretty little human girl." The sliver of jealousy in her voice startled me. It was almost comical, as I stared up at her goddess-like form, and she stared down at me.

"Is Caroline okay?" Jade interrupted us. I was glad for it, though I still wondered who the hell Camilla was to Scarlett.

"Darling." Camilla's reply was soft and chastening. "She is the least of our problems."

Jade swallowed thickly, and I sensed her isolation, a feeling of being far away, a differentness I had experienced a million times back in New Hampshire. Like the others, to Camilla, as much as she was an ally, humans, people like me, were insignificant.

"Do you know where Scarlett is?" I kept my voice steady and soft, trying to avoid being rude while I attempted to break the tension flickering softly between the two vampires.

"She's in the bunker of course." Camilla's perfectly sculpted body heaved under the weight of the sigh she released. She sat down beside Jade and slid an arm around her shoulders. "She's gone to try to fix all this, to reason with them and force them to change course. I promised I would stay here and take care of both of you..." She shot me a significant look, perhaps further accusation of our relationship potentially being disastrous for Scarlett. I couldn't deny the truth in it. "Until she returns."

The last part seemed to be added on as an afterthought. I tried to ignore the discomfort crawling up my spine at the thought of Scarlett in the concrete prison that had been my home, the first few weeks I had arrived in Vires.

MY NECK ACHED. My eyes were sore from a sleepless night spent propped up against the steelwork headboard of Scarlett's bed, with Jade by my side. Scarlett hadn't come home. As I walked into the packed Market Square after a tense car ride with Camilla, her absence was grating on me with every weary step. Jade's cold hand wrapped tight around mine when we exited the big black car that was the customary Pearce transportation. Feeling hundreds of eyes turn toward us as we headed around the crowd, I was thankful I'd had the presence of mind to gently pry our fingers apart, sure that being seen holding my hand wouldn't help Jade's case.

Bodies reached from one side of the square to the other, and I was surprised to note most of them were dressed in high-end casual but clean clothes—the clothes of vampires. Part of me had expected a sea of dirty beige to await us, an army of humans come to enjoy the rare day one of their captors was made to walk in their shoes. Perhaps they weren't allowed to attend? A few neutral-colored shirts dismissed this theory, and the thought that maybe they just didn't want to caused my chest to tingle with a momentary appreciation for humanity.

Every step we took, counted out by the sound of Camilla's ridiculous heels against the cobblestones, felt like a death march. I tried to keep the previous night, Jade's near-constant tears, her dry, sore eyes after she had cried them all out, and Scarlett's absence out of my mind. It was all still surreal, as like to a dream as any nightmare could be. Part of me still didn't believe it was actually going to happen. Another part of me, the part steeped in all the blood and the breaking I had witnessed since my arrival in the city, already snarled in anticipation, hackles raised at the thought of anyone hurting Jade.

I had to believe Scarlett had fixed it. Her standing by and watching her sister be punished went so much against the grain of all I knew about her, all I had felt from her. I knew she would be here, and I hoped whatever plan she had hatched could get Jade home safely.

I almost bumped into Camilla, my face coming dangerously close to the curve of her shoulder as she stopped abruptly in front of me. We were near the stage. A strangled noise from behind me made me whip around, terrified someone had come for Jade, but she just stood there, her eyes locked ahead on something I couldn't see. I stepped around Camilla's taller form and pushed my body closer to the front of the crush.

My heart jumped up into my mouth and tumbled down through my throat, taking my stomach with it and hitting the cold hard cobbles beneath my feet. Fear and panic, rage and shock made for a heady cocktail as they spilled into my blood. Tears stung my eyes.

Staring back at me, her eyes locked dead on mine, was Scarlett, up on the stage lashed to a tall wooden pole.

Camilla's hard arm closed around my waist the moment I surged forward, holding me in place. I pushed her away with a force that scared me, though I didn't stop.

"You knew she was going to take her place?" Her dark eyes were on mine and I scoured them for the truth. It came to me as her tongue slicked across her lips and she looked away. "You fucking knew?" The curse exploded off my lips. Behind Camilla, Jade sobbed silently.

"Of course I knew, but what good would telling you do?" Camilla came alive in front of me, her cool arms still holding me, a stone prison. "Do you think I didn't try to stop her? Do you think I want this for her?"

Sadness tinged her voice, and with the shock, the anger, the panic still thick in my blood, I forgot to hold back.

"What the hell are you to her? Why do you care?"

The vampire paused, her lips twisting as anger crossed her face before it fell back into sadness.

"Not you."

Understanding crashed over me. Camilla wanted Scarlett. Scarlett somehow wanted me, even with the offer of Camilla. And now Scarlett was about to be punished in the square for all to see.

"How do we stop this?" I let my tone be the only apology I was able to muster for the moment, though I wasn't sure if I was truly sorry at all that Scarlett seemed to have chosen me. Did she ever know Camilla was a choice?

"We don't."

Her answer wasn't good enough. I shook, adrenaline making me sick and unable to stand still. I shoved Camilla off me completely and turned to find odd-colored eyes watching us, the smallest hints of amusement creasing pursed lips.

I wondered if Scarlett knew my heart was breaking, twisting itself inside out at the thought of what was about to happen. I still saw that single crack in her cheek, the stagger in her step, the dimness of her eyes, as she'd limped toward me in New Hampshire after she was attacked by the guards.

Leave, my love.

Her voice in my head startled me. For the first time, it was a suggestion, not an absolute command. Part of me was aware she wanted me to leave, but the urge to follow her request wasn't as potent as it had been every other time she'd communicated with me like this. I could feel her intent pushing me, but for the first time, I also knew I was easily able to decide.

Her eyes were cold but curious and I held them, reaching out to her across the insanity that had become my life. My blood-stained savior, the woman who had brought me to life, and then showed me mortality and brutality in ways I had never dreamed I didn't already know. My father had been the worst of my old world. Here, in Vires, she was both the best and the worst, and everything in between.

A rough jolt to my shoulder broke our eye contact, and I glanced up to see Evan Chase blinking down at me, before he looked back to Scarlett, the confusion in his expression easily shifting into a sneer.

"What do you want, Evan?" Camilla stepped into his personal space and looked down at him from her height atop her heels.

"Camilla, how nice to see you. I've been well, thank you, how've you been?"

"Better before you showed up here."

He didn't waste a beat in delivering a reply.

"Well, business it is then. I just stopped by to assure you lovely ladies the punishment will be handled with the utmost tastefulness. One of my workers valiantly volunteered for the task. He was the only one, can you imagine that? It seems nobody else in Vires is feeling particularly suicidal today."

He laughed at his own joke and I fought the urge to punch him in his smug weasel face.

"Oh, I don't think it's the puppet who needs to be concerned, Evan, I'm sure she will take far more exception to the master who sent him." Camilla's eyes glittered with the threat, and though Evan tried not to look rattled, he failed.

A gleeful sneer replaced the flash of surprise, rising to try to cover his being caught off guard.

"This is the beginning of the end for Scarlett Pearce. Enjoy." Before any of us could respond, he was gone.

From my time in his employ, I knew he was all sweeping declarations and dark narratives with minimal follow-through to match. Though the drink situation at the party made me more nervous. I wished desperately to talk to Scarlett, be closer to her, save her from all this.

Leave.

She was in my head again and I looked up at her, tears in my eyes. A man stepped onto the stage in a dark robe and with a mask covering his face, the features pointed and angular. I expected her to look scared, concerned even, but the smile she gave him was lazy. All I felt from her was white noise with one discerning suggestion.

Leave now, before you see something you can't unsee.

Making up my mind, I offered her a silent apology, before I turned and grabbed a still-sobbing Jade by the arm. I tugged her back the way we had come. We made it about three steps before I felt her pull back. I turned to see Camilla had taken her other arm and was keeping her in place.

"She needs to stay. This will never die if she doesn't." Her apology was in her voice, but it didn't decrease the frustration that swallowed me whole as I realized she was right. I couldn't stop this, I couldn't save Scarlett, I couldn't even keep Jade out of harm's way. I tossed Jade's arm away from me as if it had burned and I turned and ran.

MY LEGS WERE numb from sitting on them too long, and my fingers ached from the cold. The thin sheer shirt I had pulled from Scarlett's closet that morning, worn on top of my blue jeans, was not enough to keep the chill of the wind at bay. The sky over my head was heavy with clouds and I wished for rain, to be drenched, soaked in a way that might wash me clean, or wash away the events of the past two days and take me back to the tower when it had been our haven, back to Scarlett.

"Well, you look cheerful."

A voice startled me. I whipped around, wondering who could have found me, my back against the heavy stone of the rear of Pearce Tower, hidden between two of the family vehicles. I looked up khaki-clad legs to find the girl who had accompanied Jade staring down at me.

"Caroline, right?"

She nodded and slid down beside me without invitation.

"Whatcha doing here?"

I studied the dirt under our feet, wanting nothing more than to be alone, too worn out for company, for the presence of anyone but Scarlett.

"I didn't want to stay at the square, I walked back and now I'm just—" I shrugged, not wanting to look at her, afraid she would see part of me wished Jade had whipped her, beaten her bloody like Scarlett had instructed, so she would be saved from all this.

Caroline was silent for a long time, and though I waited, my invisibility didn't come back, she didn't get bored and look through me or fade away. I momentarily wondered if I had lost the power since I met Scarlett and she showed me to this new side of myself—a side that runs away when the person she loves is hurt, apparently.

"What are *you* doing here?" The words came out harsher than I intended, but I didn't take them back.

"Honestly, I've been hanging around since we heard all the commotion in the square ending, trying to find out if Jade's okay. Now, I figure you're my best way up there." She lifted an index finger to the sky and I let my head loll back against the cold wall to look up and up to where the tip of Pearce Tower seemed to disappear into the clouds. The thought of going inside made me feel sick.

"Why are you hiding out here? Shouldn't you be in there with your lady?"

My eyebrow raised automatically at that. It was hard to imagine Scarlett being anyone's "lady." Their universe, perhaps.

The silence stretched long between us again, but Caroline didn't seem to mind. I couldn't decide if I liked or hated that about her.

"I ran away... I mean, she told me to go but part of her wanted me to stay and I just ran like a coward." The words spilled out of me in a rush and I let them, setting them free before I could force them back down.

She seemed to consider for a long moment, combing her fingers absently through her hair, her softly rounded face relaxed as she stared at the shiny alloys on the car beside us.

"When Joseph was pulled out and brought to the punishment center, I knew. Half the Fringe came looking for me. It's customary for us, no matter how much you hate someone, no matter the history, if someone's family gets taken or into trouble, you look out for them."

I had no idea where she was going, but I hoped it wasn't another lecture on how evil Scarlett was because, today, I just couldn't handle it.

"So, I knew it was happening, and I thought maybe I should go. We can be excused from work anytime to go and spectate. Some of the older folk who can't work anymore— that's how they spend their retirement, watching Scarlett do her thing." She laughed a humorless laugh, her gaze on mine, searching for a trace of understanding. Perhaps she was trying to make me feel guilty; perhaps she had no idea that I already did, I had from the first day I'd heard a whisper of what Scarlett did.

"Anyway..." She seemed to remember herself, her dark eyes finally letting me go. "I thought maybe I should go down there, be there in the stands so if he looked up he would see me, and maybe I could give him strength or something."

"Did you?"

"No, and when he was better, Joe said it was the best thing I ever did for him. He never wanted me to see him like that, and there are some things you can't unsee, you know?" The words felt like déjà vu and I nodded on rote.

"In the end, what meant the most to him was that he kept his dignity in my eyes, and I was there afterwards to take care of him, when he needed me."

The message was clear.

"Why are you telling me this? You hate her."

Caroline nodded.

"I do, but Jade doesn't, and you don't. I think she's a sick son of a bitch, but she's also the woman who raised Jade from the sounds of it. She's the one who was out there today in our place. Do I hate her for what she did to Joseph, what she does almost every night to people I know and care about? Yes, I absolutely do. But maybe it's not so black and white, not anymore."

For the first time in so long, I felt vindicated. If even Caroline could see there was more to Scarlett than what she had done, who she had hurt, then perhaps I wasn't completely crazy.

"So, can you get us up there?"

I nodded, a small smile on my lips to mirror her own.

"Did I just get played?" Though she grinned bigger in response, lifting her shoulder as if to ponder my question, the sincerity in her eyes told me her words had been honest.

I led her around to the front of the tower, and into the lobby, where I pushed the cool steel button to call the elevator.

Vampires stepped out from behind the pillars and I tugged Caroline closer as they studied us for a long moment. My heart beat hard in my chest, nervous, and I wondered if they would even call Scarlett to deal with intruders or if we'd be dealt with without her ever knowing I'd tried to come home.

Caroline let out a delighted guffaw from beside me when the men, seemingly satisfied, stepped back. The elevator dinged open.

"Looks like your psycho gave you a key. Big step, Blondie."

As the steel doors rolled closed, even under the weight of all that had happened that day, I couldn't help but smile.

WHEN MY FINGERS closed around the handle of the door to Scarlett's bedroom, without Caroline beside me, the chill of the day's events began to creep back over my skin. Soft voices floated down the hall, Camilla, Jade and now Caroline, reminding me I was alone with whatever I would find behind the door Scarlett had refused to open for anyone else—assuming she did for me.

Before I raised my fist to knock, I heard the soft click of the lock. I pushed the door open, forcing myself to be brave, steeling myself for what I might find.

She was perched on the edge of her bed, her face free of makeup but lacking the beauty she always had when she woke up that way. Her eyes looked dull and cold, her cheeks pale and sallow.

"Hi."

The word sounded too loud in the silence. She didn't look at me, and on closer inspection, I realized she wasn't even breathing.

"Scarlett..." Her name left my lips in a whisper and I stepped toward her. I moved tentatively to stand just in front of her and reached out to touch her arm. Finally, she turned her head to regard me. The movement was accompanied by a hiss that made me yank my hand away in surprise, afraid I'd somehow hurt her. She held my gaze for barely a second before those mismatched eyes looked away, stormy. Carefully I lowered myself to sit on the bed beside her, not yet daring to peek behind her.

"How bad is it?"

Silence stretched out with only my uneven breaths to break it. She was withholding from me. Her emotions swirled around and into me, but I felt them as if I was looking at them through the surface of a pool. They shimmered in and out of my view, leaving me unable to fully pin them down. I reached across the small space between us and slipped my hand into hers, choosing to ignore her bloodied, split knuckles as I squeezed the tips of her cold fingers in mine.

We stayed like that for too long. I argued silently with myself as to whether I should take control. Perhaps she was in shock and I ought to order her downstairs for a cup of sweet sugary tea. Perhaps I was totally out of my depth and needed to go call Camilla and Jade, but somehow that felt like a betrayal. She had chosen to let only me in.

Just when I was about to break the silence, to suggest the tea, or ask if she needed medical help, she exploded. The emotion bursting out of her and washing over me knocked the breath out of my lungs. All I could do was gasp, blinking back tears as one hundred pounds of sobbing vampire crashed into me.

I slipped one hand behind her neck, let the fingers of my other thread through her hair, and held her while she cried for what felt like hours. My heart broke.

When she finally pulled away, her face was ashen, and she avoided my eyes. The void in my chest ached, my world bursting open at the seams at the sight of the strongest, fiercest, bravest being I knew coming undone. Cold fingers twisted a strand of my hair that hung loose by my face, tucking it back behind my ear, then she was gone, leaving only the ghost of a breeze on my cheeks and the click of the lock on the bathroom door.

By the time she returned, the stress of the day had caught up with me but worry kept me awake as I lay on her bed that had become ours. Wet hair framed her face as she shuffled toward the bed, her usual smooth ground-covering gait replaced with a measured and careful stride. I wondered exactly how bad it was, how much she was hurting. She settled herself beside me, lying on her stomach, her head resting on her arms facing me. Only the slight curl of her lips betrayed how badly hurt she was.

I watched dark lines on the back of her gray sleep shirt grow and become thicker. It turned my stomach as I realized they were blood.

"Here."

I pulled up my own sleeve and offered my wrist to her, the single little scar translucent in the late evening glow of the setting sun.

"Last time it helped you." I felt stupid for not remembering sooner how my blood had healed her after she had staggered, broken, back into my life in New Hampshire.

"I can't." Her voice wasn't its usual rough aphrodisiac, it was jagged, hoarse. Her eyes softened the sting of the rejection. "If I heal too quickly, they'll know, and I'm not to drink for ten nights—their idea of making sure the punishment is effective." She heaved a heavy breath. It turned into a hiss of pain at the action, then, once again, the sound of my breath was the only thing breaking the silence.

"Can't you have just a little?" Heat tinged my cheeks in my self-consciousness. My pushing for her to drink from me left me embarrassed but unsure why.

She blinked, slow and catlike in her acceptance, before she slid one arm from under her head and pulled my wrist to her mouth. The pain this time made me jump, different from the usual bite. The quick sting I'd expected was replaced with a messy burn. When I looked back to her, my wrist was pressed against her lips, though there was no pleasant tug through my veins. She simply held it there and let my blood run into her mouth. I ignored the part of me that wanted her to take more, knowing the consequences of being caught would be devastating.

She stared up at me with a familiar contentment, lazy and sated, and I hoped this was relieving at least some of her discomfort.

"How bad is it?"

She let the blood run down my arm as she answered me, not seeming to mind its slow descent toward the sheets.

"Bad enough."

She licked the little trail like it was honey and went back to her passive consumption, though I could feel the question had darkened her.

"If it's so bad, why do you do it to others? Why do you go to the punishment center?"

I half knew the answer, and even if I was able convince myself she was doing it purely out of obligation and to protect herself and Jade, there was one more question, the one I had really meant to ask.

"You enjoy it."

As I said it, I realized it wasn't a question at all.

"I learned to, yes." Her tongue licked lazy circles around the puncture on my wrist, leaving me hot and dizzy. I looked away and tried to find a way to navigate through this difficult conversation, the crux of my guilt for loving her.

"Think about your father." Her words weren't quite a command, but soft as they were, they compelled me, and for the first time in a long time, I did. "All the things that happened to you... I imagine the night I met you wasn't the first time." Her voice was hypnotic, and I shook my head, feeling the glow of her determination as she tried to lead me down a path she wasn't sure I would follow.

"I bet you fought it at first, even just in your head. You didn't want to resign yourself to that being your life, to being helpless, feeling alone, not knowing when it would happen next, being out of control." Her words were transporting me, taking me back to my mother's funeral and then flashing me forward through all the long, painful years that came after. I remembered, and she was right.

A finger over the wound on my wrist made me jump. I didn't turn to look at her, already feeling I was about to be enlightened in a way I wasn't sure I wanted to be. What she did was wrong, awful, terrifying, and the idea of coming to think otherwise in any way scared me.

"So first comes the fight, and then comes acceptance." Thankfully she didn't make me relive all the years I had learned to stay down, to be still and quiet, and just wait for it to end. "Imagine fifty years of that, imagine one hundred.

Imagine your lifespan twice over, no escape, not without leaving the only thing you care about to be broken and twisted to take your place. What do you think comes after acceptance?"

For the first time, it struck me to wonder how old she was, and I felt dumb for never asking.

"I learned to live with it, and then to yield to it, and eventually, I learned to revel in it. This is my life, for better or worse. It's bloody and violent but it's who I am, and until I met you as far as I was concerned, it was all I would ever be. Why fight it anymore?"

I swallowed thickly, looking up at the ceiling, not wanting to see the fire in her eyes—or hear the passion that burned in her voice.

"Was I always this way? No. Did I fight it? Yes. Have I cried and begged and crawled to try and escape it? Yes. But did I learn to love it?" The seduction in her voice pulled my eyes to hers, magnets finding their opposite without any need for consent.

"Oh yes. Power is a beautiful thing, control makes me feel whole, blood and pain can't hold me like they did when I was young, and having Jade safe, keeping you safe because I'm the biggest, baddest bump in the night this city has to offer, that's also fine by me."

It was the most I thought I had ever heard her speak at once, and the barest she had ever let her soul be to me. I was speechless.

"Do I love you? Yes. Do I see you looking at me with those big blue eyes and wishing me into something I'm not?" For the first time she looked away, and she seemed tired. "You have no real concept of what your life here would be like if I was anyone other than who I am, if I did anything other than what I do. Your naivety is beautiful, but do I wish you could, for once, just look at me and see me and accept me for all I am, even the parts that keep you awake at night and make you feel this...guilt. I wish it was real, that you would love me without—" She looked down at my shoulder, hiding her eyes from me but not her emotions.

Tears I hadn't noticed forming in my eyes tracked down my cheeks. She was right. Guilt gnawed at my insides, but not for the usual reason, not because I felt guilty for loving someone like her, but because I felt guilty because she knew. I had been loving her with one eye closed, one foot in the door. For the first time, I wondered how much it must hurt her, yet until now, she had been silent, happy to accept whatever I gave. In hindsight, I realized it was not enough.

She didn't look at me as she let my wrist go, leaving the blood to tickle a trail down the inside of my arm as she brought her own palm to her mouth, then pressed it bloody over the wound. I watched fascinated as she peeled her bleeding palm away and below it, my little white scar emerged, healed. She dragged her palm up the still wet trail of blood beneath it then held it up. The jagged cut I could only assume she had made with her teeth had already closed over, a thin red scar I knew would be faded by morning in its place.

"Magic." Her voice was dry and humorless. I sensed her want to move closer to me, though she held herself back. Whether it was because she was afraid to move and hurt her bloody back or because of her earlier conversation I didn't know. I scooted carefully closer until her head rested under my chin, drifting as her intermittent breathing moved her in my arms.

"I do love you, more than anything." It was the only thing I eventually thought to say, and the rest, I knew I would have to work through.

THE CLOTH BETWEEN my fingers snagged on the raw edge of one of the many lashes crossing Scarlett's back, and she hissed her discontent. Looking over her shoulder, I breathed my apology, noticing her knuckles balled into tight, white fists on her lap.

Tired and discouraged, I tried again, carefully running the antiseptic-soaked washcloth over the angry wounds crisscrossing her back. The sickness I felt at the sight of them had waned days ago, leaving only fear and anxiety in its wake. Even after feeding from me on the night of the punishment, and twice since, Scarlett was not improving. When I was finally done, she pulled on another large shirt and moved into the shadows, grumbling at me to close the drapes I had insisted be open for at least a little while. The brusqueness of her request didn't sting like it had the first few days.

This had become my life, a monotonous never-ending battle against wounds that didn't seem to be healing and a grumpy vampire who had retreated somewhere so deep inside herself even I couldn't find her some days. She had visited with Jade and Camilla briefly, and since then she'd been unwilling to permit anyone but me to enter her room, where she spent most of her time holed up and trying to heal.

"It's been six days, shouldn't they be looking better?" I asked the question gently as I closed the thick drapes, demoting us back to only artificial light. Scarlett didn't seem to hear me, her face haunted as she flicked through something on her phone. I sat down beside her and pushed the device into her lap, forcing her to look at me.

"Do you want to drink again and see—"

"What's the point?" Her tone was lifeless as she cut me off. "We both know it won't help."

We sat there in a stilted silence until she repented and pulled me to her. I went willingly onto her lap and buried my head in her neck, fretting silently over how much pain the action must have caused her.

"I'm sorry, Princess." She uttered the words quietly into my ear, and I knew they were an apology for more than just today. Her mood had been sour and distant since day two when things had not improved as much as she had expected.

"Something's wrong."

Internally, I breathed a sigh of relief. Finally, the truth that had been hanging over the entire thirteenth floor of the tower, from Jade down the hall, to Camilla who had taken up residence in the guest room, was spoken aloud.

"What are we going to do?" I didn't ask her if she knew what was preventing her from healing—her frustration this last week was answer enough.

"I don't know." She held me tighter, her lips feeling warmer than usual as she pressed a kiss to my forehead before she rolled over and slid down beside me on her side. "I just don't know." Her dark eyes searched mine, and I was engulfed by her vulnerability. It scared me more than anything I remembered, more than her display in the punishment center or the announcement at the party or the day in the square. Long after she fell asleep, I lay awake, my mind spinning.

I don't remember when I drifted off. I woke veiled in a sheen of cold sweat, my heart beating a pounding staccato in my chest, hammering my insides. I gently moved Scarlett off me and slipped out of bed and out of the room, only allowing myself to break into a run once the door was softly closed behind me.

I banged on the door to the guest room twice, not waiting for an answer before I burst in. Camilla looked up in surprise, dark eyes narrowed at the sight of me dressed in only a large T-shirt and panties. I couldn't even find the time to be sorry.

"I know what's wrong with Scarlett."

Whatever she had been reading was immediately abandoned, and she was across the room in a blur. She pulled me inside and slammed the door behind me.

"Well?" Suspense made her tone hard, and for the first time, I wondered if I could be wrong, if I could really have the answer when all week Camilla and Jade had been trying to find it and failing.

"It's Evan." The mere mention of his name made me sure of myself. "He hates her, he hates all of you, actually, but her especially. He almost seems jealous of her."

"Old news," Camilla chimed, crossing her arms, impatient.

"When I worked at Chase Tower—" She scoffed, I guessed at the word "tower" when referencing Evan's huge home, which was positively humble compared to Scarlett's, and likely her own. "He kept on talking about how she needed to pay, about his father and some secret weapon he had to fix all that is wrong in Vires. I don't know how I didn't see it before."

The pieces slid together to form the answer that had eluded me all week. I moved past Camilla to perch on her bed.

She watched me with uncertain eyes, and my focus moved from understanding to trying to present it in a way that would make her understand too.

"His father was a scientist, right? He discovered the Delta gene." This was just like an essay at school; state some facts first and gain some credibility. "At the party, he tried to give Jade a drink, and I saw him fiddling with this little flask, like he had spiked it or something. He was furious when I stopped her from drinking it. I knew I had seen those flasks somewhere before, but I didn't remember where, until now." I moved my hand up to touch my cheek in memory of the day he'd struck me. "In his room, he has a safe hidden behind a painting, and he lost it when he thought I'd realized there was something back there."

Camilla continued to look skeptical. I ran my hands through my hair and pulled it away from my face, frustrated that she wasn't following.

"Remember at the square, what he said?" She nodded, still unconvinced. "Okay, so here's what I am going on. Evan hates Scarlett, he says his father, the scientist, had some secret weapon to solve Vires' societal problems—which he pretty much seems to blame on Scarlett. At the party, he tried to give Jade a drink spiked with something from a weird silver flask thing—a sciency-looking flask that he keeps a stash of in a safe in his bedroom. Then he acts like this whipping is the end of the world for Scarlett, and to boot, one of his people was the one to actually do it."

"So you think what—he poisoned her with something his father made?"

I shrugged, relieved that, finally, she was connecting the dots I hoped were more than just random happenings my desperate imagination had pulled together into a chain of guilt for Evan.

"I've never heard of a serum that prevents us from healing," Camilla mused, "but then again, why would I? What would he stand to gain by keeping her like this? If he wanted her job, he would have taken it by now."

"I don't know." I simply hadn't got that far. The ground I had covered was still fraught with pitfalls and possibilities, but it was better than the waiting and wondering and watching Scarlett suffer. I went back to what I knew.

"When I worked for him he wasn't very smart. I saw notes he'd made as well as the safe, and I heard him talk about it. He described it as a weapon, something only he had the cure for, a way to cleanse Vires and restore it to its former glory."

"That sounds like the anti-Government movement talking. I'm sure Evan's sad little brain wants many things but why would a slow, painful death for vampires be one of them? Though they did take his father..."

Camilla stared at me for a long moment as she seemed to piece things together in her head.

"You could be right, nothing else explains it."

I nodded. "The more I think about it, the more it makes sense. Did she take any drinks from him or anyone before they whipped her?" It still stung me to talk about it, but I pushed on. "Obviously nobody tried to inject her, or we would have already found the body."

"Have you talked to her?"

I shook my head.

"You have to, ask her, tell her what you think. She knows more than anyone in this city what the Government does in that bunker. Maybe she knows something about Mark Chase we don't, something that can confirm all this before we go around accusing people." Her eyes were alight now, dancing as a plan formed in her head.

"Why do you care so much—about her, I mean?"

The question stopped her dead, though I held her gaze, no longer embarrassed, not wondering from a place of insecurity, just genuine curiosity.

"Who are you to her?"

"We've been friends for a very long time. We were children together, she was turned two years before me. Prior to that, we were both bored little girls at our parents' fancy parties. Later she became my friend, and for centuries we were lovers between lovers, or between bouts of darkness and brooding, depending on which one of us you're talking about." She shrugged, unapologetic. "Before you ask, we haven't been together since she met you, and not for years before. I care because beneath it all, she is a good person. I still remember the little girl with so much love for life. She's been there for me when no one else has. Once Scarlett loves you, she loves you without limit or condition, but you already know that."

Realizing it was open, I closed my mouth. It was hard to believe Scarlett wanted me when she could have someone like Camilla. Almost six feet of glamorous, effortlessly beautiful, smart and complex if somewhat pretentious vampire.

"I love her, as I have for many years. Some days I think perhaps together we could accomplish great things, and she would be saved from whatever disaster will follow the exposure of this relationship with a human. Other days I think we would destroy each other and I remember that in all my years I have never seen her look at me the way she looks at you, like you're the sun and the moon. I care about Scarlett, she's my oldest friend, and by extension, I am forced to care about what happens to you."

She sniffed at the admission, and I wondered when I would ever stop being blindsided constantly by these vampires and their grandiose declarations.

"That's why you have to talk to Scarlett about this Evan Chase business, and do not say a single word to anyone else until you have."

Chapter Fourteen

THE WEIGHT OF the night before hung over us still when I woke up to find Scarlett sitting beside me, staring down at me. My grand discovery that Evan was behind her illness had not gone down well.

"How did you work it out?"

Still half lost to sleep, I yawned and rolled to wrap my arm in careful fashion around her waist and bury my face in her side. I once again recounted my experiences at Chase Tower, now the rage had died down enough for her to actually take in what I was saying.

She was silent for a long time, occasionally cursing softly under her breath. When she pulled away from me to move off the bed, I watched her go. For the first time in over a week, she stalked to the closet and began to dress in clothes fit for the outside world, though not without obvious difficulty.

"Where are you going?"

The urgency in her movements spurred me on. Immediately, I rolled out of bed and began to pull on clothes of my own, determined not to leave her side, injured as she was, with a psychopathic vampire gunning for her.

"Evan Chase has something I need. I'm going to get it."

I pulled up short, one leg in my jeans, one out.

"Scarlett, you can't fight right now, and if you go there, who knows what he will do. That's probably exactly what he wants."

She glared at me with a fiery gaze but continued to dress. Snapped out of my surprise, I continued to do the same. I pulled one of her warm cashmere sweaters over my head and moved to the vanity to brush out my tangled hair.

"There's no other way. I wait here and...who knows what, or I face this." Her words lost all their gusto when her face crumpled into a mask of pain as she bent to slip on her jeans and stretched the infected lashes across her back.

I moved across the space to take her arm and stop her, forcing her to listen.

"Scar, you can't do this. There has to be another way, a better way than you hurting yourself even more and walking right into whatever he has waiting."

The nickname surprised us both, though the slight upturn of Scarlett's lips told me it wasn't necessarily a bad thing, and I resolved to use it more.

"Come talk with Camilla, even Jade. Let's think of something together."

She smiled a sad smile but shook her head, struggling again to bend down to put on her heeled pumps.

"One, you're crippled, and these, really?" I knelt before her waving one patent leather shoe. "And two." I steeled myself for what I was about to say, because the thought terrified me, but for her, I would do it. "Let me go to Chase Tower. Hear me out. I think I know what we're looking for and where it is. I know a lot of his staff... I think I can do it." That was the lie of the century, and Scarlett seemed to know it because she stared at me as if I had just spoken in tongues.

When her reaction finally came, it came without warning.

"Are you *crazy*?" She hissed the words, tugging the shoe out of my hand and pulling me up to my feet. "Do you really think I'm going to let you run off right back to where it took me over a month to get you back? Do you think I would risk you like that?"

I pulled my hand from hers, touched but still frustrated by the sentiment.

"I'm not a piece of property to be allowed or risked or saved at your whim." I softened my tone and forced myself to relax my stance, knowing this was a moment to choose my battles. "I want to do this, I think I can do this, how does you charging over there while you're hurt make any more sense?"

She was silent for a long moment, the colors in her eyes fractured and spilled open, swirling into an abyss that tugged me down and drew me in with little effort. I wondered what was coming.

"You want to do that, to walk back into that bastard's clutches, and risk your life for me?"

"Yes." My answer was immediate, and I reached up to touch her beautiful face. I traced my thumbs over the cheekbones that had become far too prominent of late. "I want you to be safe, and better. I want to do this for you."

I felt her soften, her emotions twisting around my chest and slipping into me as if they were my own—disbelief, gratitude, love—before something darker tainted them.

"That's what you think you want." She whispered the words and my heart dropped at the arctic blast accompanying them. I recognized its feel. It was the something she always held back, even at our most connected. There were pieces of her she never allowed me to touch, and this was one.

"It's what I know I want, I want you, healthy, safe. We're...partners. I want to help you like you helped me." I tried to smooth this over, to reassure her, to skirt the storm I could feel coming, but Scarlett was crashing and crumbling in front of me. I was a boat, lost on her stormy dark sea, and

I steeled myself for the moment all the ice-cold water would crash inside me. It came with her next breath.

"You have no idea what you want, Princess. You want what I tell you, you feel as I wish you to, you have since the minute you blacked out at that house in the human world."

My blood turned to ice. Her voice in my head was dark and heavy in a way I had never felt it before. When it commanded me to kneel, I shrank down before her, having absolutely no choice. A far-off part of me knew I wanted to fight, but I couldn't even bring myself to try. Her will consumed me. My chin lifted without my consent and I was staring her dead in her tear-filled eyes.

"You don't love me." I felt every blow as her words broke her own heart. "It's all been a lie. We're blood bound, sweetheart, you're my perfect little daydream. You love me because a part of me wishes for it, desperately."

"No." I had no idea why I was protesting, but my world crumbled from the inside, spilling out to ruin me, as I tried to wrap my head around the fact that she had been controlling me all along. Betrayal burned me alive as I watched her fix her mask, her brokenness replaced by the cold hardness she wore for every punishment. I felt a brief second of her agony as, finally, she decided she would set me free. I flailed in the face of it, not wanting to go, to be let go, even now.

"Think, Rayne." My name in her mouth cut me to the core. "Remember, the times you've been compelled, the times I've judged your mood perfectly. Drinking your blood gives me a direct line into your mind. I know you inside out, and you become hardwired to want to please me."

She said all this like it was a revelation, like it was some big, surprising reveal. I used her distraction to get myself back under my own control and scrambled to my feet.

"I remember." I looked her dead in the eye, feeling my body inflate in an unfamiliar way, anger replacing my fear, rising to her challenge.

"I know exactly what you mean because it runs both ways. Why the hell do you think I stayed? Why do you think I loved you? I know you beyond what you let anyone know, I know you're more than this. I'm in your head every bit as much as you are mine." I spat the words with a venom that surprised me, furious she had known so much about this all along, had thought she was keeping me captive against my true desires and had continued to do so.

Scarlett was caught off guard, her mask slipping, her dark eyes wide and confused. My words about this running both ways struck me, and without thinking I let my anger fuel my desire and willed her to fall on her knees, just as she had me. I let the want consume me until nothing more in the world would sate me in that moment. A strangled noise of surprise left her. She hit the floor and her grunt of pain took the edge off the darkness that had momentarily gripped hold of me.

"Still think you've been controlling me all along?"

She tried to stand, and I concentrated on keeping her down, though somehow, this time it failed.

She looked at me with keen dark eyes now, like I was suddenly fascinating to her.

"That's not the way, Princess, you can't just will it. You have to want it, want it with every piece of you, let your happiness depend on it."

I did as she suggested, and instantly she hit the floor again, cursing through her teeth.

"We're blood bound. Ever wonder why a vampire's most absolute law is that we have to kill what we eat?"

She had my attention. I let her get to her feet, if only to allow her to continue to explain.

"When we don't kill the human we drink from, an unnatural connection forms between us. Some call it nature's revenge. We are the ultimate predator, after all." She smiled a sharp-toothed smile that I resolved not to be intimidated by.

"Little is known about this connection, it's been forbidden for so long the details are blurry. What I do know is my happiness becomes innate to who you are, you want it with all of you. I only have to convince myself your doing something will make me happy and you're hardwired to want to do it." She paused for a moment. "It seems we're both bound to pleasing the other."

My head spun, but I noted her surprise at this part. We were silent for a moment, the ashes settling around us, a stone wall between us, as I was careful to very explicitly want her to have no idea what I was feeling. I hoped it would work. I needed to process privately, and the slight tip of her head told me it had.

"You don't want to go running into Chase Tower to find an antidote for whatever this is. You don't want to stay here with me." She was winding up, working herself into a frenzy, and I stood taller, ready to weather the coming storm coming. My head reeled and my mind raced with it all, but somehow, even through the fog of it, I knew we were more than this, more than just blood bound. I loved her.

"You don't even love me, you just think you do."

Her final admission whipped the wind out of her sails and she seemed to deflate. I saw all the tells that, from being connected to her emotional feedback, I had come to know so well. I watched her sink into self-loathing, loneliness, vulnerability as she waited for me to respond.

Everything caught up with me, moving too fast and too slow, and the last few months spun before my eyes. This new revelation cast a different color on all my memories, the good and the bad, the ones I wished to forget, and those that were so very precious to me.

I stepped forward on reflex, forcing Scarlett to raise her chin to look at me. I held her eyes, letting the feeling in my veins fill me up, searching for the words until they exploded off my lips.

"None of this, being blood bound, or having a connection, or whatever you want to call it is the reason I love you, you stupid, deceitful, insufferable vampire." The release was so cathartic it was impossible stop. "You kept me here thinking it was all against my will? Thinking I was some kind of mind-slave who only loved you because that's what you wanted?"

She just stared at me ashen, but I didn't need any more fuel to continue letting the fire burn me and pour from my mouth.

"You knew all along, and you said nothing, after everything we've been through. And the worst part—" I paused to suck in a breath. "The absolute worst part is I know all this comes from you being a stupid insecure idiot and thinking no one could love you, or you're not worthy of love. If you stopped for just a single damn minute and looked at things, maybe you would see that I am in love with you. I've been in love with you since before you drank from me, and even while I have loved you, there have been times we have wanted different things and I haven't automatically fallen to my knees and said, '*Yes, Mistress*'!"

My voice had risen to a volume that was suddenly too loud in the small room, and I forced myself to stop, to look away and collect myself.

"You had my blood the night I found you. How do you think I saved you?"

I looked back at her, surprised to see fat tears leaking down her cheeks, all the turmoil that lived beneath her perfectly dark and polished exterior finally spilling to the surface. This was the admission she found the most damning; the one piece of evidence I was sure she had touted to herself over and over in the past few months every time she had begun to believe what we had might have been real. The thought bowled me over, saddening me right down to my bones and tainting every beautiful memory I had of her, as I wondered if this insecurity had been hiding behind each rare breathtaking smile.

"Scarlett, I can tell the difference. I know what's yours and what's mine. I can sort between the two, and I know when something from outside me is pushing me to do things. It feels different. Not all of this has been your influence, it has been real. While you wanted me to fall in love with you, I was doing it anyway, all by myself."

She said nothing, saline still falling from her eyes.

"Besides, how do I know this doesn't work the other way, that you haven't just kept me around because we're blood bound and it's what would make me happy? Why on earth would you chose me when you can have someone like Camilla?"

She hissed, her lips peeled back over her teeth for a split-second before she caught the reaction and put it away. Her hands were cool against my cheeks, still burning from the argument, and her touch felt like the first rain of fall, so welcome.

"Never doubt that I love you." In that moment I swore she could see into my soul, and I let her. When she let me in in return, it took my breath away.

She leaned down and my eyes closed on muscle memory. I was sure she was going to kiss me. Her breath was cool on my parted lips, and as she spoke, I opened my eyes to watch her.

"I'm not what you want, Princess, I'm not what you deserve. I've watched you struggle with who I am, and who I am will never change, no matter how much either of us wants it. Not even for you."

She was crying again. I stepped closer to her, confused as to what turn she had taken without me, how we had been derailed from what finally felt like the beginning of a resolution to all this.

"You don't love me, Rayne. You never have. In time you'll come to realize that. The literature is vague, but I believe when my blood leaves your system and you can think for yourself, you'll feel differently about all this. And I don't want to be here to see that."

"Scarlett..."

Frustration weighed my voice down. I was so tired of trying to explain to her that I loved her, and since our last serious conversation, somewhere between the punishment and the pain and the fear of losing her, I had come to let go of whatever had kept me from giving into the fact that I did, without a doubt, love all of her.

"No." Her voice was cold and commanding and it shocked me.

"I can't do this anymore, I don't want to. Things are bad enough without this...lie."

The word cut me deep, hot traitorous tears springing into my eyes.

"At dusk, I will be back, and I will take you home, back over the wall, away from this and from me. It ends tonight. Neither of us can live forever in this lie."

Before I had a chance to respond, to work out where this had all gone so desperately wrong, with a pained hiss and a soft breeze against my wet cheeks, Scarlett was gone.

Chapter Fifteen

THREE HOURS LATER I banged hard on the guest room door, hoping beyond hope Camilla would still be there. My eyes had finally dried, and I had pried myself away from the room that over the past weeks had somehow become mine before Scarlett had taken it all away.

Anger and rejection had turned to bitterness and bloomed back into a fierce determination not to let her do this, tinged with the voice in my head that had been practical all along, waiting for this day, for her to realize I wasn't enough. Waiting for it all to end. A part of me was determined to acquire Camilla's help and get into Chase Tower, to make sure if Scarlett had gone there she was safe, and to find the antidote. If I really had to leave, I would not leave her broken.

The thought of going back to New Hampshire, back to the empty house that had probably fallen into total disrepair in my absence, back to the bills, and my father's mysterious disappearance, crushed me. I momentarily wondered if anyone had even noticed I was gone? Was my face on the news, were there posters at the school? I realized I didn't care. I had outgrown my old life, and I wouldn't go back, not without a fight, not without fighting for Scarlett, for everything we had that I knew was real. At the very least, I would leave things better here if I had to go, a monument to this new life I would be leaving behind.

The door burst open and Camilla took a long moment to study what I could only assume were my red, swollen eyes.

"You told her then?"

She stepped aside to let me in and I nodded, ignoring the beginnings of a headache wrapping around my temples.

"I assume she took it badly?"

She looked perfect as always, her dark hair poker straight, tight faded blue jeans clinging to her lean figure, and in that moment, I envied her beyond belief. I wished I was as easy of an option for Scarlett as she could be, wished things could be so uncomplicated for us.

"Where is she?" The softness of her tone made me silently guilty for the resentment in my stomach, and I let it fall away.

"She got mad when I suggested I would retrieve the antidote and she left." Something inside me warned me not to mention the rest. I knew better than to tell anyone in Vires Scarlett had drunk from me. Somehow, I thought me leaving the city would be exactly what Camilla wanted, what she believed was best for Scarlett, and I didn't want to give her any ammunition to turn down my next proposition.

"I don't know where she went, but I'm afraid she went to Chase Tower to try to get the antidote herself. I want to go there and check. Even if she isn't there, I know where it is. I can get it for her."

Camilla studied me, her head tilted to the side.

"Foolish girl. If you're right and there's nothing Evan Chase wants more than to hurt Scarlett, what makes you think he won't start by killing you?"

The thought sent chills down my spine, but I shrugged nonchalantly.

"That's why I won't go alone, we can go together, tell him Scarlett gave me to you, or something that makes more sense with how you trade us like we're property. Either way, we make him believe I'm with you now, then you distract him, and I'll slip away to look for her and get what we need."

She laughed, long and hard and throaty.

"You actually want to do it?"

"Why else would I be here? How else is she going to get well? Do you think he's just going to get bored and give her the antidote, or that if she goes over there, she's not going to lose whatever stupid fight she starts when she's as hurt as she is?"

The thought seemed to sober Camilla.

"You're brave... Naive, but brave. If we get caught, I can't afford to go down for this. I will deny ever knowing what you were doing. The way I see it, there's little risk to me. Evan Chase doesn't scare me one bit, but if you succeed, this could help Scarlett, and hell knows I owe her that."

My heart beat fast. It was one thing when all this was some fantastical plan, and another entirely now it looked set to go ahead.

"So, you'll do it then, you'll take me over there?"

She smiled a toothy grin at me, seductive in a completely different way than Scarlett's.

"When are we leaving?"

WITH CAMILLA, THERE was no preamble, no "call me mistress" or "show me respect." I simply followed behind her as she waltzed into Chase Tower as if she lived there herself. The familiarity of the lobby struck me, transporting me back to a time when my life was simpler but even more messed up than it seemed to be now. The thought reminded me that for better or worse, I wanted Scarlett and I never wanted to go back to living the strange half-life I'd had before she had found me.

We made it into the elevator with ease, and silence surrounded us as we ascended. I knew in the floors and corridors around us, the news of our arrival would be spreading like wildfire. I had no doubt Evan knew we were here mere minutes after we stepped foot over the threshold. I tried to keep my breathing steady, nerves already climbing up my throat, threatening to choke me, as I wondered if Scarlett was here and if I ought to have planned more thoroughly on how exactly I would get the antidote. Convincing Camilla, in retrospect, had been the easy part. Now my idea was becoming action, the sheer responsibility hanging around my neck daunted me.

I jumped as the steel doors dinged open, and Camilla eyed me skeptically, before she was off, long strides covering the ground to meet Evan who waited in the hall. All I could do was bury my doubt and follow, out of time to wonder whether I could do this.

"Camilla, to what do I owe the pleasure?" Evan's sandy hair was ruffled, the bottom two buttons on his shirt undone, as if he had rushed to throw himself together to meet us.

"You can stop with the formalities," Camilla's reply was cool, but not hostile. "Surely you know why I'm here? The bunker is almost full, the punishment center has been empty for a week, and as we are the foremost families in this city, I decided it is up to us to address the issue."

His beady eyes lit up like twin Christmas trees at the mention of the bunker, and a small part of me felt sorry for him, twisted as he was from the loss of his father. Camilla's lie impressed me, and I wondered if she had planned it on the way over or come up with it on the fly.

A smile was just forming on his lips, his body turning to lead us back through to what I knew was the living room, when his expression iced over.

"You..." He hissed the word. Camilla stepped between us, cutting him off.

"Mine. Scarlett finally grew bored with her and she's too pretty to kill. Now, shall we?"

His eyes met mine over her shoulder and I held them for a few seconds, accusations itching their way up my spine, before I forced myself to swallow them down and lowered my gaze respectfully. Drawing attention to myself was a surefire way to make sure I never got out of his sight. Mollified, he led us on.

Camilla turned to give me a withering glare before she followed him. As we walked, I felt for Scarlett, any trace of her. The quiet of the tower combined with the total lack of feedback convinced me she wasn't there—at least that much was good.

In the living room, the vampires talked and talked, their meeting conducted like some slightly less formal board meeting, though still full of etiquette I didn't quite understand. Impatience and nerves turned my stomach and, watching Camilla's crystal glass full of blood shimmer in the light from the fireplace, I wondered if she had forgotten our plan altogether.

"Girl." Her eyes snapped to me so unexpectedly it made me jump. "We need a drink to celebrate. I have a feeling that a conclusion is close at hand." She gave Evan an appreciative smirk that I was sure would have melted many a man. Her dark eyes, so warm and full of promise, displayed the predator she was in all its glory. Scarlett was violence and dark seduction, Camilla was warm and fortified and had somehow made Evan believe together they would step to the forefront of society, all with an hour's preparation, maximum. It staggered me.

"Go back to the tower. Bring the '69 vintage, the one I've been saving. Ask Dimitri, have him call me if there's any issues. Bring it back quickly."

I nodded dumbly, adrenaline shooting into my bloodstream as I realized this was it, this was my out. She wasted no time in reengaging Evan in conversation, and he was too busy basking in her promises to even look my way as I left the room.

I headed straight for the elevator, holding it together until the doors closed behind me and inside, for a moment, I crumpled. The mirrored glass was cold on my forehead, and I allowed myself three deep breaths before I was upright again and hitting the button that would take me up to Evan's living floor two stories above. The Hawthorne Tower was close to Pearce Tower, based on what I knew of the layout of the City. I calculated I would have had about a five-minute walk there, maybe five to retrieve the wine, and five back, giving me a fifteen-minute window to get the antidote and report back to Camilla with a good excuse as to why I was empty-handed as far as the drink went.

The elevator doors slid back, and I stepped onto Evan's personal floor, relieved to find it as quiet and devoid of life as I expected it to be this time of day. I moved silently down the long corridor, the back of my neck prickling with anticipation, fear of what would come next, and what would come if I was caught. My heart was in my mouth, hot and heavy and making it hard to breathe as I stepped into his room and scanned the space.

My fingers were slick with sweat as I tugged the gilded frame of the painting, remembering how it had swung outward, feeling and fumbling until I grazed a small bump.

I pushed it and jumped back as the artwork swung toward me on hinges invisible to any bystander.

Staring back at me was the safe. My plan crashed around me, panic burning its way through me as I realized it had one fatal flaw—I had no idea what the combination was. Clinging to the shred of hope I had left, I tried the door and my stomach plummeted. Of course, it was locked. This had all been too easy, too simple. I reached up to touch the lock, knowing spinning the thing was unlikely to lead to it miraculously opening like in some poorly scripted movie.

"Girl?"

Adrenaline shot straight to my heart, singing in my blood, its beat roaring in my ears as I spun around to face whoever had caught me.

"Cece?" My voice was ragged and pitchy with nerves. The old woman hovered in the doorway, a frown creasing her brow.

"You're back." She stated the fact, both of us momentarily ignoring the situation she had caught me in. "I thought you were Scarlett Pearce's now?"

I nodded, unsure of how to approach this. Part of me ached. In those weeks stuck in this very tower, between her gruff remarks and taskmaster drive, Cece had saved me, becoming my constant in a sea of uncertainty. In the face of my plan being shot, her presence made me want to crumple and cry and go back to being the skinny girl she had pretended was such a burden on her in our time together.

"Why are you trying to get into the master's safe, Rayne? Is this some errand she sent you on because, you know, if they catch you, you will die."

Her words gave me hope. They hadn't caught me yet, only she had, and perhaps those two didn't have to be one and the same.

Panic froze my reply in my mouth and I floundered for a good enough story or a way to explain the truth that would make her more likely to let this go, to disappear and never recount this to a soul.

"Scarlett's hurt, Evan hurt her, and there was no way she would get better unless I could get an antidote. I was trying to save her."

Cece studied me long and hard, while internally I berated myself. Citing the woes of Scarlett Pearce to anyone in Vires, human or vampire alike, wouldn't inspire much sympathy given her reputation. I wanted to say something else, to change tack, but I just stood there, hanging my head, ashamed once again under Cece's watchful gaze.

"Let me tell you something about Scarlett Pearce, girl."

I forced my eyes upward, determined to give this woman who had once been my only friend the respect she deserved as she recounted whatever sordid and horrible thing Scarlett had done to someone she knew, perhaps even to her. The thought turned my stomach. In the back of my mind, the clock ticked on. With no watch, I had no way to judge how long I had been gone, how long until Evan came looking and all of this was for naught.

"Nineteen years ago, I worked for the Hawthornes, cleaning and maintaining the tower. I lived for them, as I do the master here." Her cloudy eyes held mine with an intensity that made me wonder where all this was going. "There was no pay, and our living conditions were deplorable. This was before Miss Camilla came of age and her father stepped back. I hear things have improved since then." She dabbed her wet eyes with her fist, and I waited for the connection between all this and me being caught with my metaphorical hand in Evan's treasure chest.

"To keep things brief, I fell pregnant. The baby came on the servant floor, a beautiful little girl. She fell sick with whooping cough, and a fella in the market had the medicine she needed, but I didn't have the money. I stole it from the Hawthornes and I saved my baby's life, but I was caught."

My heart broke for her, to imagine her as alone and scared as I was on the servant floor of Pearce Tower, constantly in danger and with a baby.

"My punishment was decided. They would take my daughter, Grace, and you can imagine the rest. I was told it would be the Pearce girl who would dispose of her, their words." She paused to wipe eyes now brimming over with tears. "I hated Scarlett Pearce for many years, but my life went on. I eventually got a new job here, with a lesser family, not Deltas, but still, the old master was kind enough and the conditions are better, but every day I was bent out of shape, twisted up inside over what the Pearce girl had done with my baby. Some said she drank her dry, others that she just buried her, still crying."

Saliva filled my mouth and I had to swallow it down, fighting the urge to throw up all over Evan's plush carpet.

"Three years after the day she was taken, a picture arrived with the master's mail. A little girl with two adults. To anyone else, it would be a meaningless photograph, but those little blue eyes were something I would never forget. Three years later, another one came. My Grace wearing a strange outfit, they call it a uniform. It was her first day at school, a real school outside this wall, and she was happy and safe."

She sobbed once before her hands covered her mouth. The sound fractured my heart, hope and warmth and joy spilling out, goose bumps rising on my arms.

"All those years I had hated Scarlett Pearce, wished a true death upon her, wished to see her suffer and hurt, and she gave me this gift, she gave my Grace a life outside these walls, and she even went to the trouble to let me know, to give me happiness, give me closure. Scarlett Pearce, the monster under everyone's bed, as sick and as twisted as she is, she did that for me."

I crossed the space without thinking and wrapped my arms around her tired body, hugging her tight, my tears soaking into her shirt.

"I imagine my Grace has a good life out there, and I hope she's grown up to be a young woman something like you."

I squeezed her tighter, tears pouring down my cheeks as I ached for her loss, and burned with a new determination to save Scarlett, to cling to my life here with her and give her a little piece of happiness that was hers alone, as she had done for Cece.

Cece pulled away. She held me at arm's length and searched my face for something I couldn't name.

"She's bad news, girl. She's dangerous and her temper is the talk of the town. What she does at that bunker turns my stomach and I won't excuse it. But she saved my girl, and for that, I will always be thankful. Fifteen, thirty-one, sixty-eight, turn the dial twice before you start to reset it. I hope this doesn't cost you your life, Rayne, and I hope she's worth it."

She pinched my cheeks hard enough to bring blood back to them, and then shuffled away, picking up her mop as she went and disappearing down the hall.

Shock froze me where I stood. Three long seconds ticked by and I stared at the empty doorway, my brain struggling to process all that had just happened. The moment it did I was skidding across the carpet. I turned the little black dial twice then carefully spun it to the numbers now forever emblazoned in my psyche. Fifteen, thirty-one, sixty-eight. A click sounded my success, and I greedily studied the little canisters inside. The first row was the same glowing silver I had seen in Evan's hand at the party. The second was a darker metal, titanium perhaps, and a slightly different shape. I grabbed one without thinking and shoved it deep into the pocket of my jeans, before yanking it back out and securing it under the strap of my bra between my breasts, confident the loose sweater I wore would hide its shape.

Everything felt surreal as I closed the safe, not daring to take more and hoping one canister would be enough to save Scarlett.

My footsteps were too loud and my heart battered me from the inside as I stormed back down the hallway, called the elevator, and hurried inside. I had no idea how long I had been gone. All concept of time was lost, my brain addled by the fact that I had done it; somehow, against all the odds, my plan had worked. All that was left was to make it out alive.

The doors opened, and I almost tripped over my own feet as I rushed back into the room. Evan and Camilla spun to look at me in unison.

"Well?" Camilla said.

"Miss Hawthorne, there was a problem I... Dimitri, he was bringing the bottle out and he tripped and it smashed. I think he needs stitches."

Camilla stared at me as if I had two heads. All I could do was stare back at her in terror, hoping my lie was good enough, feeling Evan's eyes on me.

"Well, did you bring the '72 instead?"

"Ma'am?" I played dumb, hoping our audience was buying this.

"The '72 vintage, you idiot. Didn't it occur to you that since you were completely incapable of bringing me what I wanted you should bring me at least something?"

I shook my head and she stared at me, mouthing "did you get it?" silently. I let my chin drop slightly, offering her the ghost of a nod as I looked away.

"I'm sorry, Miss Camilla, I..."

"Enough."

She cut me off with a wave of her hand and turned back to Evan.

"My apologies. It seems I have matters of my own to attend to this evening. Shall we meet again later in the week to continue with our planning?"

He stood, all too eager. "Perhaps tomorrow? The way I see it the bunker is filling and all too soon it will be overrun. We need to get inside as soon as possible. The Government could use our help after all."

I almost rolled my eyes at his last sentence, as if it wasn't glaringly obvious he had his own agenda to get inside the bunker to look for his father.

Camilla nodded and agreed to contact him later to make the arrangements, then, with her hand on the back of my neck, half led, half shoved me into the elevator. The doors closed on Evan Chase's smug face and I almost cheered. Long nails bit into the soft skin behind my ear, keeping me silent until we were out of the lobby and walking down the street in the crisp October air.

"Don't say a thing. But you have it?" Camilla asked, her face alight with the hope that had already exploded into the sweet high of victory inside me.

Daring to smile for the first time, I nodded.

Chapter Sixteen

THE VIAL HAD been growing warm in my hands and I forced myself to put it down. The sun was long set. It had disappeared behind the horizon as I'd watched from Scarlett's window, yet there was no sign of her.

Her words from this morning were still haunting me, stifling the elation that had come with successfully stealing the antidote from Evan Chase and leaving me cold, scared. The bitterness of the evening pressed in against the thin glass separating me from the rest of Vires, the crazy, bloodstained city that had somehow become my home. In the moments I stopped to think about it, to really think of what my life become, it was surreal almost. Yet I couldn't deny, somehow, I belonged here, more than I ever had in Jaffrey.

I detested the politics, the fate of the families in the Fringe, the violence the entire society was built on, but I loved Scarlett, and Jade, and even Camilla and Cece in their own ways. Vires frightened me, but I was more alive here, more myself than I knew I ever could have been on the other side of the wall.

This was my life, and Scarlett, for better or for worse, for all that she scared me and disgusted me had also saved me and showed me myself, and everything else in a new light. I had to find her.

With the vial slipped carefully into the pocket of my jeans I took the thick winter coat Camilla had brought for me and pulled it on. I set off down the hall, unsure of where I was going.

"Did you find her?" Jade's voice was lighter than I had heard it in days. She'd almost bowled me over with a hug when I had returned to the tower with Camilla once our mission was complete.

"No, she hasn't come back yet. Have you heard from her?"

Dark brows pulled into a frown.

"No, but try the roof, she goes up there to think sometimes. Do you want me to come?"

It was clear she wanted to, and I hated to deny her. For a moment I briefly wondered if that desire was from my own relationship with Jade or Scarlett's. Either way, I shook my head apologetically.

"It's cold out there. You should stay in here, we'll come by when we get back."

I hoped my optimism wasn't as hollow as it felt. Jade laughed lightly as I tried to smile, and I wondered if I would ever see her again, or if Scarlett really would take me back over the wall the minute I found her.

"Rayne, I'm a vampire, and you're the one worrying about me getting cold?"

I let her humor lighten me momentarily.

"Well, you do get cold, don't you?"

She pouted at the fact, though we both knew she was definitely the hardier species.

"Come back soon, okay?"

Something in her voice told me she knew more than I had told her. The thought broke something deep in my chest, and it stung, smarting even as I forced my lips into a smile.

"Of course."

I left before she could reply, or before I could turn around. Stalling would get me nowhere and Scarlett still needed the antidote, she was still probably suffering.

SHE WAS SITTING when I found her, her back to the city lights illuminating the dark that had settled over Vires. Standing in the doorway that led out onto the roof, I watched her. She rested her chin on her shoulder, looking off to somewhere I couldn't see. Dark hair fluttered in the breeze, her pale skin was almost translucent, and she was so still it was startling. Hurt peeled off her and sunk itself into my bones, physical, emotional. She was tired, oh so tired, and my heart ached for her, my stupid, selfless, destructive vampire.

"Staring is considered rude here. Don't know what the protocol is over the wall." She barely moved, not looking at me as she spoke. The mention of the wall turned the blood in my veins to ice.

"What does it matter?" I fingered the vial one last time, then produced it from my pocket. "My home is here."

The threat of rejection hung close around me; the wounds from our conversation this morning were still bleeding. I forced myself to let my guard down anyway, to soften my voice.

"My home is with you."

Dark eyes, green and brown, turned to meet me. I watched her shoulders rise as she sighed out the first real breath I had seen her take since I'd found her. Dark circles shadowed her eyes, her cheeks were drawn, and she sat still, slightly hunched forward, hands on her elbows, holding herself together. I wondered how bad the pain really was. The thought of the lashes turned my stomach. Last time I had seen them, it had not been pretty.

She didn't speak, studying me furiously, as if the answer to all the problems in her world might be painted across my face.

"I thought you could use this."

Raising my palm, I let the smooth titanium vial glint in the moonlight. Her jaw dropped open.

"Rayne..."

My name was like a symphony on her lips, and I ached to close my eyes and throw back my head and savor it, all the raw disbelief, the gratitude, the love that poured off her and drowned me.

She stood up slowly and walked toward me, her gait stilted, one arm still wrapped across her middle until we were standing face to face. Her eyes were large and glassy, and even in her disrepair, she was heartbreakingly beautiful.

"He could have killed you..." I tasted her fear at the mere words, bilious in my mouth, and quickly reached out to press the antidote into her cold palm.

"But he didn't, and now he won't kill you either."

Her lips quirked at my choice of words, and she opened her mouth to reply, but all I heard was her silent desire: *kiss me, kiss me, kiss me.*

My fingers twisted around the thick collar of her black wool coat and I inched myself up as I tugged her down just barely and kissed her with all the courage I had gained since she found me. Her mouth tasted like whiskey and rust and she melted into me like she was made to fit against me.

"I love you." The words fell out between kisses. "And the reason I love you is not because we're blood bound, that's just the reason you let me."

Her lips held mine for another long moment, everything falling gloriously into place, before she pulled away, tears shining, unshed in mismatched orbs.

"I can't change who I am..." She whispered the words, fearful, and I nodded, ignoring the pang of regret that came along with the revelation as I realized something.

"I never wanted you to change who you are, Scarlett." Her name tasted like stardust in my mouth. "Maybe what you do, but who you are, who you really are..." I pressed my palms to her chest and breathed her in. "I love you."

"I enjoy it." Large twin tears spilled from her eyes as she spat the admission out desperately. "What I do, I don't dislike it, I'm not a scared little girl anymore. My hand is still forced at times, but when I get to the punishment center, something takes me over and I—I like it, I will probably always like it... But I love you, I do love you." She looked heartbroken, devastated by her own admission.

I nodded soberly, smiling through my own tears. Her words didn't gut me as they once might have.

"Neither of us is perfect, and by the end, before you came, I was indifferent to being hurt most days. Maybe given another few lifetimes, I might have even learned to enjoy it too because there was nothing else."

She looked at me, horrified. I squeezed her collar and pulled her carefully closer to me.

"I understand you. Does it terrify me that you can be cruel and sadistic and wreak the kind of havoc you do? Of course, it does, but not enough to make me dumb enough to believe my life would be better without you in it."

She seemed shell shocked by the admission, and all I could think to do was kiss her again, so I did, long and hard, until she was holding me tight to her.

"We will figure this out, together, but you don't get to send me away, you don't get to threaten me with that again."

My tears finally broke through into my voice, and she pulled me against her, laying my head under her chin and kissing my hair, her tears soaking into it like rain.

"I was trying to save you...from me."

I pulled away from her and cupped her face.

"You don't get to decide when I need saving or I don't, or if I can or can't love you." My voice was strong, and she nodded, lowering her eyes. "Promise me. Don't try to send me away again."

"I chase people off when I'm..."

"Scared." I finished the sentence when she couldn't. "Be a bear, grumble and gripe, have a bad day, but no more trying to take me over the wall at dusk. Going back would be my decision to make, if the day ever came where it was a possibility."

She blew out a long breath.

"You'd be safe there." It was a feeble attempt, but I knew she wanted to try, if only so she could convince herself she had.

"Safe? Like when you met me? Like all those weeks when you were just gone?"

"You were blood bound, Princess, that's the only reason you wanted me."

I squared my shoulders, ignoring how much the accusation, fact, hurt me. Back then she was just my beautiful savior to whom I had an inexplicable connection.

"And now, I can't... Life without you wouldn't be much of a life at all."

I laughed softly at how corny I sounded, barely catching my breath before she kissed me, recklessly, the kind of kiss that made me lose my head. By the time she pulled away, I could taste her tears. They tasted like copper in my mouth. She studied me with equal parts disbelief and joy, and she almost looked like her old self again.

"Drink up." I tapped her fist that still held the antidote.

She smiled bashfully, and I smirked, realizing she'd forgotten all about the reason I had come up here, to begin with. Long fingers unscrewed the cap. She sniffed the liquid inside and wrinkled her nose, before throwing it back in one long swallow.

I released a breath I hadn't meant to hold. Somehow, she looked healthier already, her complexion a little less gray.

"Thank you, Princess." She slipped the vial into her coat pocket and wrapped her fingers around mine, then tugged me back toward the door leading down into the tower that had become my home. She stopped on the threshold and picked me up, swinging me into her arms like I was little more than a rag doll. I couldn't help the giggle of delight that escaped my lips as she gazed down at me, life coming back into her eyes for the first time since the party where everything had gone so horribly wrong.

"And for the record—" she looked at me seriously, hovering in the doorway "—I promise."

LIFE WAS SOMEHOW beautiful again, more beautiful than it had ever been before. Jade's green eyes glittered like emeralds in the soft light of the setting sun as she watched us.

"So, all Rayne has to do is bat her eyelashes and suddenly my workaholic sister can stay home a night?" She was fighting a laugh as she said the words, Scarlett fingering the dough I had just finished, her eyes down, hiding the bashful smile I knew kissed her lips.

"It was the pie. Who would have thought big bad vampires just can't get enough pie?"

Definitely not me. The best thing I had taken away from Jaffrey High was Mrs. Tillman's pie recipe. It had gone down a treat earlier, so much so that it was being put to use again, not even a day later.

"You caught me, Princess."

Strong arms wound around me and I allowed myself to enjoy it for a moment before I squirmed out of Scarlett's clutches, ready to roll my much-abused dough and lay it in the pan.

"Have you heard from her at all?"

Scarlett's question immediately dimmed the soft familial glow the evening—the last few days—had so easily taken on.

"No. No one's heard from her. If you'd just let me go to the Fringe..."

I was so tired of hearing the argument. It was obvious Jade and Caroline had become important to each other, and it was obvious Scarlett was about as likely to let Jade go running off into the Fringe to look for the missing girl as it was for the Government to throw a tea party.

"We've looked, I've looked, Jade." Even with her pale fingers still dusted with flour and a white streak down her black shirt, somehow Scarlett still managed to look haunted. "Have you ever thought maybe she doesn't want to be found?"

"Are you blaming this on me?" Jade's words were a whisper and I opened my mouth to step in before things went sideways, again.

Scarlett denied the accusation at the same time Jade continued.

"If she is avoiding me it's because of you! Because of what you did to Joseph, because you can't just let me grow up, and be free!"

The emotional ricochet from the words made me drop the rolling pin. It landed with a dull thud on the soft dough before it rolled off the counter and clattered to the floor.

Two sets of dark eyes turned to look at me, and then Jade's turned to Scarlett, understanding.

"Scarlett, I didn't mean it... I just... I'm sorry."

She sounded about as heartbroken as I knew her sister felt, and this argument was becoming painful to watch, literally.

"You're worried about Caroline. A lot has changed around here lately, and we all need time to adjust."

I tried to offer the words as comfort and to diffuse the hurt radiating off the sisters. Jade's big green eyes filled with tears, and I moved around the counter, abandoning my baking to wrap her in a tentative, floury hug.

I sensed Scarlett's eyes on my back but knew nothing of how she felt other than stung by her sister's words.

By the time I got back to the counter, the rolling pin was in Scarlett's hands and my piecrust looked like a crepe, paper-thin and limp. Her hand was cool as it grazed mine, and the silence in the room was heavy.

"I really am sorry, Scarlett. I love you, I just... I want to see more, do more."

"You want to go traipsing around the Fringe alone at night?"

Scarlett's voice was laser sharp as she cut her sister off, and it occurred to me for the first time what a strange relationship they had: siblings but also parental.

"I'm a vampire, what are they going to do to me?"

Jade's question was careful, but there was an edge to it saying she wouldn't let this go quickly.

"If they attack you will you defend yourself? If a gang accosts you will you fight? Will you kill them if that's what it takes?"

Leaving my mauled piecrust, Scarlett made it across the room in three long strides to hold Jade's face in her hands.

"I will look for Caroline tonight, I promise, but I cannot lose you. I can't."

A slow clap interrupted whatever she was about to say next. My eyes shot to the doorway where Evan Chase waited. Cold dread spilled down my neck and pooled in my stomach.

Even in just a loose shirt and the shortest shorts I had ever seen, Scarlett seemed to rise to twice her usual height, automatically inflating in the face of the enemy.

"Come to poison me again, little boy?" Her voice was smoke dragged through ashes as she spun on him, one hand reaching out to push Jade behind her, though I was the only one who seemed to notice.

My mind reeled. How had he gotten in here? He raised his bloody hands, palms up as if feigning surrender, answering my question. Alarm bells sang in my head. Evan had always been dangerous but cowardly, always determined to keep his hands clean, and in all the time I had known him, he had always shied from any real physical confrontation with Scarlett. The fact he was here, and the heavy circles around his eyes, suggested that he had finally come unglued.

"Hope you weren't attached to any of the staff. Humans, of course. The vampires are still out back—"

Scarlett's phone beeped as if on command, and Evan's face lit up.

"Yes, doing that. I expect they'll be letting you know a couple of my people are here at the back door and wanting to come up."

If Scarlett was rattled, she didn't show it.

"Oh Evan, if you've come to play, let's keep it just the two of us."

She slicked her tongue over her lips, and even with her face free of makeup, her feet bare on the cool marble tile of the kitchen floor, and wearing essentially her pajamas, she was chilling.

"Leave us."

She barked the order, not turning to look at Jade or me, but the timbre of her voice echoed in my head, beseeching me silently to take Jade and get the hell out of Pearce Tower.

"She's not going anywhere." Evan made the decision for me, his eyes burning me as he stared at me with such longing, such bloodlust, that my racing heart suddenly stilled.

Scarlett shoved Jade out the door unceremoniously, and God she looked so small. Even Jade towered over her.

"The girl belongs to me. Why did you come here, Evan?"

She was hovering somewhere between trying to diffuse this rationally and preparing to rip out Evan's throat. Her words were stone cold and measured. She was the woman from the punishment center, yet she was also Scarlett, my Scarlett in her bare feet and unpainted face, and I was terrified for her.

"You know exactly why I'm here. That bitch broke into my tower and stole from me. The fact you're not laid in bed rotting somewhere is proof of that."

Scarlett was still, so still she unnerved even me. When she spoke, her words were heavy.

"That bitch is mine, and of little consequence. You tried to kill me, Evan. Naughty boys deserve to be punished."

Her voice made even my blood run cold, and all the color left Evan's face as a sadistic smile twisted onto Scarlett's lips. I could feel her letting go, rage and insult consuming her. Evan's accusations toward me, and his confession of his crimes, were gasoline on an already blazing fire.

Pink lips peeled back to expose glistening white teeth. Evan's knees bent as he turned to run, but before the fight could begin, boots in the hall interrupted.

Three vampires almost bumped right into the one cowering in the doorway. Fear made me laugh at the scene, before dark eyes silenced my stupor.

"You brought friends!"

Scarlett lit up like a Christmas tree, and the notion that she would fight and defeat the four vampires standing before us now seemed impossible.

"The bitch stole my antidote, I have her on camera. I either kill her now or turn her in to the Government. Pearce, your choice."

"How about neither?"

"Fuck your games," Evan spat.

"And how exactly will you explain to the Government what she stole? How will you explain my mysterious illness and sudden recovery? Are you really so eager to join Daddy that you'd walk right into the bunker and announce your anti-Government scheme to their faces?"

The tightly stretched rope this entire interaction had been balancing on strained under what I was sure was Scarlett's provocation, and then, it snapped.

Evan hissed, "Kill her," at the same time Scarlett dove for me. She shoved me backward hard enough that the force of my head bouncing off the kitchen wall sent the edges of my vision spilling into black.

When I woke, cold arms were holding me, and dark eyes looked down at me.

"There, she's coming round. I told you she'd be fine. This is the least of your concerns, Scarlett."

"She's my only concern."

"And isn't that just the problem?" Camilla's voice held no note of smugness, just a dry irritation.

"You killed one of those oafs to save her, and you know Evan Chase is on his way to the Government with that glorious little piece of news as we speak. You killed one of our kind to save one of the chattels. And worse, we have absolutely no proof that he poisoned, infected you, whatever."

"Do you think I'm not aware, Cami?"

Cold fingers stroked my cheek and I looked up into harrowed eyes, one green, one brown, swirling like the galaxies.

"The question is, what the hell are we going to do about it?"

Chapter Seventeen

BY THE TIME the guards arrived, the fog that had settled over me was beginning to clear. The conversation that had carried on around me in the haze of my concussion hung in my mind. Scarlett's phone buzzed against the hardwood of the coffee table, and Camilla hissed at her to put me down. She slid me out of her arms and I sat numbly on the sofa beside her, studying her baby grand piano, remembering all our nights here as we came to know each other.

"To hell with it."

She kissed me gently and I let my fingers twist into her hair, meticulously straightened now, her lips a waxy crimson on mine, her dark eyes lined and shadowed heavily. Of course, she had donned her armor for this.

"Scarlett Pearce, on behalf of the Government we are here to take Rayne Kennedy into custody to await punishment for the crime of theft from a vampire, unless you can confirm this crime was committed on your orders as her master, in which case I'll need you to come with me instead."

Camilla made a strangled sound, and her dread echoed within me. This wasn't something either of us had planned for, not an option we'd known we would have, though I had a sinking feeling the vampire beside me had known all along and had never intended to let them take me. Scarlett would take credit for this, and again she would hurt, maybe worse, to save the people she loved.

The guards, some of whom I recognized from my arrival in Vires, waited, impatient for an answer.

"That won't be necessary."

Wilfred Pearce parted the heavily armed guards like the Red Sea as he entered the room, announced by the heavy tap of his cane. The hairs on the back of my neck stood.

"The girl had no instructions from my daughter." He turned on Scarlett, his gray eyes dancing. "Am I right? Or will you be going in while your little pet stays here with me?"

He grinned a wicked, sickening grin, and as awful as he was, I could see Scarlett in him, catching a glimpse for the first time of where the dark in her had been born.

Her panic tasted hot in my mouth, a volcano bubbling up, swirling with fear and loss and hurt, mixing with anger and getting ready to blow wide open, to blow this up disastrously. She was going to fight.

I popped to my feet, still feeling woozy from the head injury.

"I did it of my own accord. I slipped away when I was visiting with Miss Camilla. I took the...item, and nobody knew."

Scarlett's strangled denial was cut short by Camilla jumping to her feet, and my own pointed desire for her to be silent.

"Well, if that's all, I'm sure you boys have lots to do. Take her and run along. Give our best to the Government, and let them know we Hawthornes, and I'm sure the Pearces, hope this nasty business can be resolved quickly."

Wilfred Pearce's eyes shone with admiration as Camilla threw me under the bus. Hands seized upon me, and I was dragged out of the room. Wilfred followed morbidly behind in what felt like my funeral procession, as once again, I was dragged away from Scarlett. Heavy boots clunked around me as we made our way down the hall, blocking out the strangled sob of a distraught vampire, and the urgent whispers of another who had a plan.

WHEN THE THIN dark cloth was whipped off my head and I was pushed backward, stumbling until I caught myself on the edge of a table, I was half glad, half worried that I wasn't back in my old cell. The stale, moist air of the underground establishment was still familiar to me, though this area smelled less of disinfectant and more of must. The guards left the room quickly. They pulled the thick steel door closed behind them, the click of a lock audible.

"Hello, Miss Kennedy."

I screamed. A short, strangled sound I cut off before it could reach its peak, as I whirled around to see the man sitting calmly at a chair on the opposite side of what looked to be a metal foldout table. He studied me as I studied him, noting that he wasn't breathing. No wonder I hadn't registered his presence behind me.

"I'm sorry to alarm you."

He was thin and had a small build with sparse mousy hair and tiny eyes peering up at me from behind wire-rimmed spectacles.

"I'm..."

"Mark Chase." I finished the introduction for him, recognizing him easily from the portrait beside Evan's bed. He looked the same, right down to his corduroy waistcoat and bow tie.

He seemed taken aback by my recognizing him. My head pounded and, given that he seemed content to sit in his chair and look at me, I slumped into the seat across from him.

"I know your son, Evan. He's actually the reason I'm here."

Mark's brows furrowed.

"You're here because you stole from a tower, non-Delta. Are you telling me the tower you stole from was mine?"

"No. Well, yes, but it wasn't stealing so much as putting something right. Evan had used a weapon of sorts."

"My serum." His shock made the words clipped, disbelieving.

"Yes, he used it on a friend of mine."

"Scarlett Pearce?"

Seeing little choice but to tell the truth, I nodded.

"They're having me test you, to see if she drank from you."

My heart plummeted. I knew how the test would end.

"Tell me more about my boy. What on earth possessed him to ever—"

I wrung my hands, suddenly uncomfortable, wondering if the man before me was friend or foe, and knowing soon, everything would be undone. The scar on my wrist burned with guilt and I scrubbed it with my sleeve.

"He hates the Delta vampires, feels like they got everything while he got nothing. He's also been looking for you, desperately, since I met him in the spring."

His green eyes were soft and heavy with regret as he listened to me.

"He infected Scarlett with the virus, or whatever it is," I went on. "She was sick. I worked at Chase Tower for a time and I knew where to get the antidote to save her."

"And now you're here."

I nodded solemnly at the reminder, alone again in the bunker, everything I loved outside.

"I am terribly sorry for Evan's behavior. When I was...reassigned, I thought he'd finally moved on from that way of thinking, that perhaps he too could give up the politics and the pretenses and be content to further our society through science. I see now I was wrong."

I almost felt bad for him.

"So," he continued, "you succeeded in getting Wilfred's daughter the antidote?"

I nodded, wondering if I even had anything left to lose.

"And nobody knows what Evan has done? Nobody knows about the serum?"

"Only Scarlett, myself, and a few close friends."

He brought his large hands out from under the table, holding a small suitcase. He snapped it open. A thick ribbon of elastic and a needle were produced from inside, and as he assembled the sharp point onto a vial, he looked up at me.

"Can you do something for me, Rayne Kennedy?"

I was wary of answering.

"When you get back out into the City, go to my son. Tell him I'm alive and well, that this was never my choice for me or for him, but I am treated well and continue my work."

He paused to adjust the elastic around his own arm. The hard snap of it against his skin made me jump.

"Tell him he must let go of this hatred in his heart and live. If he questions the authenticity of your words tell him he's the greatest experiment of my life."

The harsh fluorescents above glimmered off his pale skin as he slid the needle into his arm, before extracting it and dropping a small amount of blood onto a plastic rectangle I recognized as a laboratory slide.

Was he going to lie for me? To say I'd never been bitten by Scarlett? Was his blood the way of cheating some sort of test? Hope flared white-hot in my chest.

"I will tell him."

"Good. And nobody, absolutely nobody must know about the serum. Evan made a mistake, but I can't help but feel responsible. I never realized how much my...absence would affect him. I will make arrangements, soon, to see him and talk with him. But nobody must know of what he has done or he'll be killed, we both will."

"Okay." I made the promise before I really thought about it. This man had been nothing but reasonable, kind to me almost, in this hellhole where I had expected the absolute worst. He didn't seem overly moved by my agreement, just nodding and giving me a grateful smile.

"If you wouldn't mind, I will need your arm for this next test."

Uncertainty ate at me again, but I offered my arm across the table. I looked away as he leaned forward to extract a small amount of my blood.

"Doesn't it make you...thirsty?"

My cheeks flamed at my own question as soon as I had asked it.

"Not anymore."

His green eyes were kind, and somehow, I liked him. A part of me even felt sorry for Evan for a fraction of second. I imagined it was much harder to lose a good father than it had been to lose my own terrible one.

I sat silent for a long time. My fear cooled to an icy dread. It clung to my skin and made my stomach ache, as I waited and watched the doctor muse over my blood. Microscopes and medical instruments I had no name for appeared from the case and those little drops of crimson were inspected again and again.

"Fascinating." He gave me a warm smile when he finally seemed to emerge from his work. "Come, we must go now, it's time for you to go back above. Do you remember what I asked of you?"

"Yes, sir."

"All right then, let's be on our way. Just remember, nobody is ever to know what my boy has done."

I nodded, offering him what I hoped was a reassuring smile.

The minute he rapped three times on the heavy door, it swung open, and once again I was plunged into the darkness of material being flung over my head. The sensation was disorienting, and I let the guards take me, practically carrying me along. With my heart hammering I dared to put my faith in the doctor, dared to hope I would see Scarlett again, that finally, all this could be over. Something small and dark inside my head laughed, reminding me things would never really be over, never easy for us, not here in Vires where society was geared to rail against everything Scarlett and I were together.

When light assaulted my senses again, it was dim, almost red, and eerie. Mark Chase stood beside me as the guards stepped back. The two plastic slides he had placed my blood on sat on one of his palms and his suitcase hung loose from his other hand.

"Greetings, Rayne Kennedy, from the Government."

My palms were sweaty as I looked ahead and slightly up to see six men sitting in a row on a raised step, backlit by red lights. I pondered if I should reply until I realized I had missed my chance as the voice spoke again.

"Doctor Chase. Your findings?"

Boldly, the doctor stepped forward and laid the two slides he had carried at the edge of the large step. He hurried back to stand beside me as one of the shadowed figures moved forward to pick them up, brought them up to their face and then carried them back to the rest of the row.

"The girl has not been bitten by Scarlett Pearce, test one."

Low murmurs broke the silence, though I could not distinguish what they were saying until a voice spoke.

"Very well, Rayne Kennedy will pay the price for theft from a vampire. At dawn in the square, as she has no family to pay the ultimate sacrifice, she will be killed."

Fear gripped me like a vice.

"A-actually," Mark Chase's voice wavered as he cut in. "Your greatnesses, there is one other thing to consider here. I hardly believed the result when I saw it either, but it seems the girl—well, she's not entirely human."

"Explain," the voice from above demanded at the exact same time my mind screamed for it, wondering if this was a trick to get me out of the bunker to deliver the message to Evan, or the truth.

"Her genetic makeup, it is distinctly human, in places. In others, she shows sequences exclusive in nature to only one species... Ours. Delta vampiric sequences, to be exact."

Before I had time to blink one of the figures was in front of us. The only thing visible below his large hood was a midnight shadow across taut lips, a thick scar running from the left side of his upper lip to his nose.

"Duck."

As he said the word, he swung and caught me hard across the face with what felt like a steel blade, though when his hands dropped back to his sides, they were empty. Something cold and wet ran down my face, dripping off my chin, staining my hands red. As I lifted them to inspect the damage, my eyes clouded with tears.

The doctor took a thick square of linen from his pocket. He turned to me and pressed it hard against my cheek, making me jolt in pain.

"She doesn't have the reflexes of a vampire."

A large hand took one of mine and guided it up to hold the handkerchief in place.

"Agreed. But genes do not lie, and she is part vampire. As such, it would be unfair to punish her as a human stealing from a vampire, rather than a vampire stealing from their own species."

The voices murmured again, and I swayed on my feet.

"Given the value of the item, a vitamin serum of some sort according to Evan Chase, if she is to be treated as a vampire she will be released with only a warning."

My fingers were growing wet and sticky with my blood, and in a room full of vampires the thought made me incredibly nervous. I tried to rationalize the situation, telling myself face wounds bled a lot, or was it head wounds? The world spun around me. The doctor took me by the arms and sat me on the cold stone floor. The spinning eased slightly.

"How could such a hybrid come to be made, doctor? For the advancement of our great city, the Government is happy to hold and assign her to you for your research into this phenomenon."

"That won't be necessary, I have all I need from her blood. My recommendation would be that she is returned to the city and completes her transformation once she is in good health."

Voices rumbled around me and the conversation escaped me, fading in and out. I pressed the handkerchief harder onto my cheek, blinking my eyes as I studied the flagstone floor, trying to keep myself in the present.

"Before we conclude, there is another attendee who wishes to partake in this council."

The click of heels on the hard ground sounded like the symphonies in E minor that Scarlett loved to play for me.

Her voice was cold and detached, but she was here. I dragged my eyes up to her, catching the last moment of her cursory glance at me before she addressed the men before us.

"Apologies for my tardiness but I was a little busy."

I noted her clothes and wondered why she had changed from one dress to another. Her makeup was even darker than earlier, though her eyes were alight, bright and brilliant like I hadn't seen them in too long.

"I had business to attend to. As you all know, the girl stole from Evan Chase. I came here to tell you it was on my orders. I also came here with this."

My heart sank as she pulled her hand from the shallow pocket of her leather jacket. Nestled in her palm were two familiar vials, one a gleaming silver, the other dull titanium. I heard the doctor's whispered plea from beside me.

"Evan Chase wasn't developing a vitamin serum and that wasn't what she stole. Evan had infected me with one of his father's vampire-harming serums. I have all the details back at my tower in the notebooks he so helpfully provided. Though these vials are all the proof you'll need."

The room stood in stunned silence.

"One drop of this—" she threw the silver vial in the air and caught it effortlessly as I watched in horror "—and you don't heal, you don't feel anything but pain, and your body begins to decay. Evan had used this on me, and I believe it was his plan to use it on all Delta vampires, perhaps on our beloved Government, to fuel his own rise to power at the expense of us all. Naturally, I killed him."

Her proclamation was gleeful, horribly juxtaposed against the strangled cry that came from the doctor.

"You, you monster! You killed my boy!"

Scarlett turned to him, and even in the dark, I saw her eyes shining with the bloodiness of it all. Silently I begged Mark Chase not to say what I knew was coming.

"How could you when you—?"

I closed my eyes. The heavy thud of a body hitting the floor beside me was more than I could bear. Hisses sprung up around the room.

"Traitors deserve to die. Threats to Vires and the mighty Government we serve must be extinguished. I take great pride in doing so."

When I opened my eyes, tears spilled down my cheeks, wetting the already blood-soaked rag further. Mark Chase was dead on the floor beside me and Scarlett stood in front of me, head bowed. I held my breath as the same hooded figure as before approached. He took the vials of serum from her outstretched hands and retreated to his post amidst the others.

"Given your exposure of this anti-Government scheme and your family's good standing, your assaults against your kind can be permitted as both were fair punishments given the heinous nature of Mark and Evan Chase's crimes. You have given us much to discuss, research, and mull over with these vials. Your loyalty and service are once again noted."

Scarlett stood straight. Her long hair fell down her back as she raised her chin to study the figures on the altar. Nothing felt real.

"Collect your servant and take your leave, Miss Pearce."

Scarlett didn't need to be told twice. Her fingers were bruising around my arm as she hauled me up and dragged me out, my feet scuffling on the rough stones. When I tripped in the hallway, she swung me up into her arms and carried me, her lips soft against my ear as she thanked a God she didn't believe in that I was alive and safe. I cried harder.

"You didn't have to kill him."

She silenced me without opening her mouth and I railed against being blood bound to her, before I sagged against her chest, wrapped my arms around her neck and cried harder. Cold air stung my face, telling me we were back on the streets.

"He was about to expose the switch he did on the tests."

"How could you know that?" My voice was raw and scratchy, and I ached for the vampire who had helped me in the bunker, even feeling bad for Evan who was ultimately a scared, messed-up boy who missed his lost father.

"I know your blood intimately, sweetheart. Think I couldn't smell the difference from a hundred yards on that bite test?"

I sucked in a breath and let my head rest back on her chest. My eyes stung and I was exhausted.

"I will not lose you, Rayne, not now, not ever."

Cold fingers covered mine, keeping pressure on my cheek as, clouded by a haze of grief, confusion, and love for the vampire holding me, I fell into an exhausted sleep.

Epilogue

THE FIRE GLOWED warm in the hearth, and I marveled that Scarlett's cheeks had a soft rose blush to them. Her dark eyes were set alight by the flames, smoldering gently as I looked down at her from my position on her lap, wondering if it was my blood in her system or the fire that had her looking so alive.

She reached up to run her finger over the thin cord of scar tissue I knew marred my face. Though it was closed thanks to Scarlett's blood, the scar was still raised and angry, tender, running diagonally across the apple of my cheek.

Contentment washed between us, back and forth, lapping gently at each of us like the tide on the shore. She kissed my chin softly. Though the trauma we had been through just two days ago was still fresh, raw, I couldn't help but treasure moments like this where I just got to be with her.

"Do you mind it?"

Dark eyes narrowed at my question, before widening once they realized what I was asking. Her thumb was cool as it passed again over the scar on my cheek.

"You're beautiful, you will always be beautiful to me."

I leaned into her embrace, listening to Jade and Camilla talk softly together, sitting a little too close on the loveseat across from our sofa. It struck me for the first time that I was aging while Scarlett wasn't. Would she still love me when I was old? The thought turned my stomach and I pushed it away in favor of eavesdropping on Camilla, who I had learned since my arrival back at the tower hadn't really betrayed me. She had been the one to give a distraught Scarlett the idea of getting the vials from Evan so she could take the blame and vindicate us both. I assumed all the bloodshed was Scarlett's idea alone.

"You know that wouldn't help her, she'd been dead for days. Her body is too far gone. I'm so sorry, darling."

My heart ached for Jade, at the loss of what she had told me late last night had been her first real friend, and crush. As I watched Camilla's long fingers tuck a lock of hair behind her ear and fold her arms around her when Jade collapsed into her chest, I wondered if perhaps Jade wouldn't be alone with her grief for as long as she feared.

Scarlett tensed beneath me, and I turned to kiss her parted lips before she could steal their moment.

"There are worse people in the world."

She grumbled at my reminder but, nonetheless, left Camilla and Jade to their embrace.

Strong fingers squeezed my sides softly, lovingly, holding me close. Just before she could lean up to kiss me again, we were interrupted.

"There you are, Scarlett. Oh, don't get up, Rayne."

The sound of my name in Wilfred Pearce's mouth was discordant and jarring. Scarlett slid me from her lap and rose to stand between her father and the rest of the room.

"Father. You heard about my aid to the Government with uncovering the Chases' plot?"

"Of course I did. Good for you. Yes, yes, well done, but that's not why I'm here."

His tone was belittling though his eyes shone with mirth and I wondered silently if we would ever get a day alone, a day with the people who had become my family, just to be happy. No Government, no Evan Chase, no Wilfred Pearce.

"I'm here to officially welcome Rayne to the tower."

My heart plummeted, and I knew instinctively the question that had tormented me since I escaped the bunker, the one I had been unable to find the right moment to ask, had been dragged out into the light.

"You hid her well, your hybrid. I must admit I am impressed. When you visited the bunker, there was one thing the Government forgot to convey to you before your abrupt departure."

If Scarlett was confused or surprised by his announcement, she didn't show it, though I knew better than most she had a fantastic poker face.

"Too little is known about hybrids, and she poses a threat to the City. She cannot remain as she is."

Blood rushed to my cheeks and something sharp ripped across my chest, panic tinged with excitement. Scarlett whipped around to face me, dark eyes accusing, and I knew she had felt it too.

"So, welcome to the family, Rayne. Scarlett, the Government has granted you ninety days to turn the girl completely. By sundown on the ninetieth day, she must be a full vampire."

Scarlett turned, gaze dark with anger but soft and questioning. A million emotions rushed through me, solutions and problems, fears and dreams. I stared into her mismatched eyes and tried to marry the racing of my heart with the sinking in my stomach.

About the Author

L.E. Royal is a British born fiction writer, living in Texas. She enjoys dark but redeemable characters and twisted themes. Though she is a fan of happy endings, she would describe most of her work as fractured romance. When she is not writing, she is pursuing her dreams with her champion Arabian show horses or hanging out with her wife at their small ranch/accidental cat sanctuary.

Email: L.E.Royal@outlook.com

Facebook: www.facebook.com/le.royal.writes

Twitter: @leroyalwrites

Website: www.leroyalauthor.com/home

Coming Soon from L.E. Royal

Blood Lust

Excerpt

"PICK IT UP."

Lazy mismatched eyes watched me. As my hand shot forward to grab the apple, I hated her a little for how easy she found this.

"You're scowling, Princess."

I dropped the apple the minute she let me and did my best to straighten my face.

The revelation that Scarlett and I were blood bound was old news, but its implications were still new to both of us. We'd been spending time when we were alone learning to overcome the phenomenon, or trying.

The vampire stretched, reclining before me on the black satin bedsheets, and I wondered if she felt me compelling her at all. I tried to recreate the feeling inside myself from the rare times I had succeeded in bending her to my will. Silently, I concentrated and willed her to pick up the apple.

She yawned.

Raindrops ran down the sleek glass doors of Scarlett's balcony, the sky a dreary gray. Even from the great height of the thirteenth floor, I saw little beige specks below that I knew were actually humans. They came from the outskirts of the city—the Fringe—brought in to work around the decadent skyscrapers that housed Vampire families, like Scarlett's. High up in Pearce Tower we could live under the illusion of safety, for the moment.

Below, the streets of Vires teemed with vampires, Deltas who were genetically advanced enough to walk in the daylight. The non-Deltas would join them at sunset.

A flash of curiosity disturbed me, pulling me back off the dark path I traveled, thoughts of society in Vires starting to consume me. Without looking I could feel her watching me, taste her curiosity. Her wish to know what was going on inside my head was clear through the emotional connection we shared. I tried to lock her out, to shield my feelings from her. She tipped her head and when I met her dark eyes, their intensity burned. I figured I was successful.

Pick up the apple.

Her voice was liquid smoke, lingering in my mind, penetrating every corner. I watched my own pale hand dart forward and grab it again. She smirked. My stupid, smug, beautiful vampire.

My fingers released their grip the moment she bade them to, and the abused fruit fell back onto the sheets.

"Your turn."

I wanted to grumble, to ask what the point was. We both knew I couldn't resist the commands she gave. We also knew she could resist mine effortlessly, most of the time. I smoothed my hands over my jean-clad thighs and tried again.

"I'm not resisting you, sweetheart. I haven't felt any compulsion to resist yet." She was amused. It danced in her eyes, in the little tug at the corner of her mouth, but I knew she was *trying* to be diplomatic, at least.

"Why is this even important?"

Also Available from NineStar Press

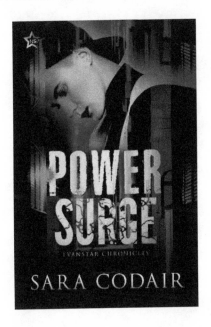

Connect with NineStar Press

Website: NineStarPress.com

Facebook: NineStarPress

Facebook Reader Group: NineStarNiche

Twitter: @ninestarpress

Tumblr: NineStarPress

CPSIA information can be obtained
at www.ICGtesting.com
Printed in the USA
LVHW102206280422
717538LV00003B/79